THE LEFT HAND
OF GOD

ALSO BY ROB ALLOWAY

Balaam's Revenge
and other uncommon tales from the Old Testament

Babylon Post
and other uncommon tales from Jeremiah

THE LEFT HAND OF GOD

And other uncommon tales from
Esther, Nehemiah and Ezra

ROB ALLOWAY

REGENT COLLEGE PUBLISHING
VANCOUVER

Regent College Publishing
5800 University Boulevard, Vancouver, BC V6T 2E4 Canada
Web: www.regentpublishing.com
E-mail: info@regentpublishing.com

Views expressed in works published by Regent College Publishing are those of the author and do not necessarily represent the official position of Regent College (www.regent-college.edu).

Cover: Artaxerxes Granting Liberty to the Jews. Gustave Doré (1832–1883)

Library and Archives Canada Cataloguing in Publication

Alloway, Rob, 1955-
The left hand of God : and other uncommon tales from Esther, Nehemiah and Ezra / Rob Alloway.

Includes bibliographical references.
ISBN 978-1-57383-437-7

1. Bible stories, English—O.T. Esther. 2. Bible stories, English—O.T. Nehemiah. 3. Bible stories, English—O.T. Ezra. I. Title.

BS550.3.A44 2008   222'.09505   C2008-906998-6

CONTENTS

PREFACE

I n 587 BC Nebuchadnezzar, king of the Babylonian empire, destroyed
the city of Jerusalem, having laid siege to it for over two years. It was
the end of Israel's sovereignty. Not everybody was killed. Somewhere
between four and twenty thousand of their more talented citizens were
forcibly relocated to serve in Nebuchadnezzar's court located at Babylon.
Whatever the actual number of exiles, compared to the roughly million
people that had left Egypt seven hundred years earlier, God's people were
perilously close to extinction.

By 550 BC, Babylonian rule gave way to the Persian empire, a world power
that endured for the next two hundred years. The Jews prospered, followed
their new masters to the capital city of Susa, retained their distinctive Jewish
heritage, and settled in to wait until their God, Yahweh, would deliver them
from bondage just as he had done once before when they had been slaves in
Egypt. Within seventy years, just as Jeremiah had prophesied, Jews started to
drift back to their homeland in small waves. The temple was rebuilt, but was
so reduced in size and substance that those who could remember the earlier
one cried in sorrow that the seat of Yahweh had been brought so low. The
Promised Land had never looked so bleak.

The Old Testament contains only three books from this period. The first is *Esther*, a fascinating tale of how a beautiful Jewish princess saved her people from annihilation. The next two, *Nehemiah* and *Ezra*, tell of how the Jews returned home and Jerusalem was both rebuilt and repopulated.

An uncontested synthesis of the historical records is just not possible. But I have done my best to sift the history and show at least how each writer was telling the truth, as he might have understood it. At no point do I intentionally challenge the canonical material. Leave aside my belief in their unique authority. There is simply no evidence to mistrust their historical assertions. As a general rule, therefore, I have followed the biblical records closely. Where I have interwoven events taken from other sources these are clearly marked, either within the stories, or by way of a footnote. Among the various ways to harmonize the details of *Nehemia* and *Ezra*, I have generally followed the conclusions of John Bright as put forth in his book *A History of Israel*. Where conjecture has been necessary, these points too are disclosed in the footnotes together with the available evidence.

These stories mark the end of Old Testament history. They have been called by one scholar "the most unattractive section of the entire Bible." They are tales of a people seeking an answer to a question that is still being asked today: *Who are God's people?* It was answered with little grace.

Deciding who is "in" and who is "out" does not sit easily within the greater story of God's redemption. But these stories are part of our canon. They are part of us.

Toronto
Fall, 2008

PERSIAN PROVIDENCE

The Queen Vashti Refusing to Obey the Command of Xerxes.
Gustave Doré (1832–1883)

T hink of me as Vashti.[1] It's what the Jews call me in their quaint little novella that is still read aloud each year at their Feast of Purim.[2] *Esther* is what they call their book, after the beautiful heroine who saved her people from the stupidity of my husband. It's a clever tale: an orphan girl becomes the queen of Persia in my place, marries my husband Xerxes, and then thwarts the evil Haman who hated all Jews, his arch-foe Mordecai in particular.

Esther is not the only Hebrew account of how the Jews almost came to be destroyed. There are at least two other versions, although one of them is more like a child's fairy tale, full of angels and incantations and even a succubus who sleeps with my husband so that Esther would not be defiled.[3] There is a certain literary justice to a demon sleeping with a demon. But despite their differences, the main point to the stories remains the same: disaster was averted! *Their* disaster was averted. What happened to the rest of us didn't matter. But it did matter — to me and to them. Let me tell you why.

I've read all the stories written about us. I was queen of Persia — how could I not be curious about the public version of our lives, mine in particular? Vanity does not stop with the body. If you want a bigger picture of things, then you'll be wanting to read how the Greeks saw us. I still prefer the Jewish versions over the Greeks'. To the Jews, my husband, King Xerxes, and all his courtiers come off just looking foolish. But when Herodotus the Greek took to writing about us, we were foolish, cruel and violent, not to mention incestuous. Well, my husband did invade *his* country, so I suppose some prejudice is excused.

In the end it seemed that each of those who wrote was like the proverbial blind man grabbing a hold of some small section of an elephant and then thinking he'd grasped the whole. One man touched a tusk, another a foot, and another the creature's broad, rough flanks.[4] Each man wrote from conviction of the things *his* hand had touched. It wasn't that any of them lied. Just that nobody could see how it all fit together. The best they could paint was a fragment, a tiny scrap of the grand tapestry that we call history. We all so desperately want to make sense of things, to see how each tiny decision — birth, death or accident — cascades out, meets up with other tiny obscure actions, collides or merges until finally we see the reason for our endings.

I will do my best to tell you the *whole* story of when the Jews lived among us, and why in the end we let them go. I buried three kings: my father-in-law Darius, my husband Xerxes, and my son Artaxerxes. All three had some part in returning the Jews to Jerusalem and I know all their stories, for their stories is my story. I outlived them all,[5] and now, in my old age, I have only one ambition left: to be understood.

The Jewish writers have only one stock reason for why things happen. That God of theirs — Yahweh — steers the whole of history in accordance with His grand design. People do things because they are pressed into the service of Yahweh. Greeks and Persians line up like so many marionettes waiting to have their strings pulled by the invisible hands of their great deity. Our gods, Ahura Mazda, Mithra — we have a pantheon of higher powers, the Jews have only one — our own gods give us more choice. Nice in the moment but the future is less certain.

For certain I was never visited by this Yahweh god and handed my lines. I've always done what I pleased. Yet apparently I'm also in the control of a god whom I do not even worship. An odd view of the world indeed; incredulous to any intelligent Persian.

I don't hate the Jews for what they wrote about me. It's correct in the essential facts, and they meant no offence, for in truth their tale is not about us Persians. Their stories are an extension of who they are — Jewish — wrapped in their own sense of destiny and oblivious to the bigger world within which they are but a small, insignificant tribe. A peculiar people indeed, for whom history is only about them. Them, their strange god that they serve so devoutly, and their holy city. That is the sum total of their world, and if some other nation is mentioned in their literature it is only to confirm that we are nothing more than bit players in the Jewish manifest destiny.

It's their very egocentricity that made them so trustworthy. They simply didn't care about the fate of Persia, much less aspire to our power. Served us well they did, and some rose to high office as a result. Esther's story is true in that detail; Mordecai did become our Grand Vizier for a time. And as for Haman, I never liked him anyway: too slimy with ambitions well beyond his station.

The Jews promoted each other, of course, but we didn't begrudge them that. How else do you think Nehemiah came to be my son's cupbearer? It certainly wasn't because they liked each other, as Nehemiah would have you believe from his memoirs. Remember when you read his book that he writes a memoir, not a history. Truth is, after the Great Treachery the Jews were the only ones I did trust. All they wanted was to go back home to Jerusalem, or to what remained of it. And by the end of it all, that served us too. Divine providence, they would say. Perhaps. But it also suited me.

* * *

Even before I married Xerxes, my blood was half royal. Power, the real power, is closely held among us Persians. Darius, Xerxes' father, was already my uncle before he became my father-in-law. There are only seven noble families whose children can marry into the royal family, and I am from one of them. It's the heads of our families that form the Council of Seven, the king's most senior advisors. Our family trees look more like one giant incestuous mangrove swamp. I'm from the household of Otanes, and after I was banished I retired to the family estates that begin a short six miles from Susa, our capital city. They were opulent quarters and both palace visitors and gossip reached me just as easily as before. My divorce had been hugely public, but not quite the humiliation you might think. I was divorced, but not disgraced, or so my friends kept telling me. For I was still the Queen Mother, and one of my three sons was the future king of all the world that mattered.

To read only the Jewish story you might think that my divorce was purely a domestic tiff that spilled over into public view: a haughty wife who stood up to the drunken demands of her husband, only to be made an example of lest other wives took courage from my insolence. Not that I mind being haughty and headstrong. Add to those the fact that I am cruel, spiteful and unforgiving, and you will respect me for all the woman that I am. But the Jews never understood the way we Persians do our politics. The real reason Xerxes divorced me was over the war. The war: that stupid obsession Xerxes had of finishing the work of his father and subjugating the Greeks once and for all. I was sympathetic to my husband's insecurities — his need for self-esteem. His father was a hard act to follow. But that is hardly a good reason to commit some mad act of national genocide, for that was how badly I feared the Greeks. And as you will see, I was not the only one who thought that way.

"Go kill more Egyptians," I had said. "Or push back our borders in India. But leave Europe alone. Your father, Darius, did not succeed. *And you, dear husband are not nearly the warrior king that your father was."* I did not say it, but perhaps he heard it just the same. So we differed. It's a state of domesticity visited on most couples.

The Jewish story talks about a banquet — six months long, if you read their story carefully. And to be sure, everyone who was anyone in the realm attended. But it was not just an elaborate extension of King Xerxes' installation ceremonies. True, the banquets were numerous and the wine flowed more freely than even our relaxed attitudes would call normal. But what the Jews missed was that the gathering was quite genuinely a council of war. Darius, capable though he was, had not secured us a victory over the Greeks. Europe, with its lush orchards and fat cattle, still lay beyond the yoke of Persia. And Xerxes was seriously considering 'completing the work of my father', as he would so often put it in public discourse. But to the Jews it was just another example of Persian debauchery, and my opposition to the war goes unrecorded. Not that their account should be dismissed as false, I hasten to assure you, just that it only grasped the public gloss of things. And if you didn't know what else was going on, you could be forgiven for thinking that Xerxes and his seven wise men were complete fools. They were, of course, but not in the way the Jews described.

I'll tell you the Jewish version; it's quite amusing, actually. Towards the end of the long banquet, having run out of royal wonders with which to impress the gathered minions, the king summoned me for the entertainment of his guests.

"Let Vashti appear wearing nothing but her crown in order to display her beauty to my nobles." It's true I am beautiful, even though it was scarcely a year since I'd given birth to Artaxerxes. But did the Jews think I was some kind of Ethiopian dancing girl? I suppose from the outside that is what it must have looked like — the cream of Persia's nobility, all fallen deep into their cups, bellowing loudly for the queen to show her tits.

"What! She won't come? Won't obey her husband? Make him out to be a cuckhold will she! Anarchy! No husband will be safe." Or as their story puts it, more delicately, "There will be no end of disrespect and discord."

And so I was divorced — banished from the king's presence in all three official languages. I was the stern object lesson to all the other Persian wives on the verge of rising up in protest against their husbands. Stability had been restored and each man was, once again, confirmed as lord and master of his household.

Divorced I was, never again to enter the king's presence, but that did not mean Xerxes and I did not retain strong feelings for each other. No sooner did Xerxes sober up and the assembled party-goers had removed themselves finally from our city than Xerxes fell into a deep melancholy. The man missed me, so much so that my spies told me that he would not remove my portrait from his bedchamber![6] Not even the excitement of the impending war and distractions of preparations could drive me from his heart. The king moped like some lovesick adolescent who, through his own actions, had banished the one woman he truly loved.

But before you begin to feel sorry for any of us, do not project your own sloppy sentimentality onto our world. There are some stories about couples whose conjugal arrangements are marked by love and tenderness — the vines of Venus growing slowly through the years entwining the pair into a mystical unity. Xerxes and I were intertwined, all right, but not by love. We had both buried that fantasy years before. What held Xerxes and me together was more like a war, two antagonists each of whom is incomplete without the other. We knew each other's faults intimately — his was unlicensed lust and mine was unbridled cruelty and we punished each other at every opportunity. Neither of us cared who died as a result of our game. And by the end, noble blood ran thick on the palace floors. There are some who say that sex brought an end to the empire. I would not disagree. But when I say "sex" do not think that I ever objected to Xerxes' harem. Men need to be men and I was glad for such institutional outlets. The gymnasium or the harem, it was all the same. It was his dalliance with the wives of other nobles that I could not tolerate. That was not sex; that was scandal.

You think I stray into melodrama? There was not a wife in the realm safe from Xerxes' attentions. That included his brother's wife, and his son's wife too. These were affairs that I could not overlook.

Xerxes' younger brother was named Masistes, a loyal enough sibling who had not contested the throne but remained a senior and capable general in the military. His wife was the first recipient of Xerxes' ardent advances, but was wily enough to escape his clutches. Rebuffed but not defeated, my husband then arranged for my eldest son, Darius, to marry the daughter of this woman, thinking that he would have more opportunity now that the families were more closely tied. But in time, Xerxes tired of the game of unrequited 'love' and fixed his gaze (along with other parts of his body) on the daughter. Artaynte was the daughter's name, and unlike her mother, felt no compunction about sleeping with the father of her husband.

Even then we might all have looked the other way had Artaynte not chosen to wear a golden scarf that all the court knew had been a present of mine to Xerxes. It is one thing to have an incestuous affair, but to then parade the proof of it — nay, to rub my nose and that of my son in it cannot be overlooked. Action was demanded of me.

I did what any aggrieved wife would do in my position. Since I could not touch my son's wife and risk his disaffection, I punished the mother instead. Waiting until Masistes was away, I took my personal guard, entered his house and mutilated his wife. Cut off her breasts, her nose, and her lips and fed them to the dogs. In the aftermath, Xerxes was forced to kill his brother along with his brother's entire family. Darius retrieved his wife; my scarf was returned to me. Xerxes and I carried on and nothing more was said of the matter.[7]

There is an old saying that it is your enemies who will always tell you the truth about yourself and it's your friends who will betray you with flattery. That was the way it was with Xerxes and me; with his every infidelity I exacted my bloody revenge. But Xerxes knew I would never betray the throne. In matters of state, I was his most honest advisor. In divorcing me he'd dismissed the one person in the world who would speak the truth to him. And since I'd counseled him against the war — a war to which he was now inexorably committed — I think he was afraid that I might be proved right in the end.

Yet by his own law — an imperial decree published throughout our empire, each copy complete with his Imperial seal — it was impossible to undo what he had done. For the first time since he'd become king he was confronted with impotent desire. Reconciliation lay beyond even his powerful grasp. The Jews say simply that he was melancholy. I will tell you he was terrified. He'd lost the one person who cared about him in any way that mattered. Perhaps we loved each other after all.

The solution, such as it was, lay in organizing an elaborate search for my replacement. Heralds, couriers and emissaries scoured the land for the most beautiful and desirable virgins who might take my place. Within a few months the harem bulged with candidates, most of whom had competed fiercely for entrance. It was to be a long, protracted contest, made more difficult by the war. And if it did not exactly engender hope, at least it was a sufficient diversion for Xerxes to rouse himself out of his lethargy and resume his usual impetuous, public face.

And that was how Esther came into our lives. She was part of the beauty pageant.

* * *

My most reliable source of palace news came from Hegai, guardian of Xerxes' harem. He was a eunuch, now well into his seventies, and I always held forth with him in the intimacy of my dressing room. There are such few opportunities for a woman to flaunt her prurience with impunity, and I took a secret but shameless delight in exposing my body to Hegai's ancient gaze. I didn't begrudge Xerxes his harem of nubile flesh that entertained him nightly. Those girls were simply titillating amusements consumed by the king the way lesser men might eat candies. But even the Queen Mother, in all her imperial haughtiness, wants confirmation that she still has what it takes for a man to breathe a little harder, even if that man is a eunuch.

I did not envy him his job — condemned to live in the presence of a few hundred healthy virgins whose monthly cycles would no doubt create an atmosphere of semi-permanent hysterics making even a eunuch slightly crazed. But we all have our troubles.

A servant announced him, and on seeing his stooped form in the doorway I turned round so that he could see me plainly. My flimsy tunic hung open.

"Come and look, dear Hegai, and tell me if you have found anyone in the king's harem that approaches my charms or can dislodge my image from the heart of my poor impulsive husband."

"Queen Mother, you are forever etched in the heart of our king. Those closest to him tell me that he still longs for both your beauty and your wisdom." Hegai advanced while he spoke.

"But your search for my replacement is now in its third year.[8] And from what I hear, every father in the Empire veritably throws his daughters at you for consideration. You've been offered everything except your manhood. You must be a rich man now, considering what some are said to have paid you."

"If only those particular rumours were true — and what would I do if they were? It's not as if I have children to leave it with." He smiled, inviting me to share in his joke. "But I keep hoping that Xerxes will see reason and call off the search for a new queen — or at least the manner in which he goes about it."

"So he still means to select my replacement from without the seven noble families?" I asked.

"My instructions have not changed. And every month I dispatch another caravan of young women to . . ." — Hegai searched for the right phrase — ". . . to attend his needs, and every month the message he sends back is the same: 'Keep searching'. I pray each day that he might take you back. You were a good influence on him."

He spoke the truth. I knew my former husband well, knew his foibles, his fantasies, his fondness for drink and the inevitable trouble that came when his intoxicated passions were left unguided. It wasn't just that at those times the royal sceptre lay below his belt instead of in his hand. Xerxes could do what he wanted for amusement and frankly, as king it was expected that his arsenal of sybaritic weaponry should have no equal. It was when Xerxes conducted matters of state with a full head of wine and visions of himself that were twice the size of the man he actually was that trouble reared its head. And I had shown remarkable skill over the years at steering my husband away from rash, capricious, and frequently incomprehensible royal decrees.

"So there are still a few at court who wish I could return?" I asked. "I am flattered to hear of it. And Xerxes will have only gotten harder to handle once he returns. The campaigns continue to go against us and the man is intolerable when his ego has been the least bit bruised. For once I am glad not to be the one to deal with him. But tell me of your search for the new queen."

"I've found her," Hegai said bluntly.

"Are you serious?" I stared hard into his face half hoping it was the beginning of another bit of flattery. His face said it was no such thing. My face froze. Divorced I might be, but up until that moment I had entertained the comfortable delusion that somehow I would be reinstated. Rejection, until then just a theoretical and somewhat transitory inconvenience, was about to take on real and more preferable flesh. I felt the sting of having been passed over in favour of another woman. If Hegai guessed at any of this, he did not comment, and at that moment it was the kindest thing he could have done.

"You will approve, I think." He continued in a quiet measured tone. "She is naturally beautiful. Even without the daily treatments, her skin is perfect. In form, she is much like you but her hair is different." He gestured towards my oiled curls that framed my face and trailed down off my shoulders. "She wears her hair perfectly straight, and much shorter in the back. But it is her eyes that you most notice. They are round with a doe-like softness."

"She is submissive then? Pliable?"

"She is gentle; not without her opinions, to be sure. But she makes them known in a way that will not threaten the king, and certainly not in public."

"Unlike myself."

"Ah, dear lady, that was unfortunate. But in the end, you had no choice. And you did not lose your dignity."

"It's a small comfort to sleep with at night, I assure you. In the end, he went to war anyway, puffed up by the flattery of fools and desperate to be bigger than his father. But all that is in the past, and we digress. This girl — the round-eyed one whose pert breasts no doubt flow with the milk of chaste humility — why precisely have you settled on her?"

"Because unlike all the others we have recently gathered into the harem and whose plaintive longings to wear your diadem fill my ears incessantly like the bleating of sheep in heat with the ram nowhere in sight—" Hegai checked himself, breathed in and out once very deeply, and started again. "Because, unlike the others, this one does not seek to be queen."

"Then she is an infant."

"On the contrary. She is not naïve in any way save the obvious. It is that she has chosen innocence over intrigue."

"But her family. Surely they press her advancement."

"She appears to have none."

"None? Impossible."

"None that I can locate, and believe me, I have tried. And she teases me by not telling me." He sighed. "It's not as if I can threaten her with torture to find out."

"I'm liking her more and more," I replied. "An orphan girl, capable of beguiling the king, yet without ambition. What is her name?"

"She goes by Esther. And there is one more thing that will make her win your approval if not your heart. She will remain childless."

"Are you quite certain of this?"

"As certain as is possible in these things. But I have observed her flows. They do not come at the appointed times, nor in the usual quantity or colour. There is something not right within. The physicians agree with me. And although Esther says nothing, I think she knows this about herself."

I allowed a small smile to flit across my face. "Then my sons are safe."

"Yes. Darius, Artaxerxes and Hystaspes remain the only heirs to the throne. And you," — he paused — "will remain the only Queen Mother."

"You have served me well, old friend. And I must show my gratitude to you." It was the wrong thing to have said. Hegai took one step backward, drew himself up to his full height and glared at me.

"I have served *Persia* well, and your husband Xerxes. A contested succession divides a kingdom, as Xerxes knows only too well. His father Darius had two queens and two legitimate heirs as a consequence. Xerxes asserted his claims peaceably enough and was successful. But empires are not always so easily passed on.[9] Not when absolute power is the prize."

"I am sorry. Forgive me. You have served us all well and I too shall do my part, just as you have done. Arrange for me to meet this Esther and, if she is as you describe, then I will show her *exactly* how to please the king."

"I will find some way to send her to you."

* * *

"Approach and let me look at you," I commanded the young girl whom Hegai had sent to me. I delivered the words in my best imperial tone — a fine blend of ice and contempt. The girl showed no signs of fear as she did as I had ordered, and stopped about three feet from the elaborate chaise on which I reclined. Queen of Persia might be her destiny but at this moment she was just one more harem trinket and I was royal blood.

She looked at me squarely, waiting for my next move.

"So you are Esther, the one Hegai recommends. He was right. You *are* a pretty thing." She was more than that, of course. Even my cynical shell was not immune to the warmth of her frank, inquisitive gaze. It was a face that invited intimacy, a face that you knew with absolute certainty would never betray you. Sensual without any contrivance, but still offering a safe refuge without reproach. It was exactly what my poor insecure Xerxes needed at his side and I could already hear him gasping, '*you are the only one who truly understands me*,' as he poured out his frustrations of a failed military campaign and a bruised ego. Esther was still silent, just kept her large round eyes fixed on mine, inviting inspection while at the same time taking in my measure.

"The king will soon return from the wars," I said finally. "Hegai thinks you should be among the first to be presented."

"He hinted as much to me," she said. "My beauty treatments are complete."

"Your skin is fair," I said. "The emollients seem to have had their desired effect."

"I smell terrible," was her frank reply. Her whole face danced into life, inviting me into the absurdity of what she had endured in the name of beauty.

"You smell the way the king likes his women to smell," I said. "Beauty is not restricted only to what the eye can see. To be truly beautiful, all the senses must be intrigued — touch, smell, even hearing."

"I know. Hegai says the same, and I have not defied him in these things," she said hastily. "But the daily baths in perfume — they are too strong and make me want to gag."

"It is the way my husband likes things. The perfume seeps deep into your skin so that no matter where he puts his face," — I paused to make sure she understood what I meant — "always there is the smell of perfume."

She almost corrected me but caught herself just in time: "*former husband*" was what she had almost said. I saw her mouth form the words but not speak them. But there was no malice in her gaze, only a desire for truth telling. I corrected myself.

"Former husband," I continued. "Which is the reason you stand before me now. Hegai thinks you will make a suitable replacement for me and bring this embarrassment of a beauty contest to a speedy end before Xerxes makes a complete fool of himself."

"I sought none of this," Esther said, but I wasn't in the mood for modesty.

"Oh, don't pretend you aren't hungry for the grand prize just like all the other girls."

"I am the king's servant," was her safe reply.

"Ah yes, Hegai told me you were modest. Modest, chaste, without the least interest in becoming a queen. Still, think of what might lie before you — the little servant girl who turns into a queen. It makes for quite a tale, doesn't it?"

"Yes," she answered. "It is just that: a tale unlike any other I have heard, and therefore one to be believed cautiously, if at all."

"Still, you will have your chance," I said. "Your one chance. And Hegai says I should help you."

"Why are you inclined to take his advice?" The directness of her question took me back a bit and she continued. "I should think you hate us — hate us all. What the king did to you was not . . . just."

At that I laughed. "You make it sound as if I was violated in some back hallway of the palace. What the king did to me, as you so delicately put it, was to be as impulsive and rash as ever. And don't expect any different treatment when your time comes. And it will, make no mistake. His counselors will see to it even if Xerxes doesn't tire of you. You are, and always will be, a momentary visitor, an interlude of amusement before the old order is restored. Nobles marry nobles and beget more nobles who ascend to the throne. And you, titillating though you are, are simply a diversion."

To my surprise, she did not take any offence at my summary rudeness. Her eyes danced as if this was every bit as funny as the daily oblations she was forced to endure.

"It's true," she replied. "I am an amusement. But if it should please you, I wish to be a good one, and there is ever so much I do not know. Hegai can only tell us so much, and we are not allowed to see any of the girls who have already slept with the king. They live now in another part of the palace under the watchful protection of Shaashgaz." She stopped herself. "But of course you know all this."

"And much more, I assure you."

We stared at each other, me trying to force her into submission and Esther staring back as if my equal.

"I need to know how to please the king," she said simply. "You asked me before if I did not crave to be queen of Persia. It's true. I do, but not for any of the reasons you think. I did not ask to be part of your world, but now that I'm caught up in it, I will make the best of it — "

" — best of it," I cut in. "You call being the most powerful woman in the world making the best of it?"

"I do not mean to insult the court," Esther replied, "and please do not confuse my frank innocence — yes, I know how people talk about me — but do not mistake me for a simpleton who does not know about power and its uses. I have already been in the palace for three years and I am not stupid."

"So why this fervent wish to please our king?" I asked, now genuinely curious.

"Because I do not want my whole life to be reduced to simply one night with a man who, by a freak accident of birth, has the power to banish me forever into the depths of a harem. I could not bear it. It is not your crown that motivates me. It is the fear of what my life will become if I don't succeed. For me, there is only one way back to any kind of freedom, and I need your help to get it."

"Being queen has many privileges," I said quietly, "but know this: freedom is not one of them. Believe me, the politics of court will be thrust upon you relentlessly. You will find that no one can be trusted. People will suck at your power like a hungry child sucks until your teats are raw. And if you wish to survive, then you too will learn how to eat, or be eaten. But since you are so sure this is the only path to your salvation, your freedom, as you so dramatically put it, I will grant you what you wish and show you how to please the king."

"And in exchange?" she asked. *She does learn quickly,* I thought.

"Esther, there are three things I love in life beyond everything else. Their names are Darius, Artexerxes and Hystaspes. One of them is our future king. And when my dainty diadem rests upon that demure little forehead of yours, you will not only publicly acknowledge their birthright, you will take care that they have no contenders and that no harm befalls them while at court. For even my influence is not absolute."

"It will be as you wish. I will welcome your sons."

"You will do more than welcome them," I replied. "You will stay out of their way of destiny. And now," I continued more sweetly, "let me tell you about Xerxes. To begin with, he hates body hair of any kind . . ."

* * *

Xerxes returned from the war and for once I was glad he was someone else's problem. The public talk was that a battalion of elite troops had been left in Europe where they would rapidly complete his glorious campaign and that Greek tribute would soon flow toward Susa like a broad river in spring-time flood. The truth was that my former husband had been roundly defeated in three engagements. Of our twelve hundred galley ships, less than a quarter of them were thought to be still afloat and were limping, like so many old cripples in small groups, toward the friendlier waters of Phoenecia. The great and glorious army — half a million when they left Persia[10] — was now at best one hundred thousand. True, they were all native Persian, professional soldiers and intensely loyal. They were also totally surrounded by Greek forces and supplies were limited. Early in the campaign, Xerxes did manage to defeat the Spartans and occupy the city of Athens. But a retreat was soon quickly forced upon him.

The glory of Persia now lay in a trail of graves that stretched from the Hellespont River to the Aegean Sea. The carnage, however, was not visible, and our own lands were undisturbed. As a consequence, the court chose wisely to simply ignore what had happened.

Xerxes now busied himself with building projects and threw himself at this new interest with great energy. We had a city — almost at the geographic centre of our empire — called Persepolis. King Darius had conceived it as a huge monument to the grandeur of our dynasty. Xerxes now took it upon himself to complete it and eventually spent as much on it as he did fighting the Greeks. The extent to which his ego and self-esteem had been damaged in the war could be measured by his architectural extravagance. The scale of his building projects spoke of a man desperate to be remembered for a greatness that remained absent from both character and deed. But what I missed — what everyone missed until it was too late — was that his judgement had been compromised as well. It was a wound he carried secretly, hidden by his entrenched penchant for impetuous behaviour.

Esther was presented to him at a propitious time, and, coached by Hegai and myself, captured his heart — or at least his fancy. Less than a month after their first tryst, Xerxes proclaimed her queen. They must have felt something for each other. My portrait was returned to me.

Esther, it seemed, was keeping her part of our bargain, for she remained childless. On my divorce, my two youngest children, Artaxerxes and Hystaspes, had been taken from me, deemed far too valuable to be left in the care of an errant and perhaps angry mother. Darius, quite a bit older than his two siblings and already married, had his own quarters within the palace.

I did not love my sons equally. Darius was the heir, and this seemed to define his character almost from birth. He cultivated a dismissive distance from his younger brothers who would have welcomed his friendship. Even I was not immune from his disdain, as if having safely whelped him, I was now useless to him. It was no wonder that my divorce was beneath his notice. He learned a little too late just what powers I still retained, but never stooped to even acknowledge what I had done to his mother-in-law. It was not just this inbred sense of entitlement that grated on me. I could have tolerated such elitism — after all, I shared it too — if it came with a sense of elegance or style. But he had no appreciation for the finer things in life, for culture or beauty, not even bothering to eat his meals with epicurean manners. Rather, he ate, much as he lived, with a kind of brutish energy — a dangerous blunt force, lacking in kingly intelligence. Even Xerxes, for all his faults, knew the usefulness of courtly manners, of rhetoric and persuasion. The rift between Darius and his father was regrettable, for Xerxes might have had some influence on him. As it was, the two rarely spoke. Darius found company in a group of dull-minded but boisterous fellow nobles who swaggered through life banging their fists loudly on table-tops, brushing aside anyone who passed too close in the street. They were too full of themselves.

It was Artaxerxes I loved. I want to say that it was because he was most like me. The truth is that he was better. Certainly we were closest, and he easily accepted my guidance and was my most reliable source of juicy palace gossip. Robust and well built, he was by no means delicate, and learned the horse and sword as good as any. He'd been born, however, with just the slightest of deformities: his right arm was about two inches longer than his left. You didn't notice it unless you were looking for it, and it posed no impediment to his abilities. Still, it earned him the nickname *Longimanus*[11] that stayed with him all his life. Perhaps it was this deformity that made him more observant of other people's imperfections and more gracious in his own deportment. Certainly he moved through life with considerable awareness of those around him, and he kept a special eye on my youngest, Hystaspes, who reciprocated the attention with utmost devotion. A shrewd judge of character, Artaxerxes held room in his heart for everyone despite their faults. He was sympathetic to how Xerxes had treated me. It did not estrange him from his father, and he accommodated Esther's presence with polite acceptance. He didn't seem to mind that his older brother would some day lord it over him, but neither was it lost on him that Xerxes had killed his own brother. There was a solidness to him; he would neither push, nor be pushed. I told you before that he was better. It was because his heart was bigger than mine.

Hystaspes was everyone's favourite, for never was there a happier child to charge through the palace corridors. Unlike his brothers, he never quite outgrew his chubby toddler fat, but rather added to it in his adolescent years. But he also never lost his natural mirth or delight in life's tactile pleasures, small or grand. If he had ambitions at all, they were to enjoy all of life to the full, and to persuade as many others as he could to join him in the journey.

Xerxes provided adequate care to Artaxerxes and Hystaspes. He turned them over to Artabanus, his Chief Steward in charge of the Royal Household. Xerxes had few direct dealings with his sons, and I was glad for the attention given them by Artabanus. They came to call him "Uncle," and he returned their affection for him with an easy affability. Most important, he allowed them to visit me as often as they wished, for which I was grateful.

But it was not through my sons that I first heard about "The Jewish Problem," as we eventually called it. Artabanus himself brought me the news in the context of seeking my help. What you first noticed about Artabanus was his nose. It consumed his whole face, looking like the prow of a large ship. The top of it started level with his eyebrows and the bottom splayed out almost to the edges of his mouth. It didn't help that he walked with a permanent hunch, no doubt acquired at an early age in an attempt to reduce his bulbous protrusion. Perhaps it had helped in his youth but by now his shoulders sagged and this only made his nose all the more impressive. By comparison, all his other features seemed stunted, sunken eyes and a chin that disappeared quickly and quietly below his mouth. The gods had not been kind to Artabanus.

But behind his grotesque beak was a keen and capable mind, which had served my husband well. It is not an easy thing to run a household staff that numbers in the thousands, and even such senior people as Hegai reported to him. Others might hold high titles of Grand Vizier, or satrap, but when it came to the actual running of the huge sprawling bureaucracy that formed the palace household, nothing happened without Artabanus' knowledge and consent. He had served Xerxes even before he was king, acting as his closest chamberlain, keeping watch over both bed and goblet of the king-elect. It is not just our kings who have cupbearers. They are assigned to all heirs to the throne at an early age. Artabanus was one of the few attendants with unrestricted access to Xerxes, no matter how the king might be occupied. And you will pardon my bad attempt at humour if I point out that he had an obvious nose for smelling trouble. As I said, he served my husband well — too well, as it turned out.

"What do you know of a man named Haman?" Artabanus asked me after we had exchanged more modest news.

"Haman, from the house of Hammedatha?" I asked.

"The same."

"Not much," I replied. "They aren't nobility, if that is what you're asking, and the estate is modest. They pass themselves off as native Persians, but the grandfather arrived from the south. I'm told that it's his wife who really is the force in the family. She does the scheming and Haman carries it out."

"His grandfather came from the city of Gaza, close to Jerusalem. When he lived there, he claimed to be a direct descendant of one King Agag."

"Who is . . ?" I asked. I raised my eyebrows, and pushed my lips together and breathed out heavily through my nose. My impatience was obvious. But I knew that Artabanus was not a man to waste his time with trivia and had no need to toy with me. Something was afoot and whatever it was, it had troubled Artabanus enough to seek me out.

"Who *was*," corrected Artabanus, "the king of a tiny and ancient tribe known as the Amalekites. The Jews conquered them when they first escaped from Egypt."[12]

"Your knowledge of history, however obscure, only adds to your stature," I replied, "but what is your point? You already know more than I do, and you've done your usual thorough job of uncovering deception, however harmless. Look hard enough and you will find that we all came from somewhere else."

Now it was Artabanus' turn to sigh. His was the long slow breath of someone wrestling with a puzzle that would not yield its secret. But when he spoke, it was as if he had not heard my question. "Haman has the king's ear these days, far beyond what is safe. On the days when Xerxes holds public audience, Haman has been granted free access to approach him. He is most frequently seen standing on the dais in front of the throne so to be included in every conversation."

"Preposterous!" I said. "That is a privilege reserved only for The Council of Seven. They, and only they, form the inner circle with freedom to approach the throne at will. Everyone else risks death if they are not first summoned. The rules are clear and inviolate. They even applied to me when I was at court."

"There is worse," Artabanus continued. "So great is Haman's status in the eyes of the king that every citizen in Susa is now ordered to genuflect in Haman's presence. It is said that he goes to the city's gates twice daily just for the thrill of seeing everyone drop to their knees like wheat cut down at harvest."

"Vanity, and no doubt the subject of much mirth behind his back," I replied, "but hardly serious."

Artabanus carried on: "If this were the only eccentric edict your former husband has allowed, I too would not care. But three days ago, Xerxes entrusted the Imperial signet ring to Haman with liberty to draft a public decree of his own choosing. Haman is drafting it as we speak, and rumour has it the final version will be ready within a week."

"What?" All posturing had gone out of me. "My husband's taken leave of what little judgement he had. But surely one of the Seven has intervened. Haman is a nobody!"

"Precisely why I've come," said Artabanus. "And you see the problem. We have a nobody, or worse, who is about to issue a royal decree that can never be recalled and whose content will no doubt serve Haman's own personal ambitions. The Council of Seven have been usurped and effectively sidelined."

"Get the ring back," I barked. "This is madness!"

"We've tried. The Council of the Seven have petitioned as strongly as they dare — have even gone so far as to go as an entire group. Yet Xerxes does not listen. 'Haman is my loyal servant,' says Xerxes, 'he seeks the welfare of the throne and is preparing the laws as are requisite to protect my realm from enemies within. Be patient and all will become clear. That is the end of the matter.'"

"Is there no one else who has the king's ear these days? What about my son Darius? He is the heir apparent."

"The two continue to avoid each other. It is rumoured that Artaynte still has feelings for the king and has yet to learn to be discreet."

"It's more likely the other way around," I snorted. "What is Haman's position at court?"

"Besides drinking with the king until neither of them can stand? He was Chief Commissary during the war; he and his ten sons pretty much ran the supply side of things to keep the army provisioned while in the field. Bought the rations and whatever else was needed and shipped it to the front."

"And probably made a small fortune in the process," I said.

"Rumoured, but never proved. Only one man ever stood up to him — the senior Paymaster of the Treasury. Mordecai is his name. A Jew of some repute within the city who had the temerity to think that Haman should submit receipts for items purchased in the king's name. He's not chief of the Exchequer, but he can approve substantial payments on his own authority.[13] They butted heads constantly but in the end Mordecai could never prove malfeasance, and Haman, even then, seemed to have the king's protection. Now, Haman is the king's highest advisor; an Advisor-at-Large, so to speak, free to meddle wherever he chooses."

"Which is where at present?"

"Getting his revenge on Mordecai. And not just for his opposition during the war years, either. They continue their public feud — this time by Mordecai refusing to bend his knee in the presence of Haman."[14]

"He'll not live long," I said.

"None of the Jews will, I'm afraid," said Artabanus. "Haman's revenge goes well beyond silencing the probity of one just man. He appears intent on exterminating all Jews who live in Persia. The edict that he drafts? It says that on a certain day yet to be determined, Jews everywhere may be slaughtered with impunity. A rough copy has found its way to me. Men, women, children, young and old; they are all to be put to the sword. They have been deemed a threat to the security of the throne, and loyal Persians everywhere are expected to do their part in ridding our empire of this distemper that has been sprinkled among us. Haman will see that his decree receives the usual circulation throughout all the provinces and I don't know a single satrap who would risk offering the Jews sanctuary. There's one more thing I've found out: Haman has promised ten thousand talents to Xerxes in appreciation for the privilege of ridding us of the Jews. I suspect he'll try and confiscate some Jewish property."

"Ten thousand talents," I repeated, trying to do a rough calculation in my head about what that amount might represent. Artabanus was ahead of me.

"It's almost a year's worth of royal expenditures. I checked. Not to be sneezed at, considering what the war has cost us."

I sat silently for a moment, taking in what Artabanus had revealed. To be frank, it wasn't the prospect of killing helpless people that disturbed me. The Persian way of solving problems usually involves the spilling of blood. It is our way of handling things. The mysterious deaths of senior court advisors, often with their families, was all too regular. The occasional impulsive execution for some trifling matter even enhances the power of the king. They were reminders that his authority is absolute. No, small-scale bloodshed was a perfectly acceptable administrative technique. Even I embraced it the odd time when I was queen.

But wholesale genocide of an otherwise peaceful and useful group could only be justified to protect against some national threat; an armed uprising perhaps, or consorting with the Greeks, or even the withholding of tax. And the Jews had done nothing like this. Their merchant houses gave honest value and were among the biggest in the city. Many, like Mordecai, had risen to senior positions within our ranks. True, their worship rituals were odd, but they kept to themselves for the most part. Such a wholesale slaughter did nothing to further Persian interests.

What disturbed me most was that the Council of Seven, essentially the executive office of state, had been effectively removed from influence. In the normal course of things, the Council would have found a way to divert the king's impulses, steering him into a more harmless display of public punishment. They had always been the voice of reason that checked, or at least mitigated, Xerxes' more outlandish administrative blunders. Now, for reasons no one could determine, Haman was leading our king around like some kind of puppy dog, making fools of us all.

But something else bothered me about my conversation with Artabanus. Nobody ever gives up information without a reason. And shocking as his news was, he had nothing to gain from telling me. Yes. That was what bothered me most. Artabanus had a scheme of his own and needed my help. Finally I spoke.

"What is it you want of me?" I asked. "You have not taken all this time just to prepare me for the fact that I will probably lose a dozen of my servants. What is it that you have not yet told me in all this?"

It was his turn to be quiet. Then, pushing his face as closely towards mine as he decently could, he said simply, "I have reason to believe that Queen Esther is Jewish."

"She's what? How do you know?"

"I don't — at least I have no proof of it. And she continues to keep her family origins a mystery. Call it more of a suspicion at this point, but there are a few clues."

"Such as?"

"Do you remember some months back, there was a plot against the king — two chamberlains who had in mind to murder him?"

"I do. Bigthana and Teresh."[15] Artabanus had caught them in the act of poisoning the king's cup. A lucky break for him since they were both on his staff. Xerxes had them hanged. But everyone suspected there were others involved in the plot, much higher placed.

"The only reason we caught them," replied Artabanus, "is that we had been forewarned. The conspiracy had already been revealed before they made their attempt, and to my shame, it was the king himself who alerted me."

"But what did they have to do with Esther and your suspicions?"

"It was Esther who apparently warned Xerxes of the threat."

"Impossible. She is too new at court to have established any spies capable of uncovering such a scheme. She's still a novice."

"I agree. And the story sounded strange to my ears, so I investigated. She credited Mordecai with having uncovered the plot.[16] There is a notation to that effect in the palace logbook. And Mordecai is certainly senior enough to have gotten wind of mischief. He has his own sources, like any of us."

"And so he tells Esther," I said. "A strange choice. You would be the logical one to have come to, or the king himself, assuming he could get an audience."

"It's a strange liaison: a queen whose origins still remain a mystery suddenly receiving intimate palace intrigue — "

" — from a Jew," I finished. "Still, it's not proof."

"Not in itself. But ever since then, I've kept closer watch. There is a eunuch named Hathach[17] who attends the queen. He's among those who personally serve her. He's frequently been seen conversing with Mordecai, sometimes in public, but on two occasions he's entered Mordecai's house. Esther and Mordecai have known each other since before she became queen. Of that, I am certain."

"Do you think Haman knows?"

"No. In fact, he fawns over Esther, hoping to further his influence with the king by the good opinion of his wife. Either that or he is playing a dangerous game and biding his time before he exposes her to the king."

"Your second thought is unlikely. Xerxes remains enthralled with Esther's charms and would not take kindly to having his toy taken from him. My own sources keep me very accurately informed on that point. But tell me, does Xerxes know that Mordecai is a Jew?"

"Mordecai makes no secret of it — is proud of it, in fact. But I do not think Haman has stressed the point to Xerxes, and it's a detail beneath the king's notice. Haman has made *all* Jews a national threat, and so hides his personal animus for Mordecai. He's attempting the pose of a wise statesman seeking only what is in Persia's best interests, however odious the task."

"It would make a strange reward for a man who saved the king's life," I mused, half to myself. Then, facing Artabanus squarely I asked the obvious question. "But tell me, why have you brought all this to me?"

"Because, to be frank," he said without a trace of emotion in his voice, "I am not sure how to proceed."

Or how to profit from all this, I thought. You are seeking some advantage but are not sure how it will all work out. And for some reason, you need me.

Artabanus continued. "Hegai has confided in me. You were helpful in establishing Esther as queen."

"What of it?" I wasn't about to give anything away just yet.

"If Haman succeeds in his goal that all Jews die, Xerxes loses a wife. There are some at court who would welcome the return of your influence over our unruly king." His voice had softened. Seduction does not always take place in a bedroom. I said nothing, forcing him to continue.

"On the other hand, if, for example, the king discovered that Haman's foment against the Jews deprived him of his beloved queen . . ."

"Then Xerxes makes short work of Haman and order is restored," I finished his thought.

"You see the possibilities," he said. "Haman is left unchecked — and Persia is without a queen once more. Who knows how the vacuum might be filled. Haman's treachery is exposed and he is safely removed from influence, but Esther remains queen. It's difficult to say what exactly is in Persia's best interests in the long run, isn't it?"

You are a clever one, I thought. You've come to see how badly I want back in the game before you commit yourself. Well, you'll get no satisfaction from me today. Should it come to that, I will bend you to my purposes.

"Artabanus," I said in a voice signaling an end to his visit, "I am grateful for your confidence. But a clear strategy has yet to emerge. Perhaps Haman will overstep himself and save us all a lot of trouble. He wouldn't be the first courtier whose meteoric rise to power plummeted with the same speed. For the moment let us only watch. And keep close attention to the movements of Hathach. Let us see how frequently Mordecai and Esther exchange news."

Artabanus left. On the face of it, he had acted in good faith. But something about his visit didn't quite ring true. He was up to his own scheming and trying to co-opt me into some bigger intrigue of his own making. I had no proof, of course, only a lifetime of experience at court and the fact that given half a chance I'd do the same to him.

It took me a while. But I finally hit upon what made me wary. Why hadn't Mordecai come to Artabanus with news that Bigthana and Teresh meant to poison the king? Did Mordecai suspect that Artabanus was also a conspirator? If so, then Artabanus would be glad to see Mordecai dead, and quite likely Esther along with him. Perhaps Esther wasn't Jewish after all, just someone who was in the way — not of my ambitions, but of Artabanus'.

Who are my true friends at court in this matter, I thought. But I already knew the answer: *No one.*

* * *

It was on the thirteenth day of Nisan[18] that Haman's decree was finally circulated. The book of *Esther* says simply that on reading the ordinance, "all Susa was bewildered."[19] It is a masterful understatement, but then, they had worse things to deal with than to write about our collective reaction.

Shock, outrage and fear — those are better words, to which I should add revulsion, disgust, and loathing when it came to how we felt about Xerxes. It wasn't until the decree went out that any of us realized just how many of our well respected and connected citizens were Jewish. Their impending removal from society would be far more than a minor inconvenience, quickly forgotten. Haman's decree would scar the entire empire.

This decree sullied us all. It is one thing to spill the foreign blood of Greeks or other barbarians who live in distant lands. To turn the royal sword inward on a people who clearly were not a threat — it was senseless self-immolation that, once started, might not be stopped. Persia was a patchwork of conquered people, each contributing their talents towards our greater glory. We did not just tolerate this colourful menagerie of tongue and tribe, it was our strength. For the first time words like "mad" and "despot" were used in whispered conversations about the state of Xerxes' mind.

The decree itself gave no specifics of the Jewish treason — only that Xerxes owed a great debt to "Father Haman" for exposing the enemy within. Everyone had a copy. It had been speedily dispatched to all one hundred and twenty-seven provinces and translated into a dozen local languages. There was ample time for all to read it and ponder its meaning — eleven months we would have before the day of destruction — the day of *Purim*, as we referred to it. Haman, it seemed, had consulted the seers and cast lots to choose a "lucky" day on which the Jews should die. That's what happens when people conduct a *purim* — they roll the dice. For Haman, the thirteenth day of Adar[20] was what the gods decreed.

Following is the decree which was sent out:

> *Xerxes, the great king, to the rulers of the hundred and twenty-seven provinces, from India to Ethiopia, sends this in writing.*
>
> *Whereas I have governed many nations and obtained the dominion of all the habitable earth, according to my desire, and have not been obliged to do anything that is insolent or cruel to my subjects*

by such my power, but have showed myself mild and gentle, by taking care of their peace and good order, and have sought how they might enjoy those blessings for all time to come.

And whereas I have been kindly informed by Haman, who, on account of his wisdom and justice, is the first in my esteem, and in dignity, and second only to myself, that there is an ill-natured nation, intermixed with all mankind, that is averse to our laws, and not subject to kings, and of a different conduct of life from others, that hates monarchy and is of a disposition that is ruinous to our affairs.

I give order that all these men, of whom Haman, our second father, has informed us, be destroyed, with their wives and children, and that none of them be spared, and that none prefer pity to them before obedience to this decree.

And this I will to be executed on the thirteenth day of the twelfth month of this present year, that so when all that have hostility to us are destroyed, and this in one day, we may be allowed to lead the rest of our lives in peace hereafter. [21]

The imperial seal was at the bottom. Like my divorce, it could not be repealed.

It would have been laughable were it not so dangerous. The palace did not sit idly by, however. The noise of public dissent and consternation penetrated even its reclusive haughtiness. Voluminous counter-propaganda descended on us in an effort to capture, if not public approval, then at least public acceptance of this madness. Old histories were dragged out and revised. Twenty years earlier the Jews had tried to rebuild Jerusalem. Darius, Xerxes' father, had not only approved of the plan but had even financed part of the venture from the public purse. For years the work had gone on quietly enough on the southern edges of our borders. True, Jerusalem was close to Egypt, a territory that was perpetually on the edge of revolt. But the Jewish enterprise itself was harmless enough. What displaced people would not yearn for the restoration of their sacred city? Even after Darius died and Xerxes took the throne, the work continued, albeit slowly. It was all contained in the Royal

Library for anyone who had a mind to go look. But suddenly a new history was foisted upon us. The Jews' real ambitions had been to reconstruct a *fortress* from which, with the help of Egyptian insurgents the peace of Persia could be attacked. Xerxes, when he assumed the throne, had not punished the Jews but chose instead to win them over with forbearance and beneficence. He had stopped the reconstruction out of military prudence, and Jerusalem remained in ruins.[22] But he had not molested them. Now it seemed the Jews were repaying his kindness with treason, and refused to recognize his sovereignty. For added strength, even the foiled attempts by Bigthana and Teresh to murder the king were now linked to Jewish masters who had subverted these two simple Persian servants to their dark purpose. Treason and sedition was now seen to wear only Jewish robes.

By the end of the first month, we all found a reason to remain silent. Silent, but not inactive. I decided to go and meet Mordecai, and see for myself why Haman hated him so.

* * *

Had Mordecai not been carefully described to me I should not have found him. He was in the fourth week of public mourning and passed more for a beggar than a senior bureaucrat. His long gray hair hung loose in matted strands down his back. Dirt or ashes, I couldn't tell, lay etched in thick black lines everywhere his wrinkled skin gave opportunity. The tunic he wore was ripped so that his chest was exposed almost to his navel. His collar-bones bulged out, threatening to pierce his thin skin, and the rest of his torso receded inward from his neck. Whatever muscle he might have once possessed had melted away, leaving only the sunken chest of a man who had grown old quickly. He smelled terrible, as if his clothes held vomit, or worse.

But when he spoke his voice held the commanding elegance of a man who had lost neither wit nor authority. In mourning he might be, but that would not stop him from discharging his Imperial duties. He sat behind a small escritoire in an open square close to the palace compound. To anyone seeking payment from the king, Mordecai was ready to examine the requisite receipts and approve them. I watched him for a short time from a little distance. Those who made their approach clutched a perfumed cloth to their noses. Mordecai, true to his station, elected not to notice, and received all petitioners with dignified ease. But for all his patrician manners, even I could see that he was both astute and forceful.

One man, whose dress and features marked him from somewhere in India, was greeted by Mordecai in his native tongue. It was an impressive gesture, and the merchant was visibly buoyed up by such royal accommodation to the difficulties of international trade. But despite his welcome, Mordecai gave the man's receipts the same careful scrutiny he gave everyone. I watched as Mordecai read through the bundle of papyri, stamping most of them, but laying one or two aside. The unfolding drama needed no interpretation; the merchant's voice shifted from dulcet deference to hawkish harangue when it became clear to him that certain invoices would not be paid. But Mordecai would not be dissuaded, and in the end the merchant desisted, stuffing the two offending papers back into his bag with a shrug, and, strangely, a smile. I took advantage of his departure to step forward.

"You are Mordecai, the Jew," I began.

"And loyal servant to Xerxes," he replied with a bemused glint in his eye, "who once was blessed to be married to a beautiful queen named Vashti and who now honours me with her presence." He grinned, obviously quite delighted in his own cleverness.

Neither of us was about to enquire how we recognized each other. Like two dogs who had peed on the same tree, we had established ourselves as players, each with our own sources of information.

"I see you do not approve all claims upon the royal purse," I said, nodding towards the back of the retreating foreigner.

"Ah, you saw my old friend Gedrosia present his case. He is a sly one. I had already refused one of those bills, a shipment from an earlier caravan. The goods were spoiled and he hoped I would not remember the details. A trifling sum, really, but you lose their respect if you appear feeble-minded."

"You could have stamped it," I pressed. "The man had come so far."

"Near or far, everyone receives the same treatment."

"Yes, I understand that Haman has encountered the same treatment when it came to getting paid, and he lives quite close, if I am not mistaken."

Mordecai's smile was a mixture of sadness and pain. "He was paid in the end, for everything. High friends, with more influence than I, have prevailed and overturned my judgement. It is fortunate for Xerxes that not everyone has such friends, else his Empire would be in much reduced circumstances."

"Yet he has not forgiven the slight," I said. "Hard times await you, it seems."

All trace of a smile had left Mordecai's lean face. "Do not mock me. It is not hardship; rather, annihilation is what I face; for myself and all Jews. Would that I had never been born. And gladly would I give my life to save my kinsmen."

"I have read the decree," I answered, "and am sorry for the current crisis. Xerxes listens to no one but Haman these days, or so I am told by my sources at court."

"It's true. No one is granted an audience with the king unless it has first been arranged by Haman, and he is careful with the privilege. For him, the royal sceptre is always extended. Others do not take the risk of seeking an audience without invitation. You know the rules well enough. They have not changed since you were at court. What has changed is that risks are higher. Ever since he returned from the wars, Xerxes' moods are harder to predict."

"Does he not call even for Esther?" I asked.

"Esther?" Mordecai repeated flatly.

43

"The queen," I replied pointedly, "and, I believe of some acquaintance to you."

"I know the queen from a distance only, as do many others. Never have I been seen in her presence. She has no need of my offices."

Do I confront him? I thought. I wasn't sure what I would gain. Still, I was disappointed in his subterfuge. It diminished him somehow. Well, he had not outrightly lied to me and I would not push the point just yet, only let him know that he could not fool me. "It would surprise me to learn that she did *not* know you," I said finally. "But I have not come to quibble with you, or add to your misery."

"For that I am grateful."

"I only thought how helpful it would be for you — for all your people — if you could find someone to plead your cause to Xerxes, to counter Haman's influence."

"Sadly, no such person has appeared."

"Sometimes a queen can have the ear of a king in a way others cannot."

"I would not know," replied Mordecai officiously. But then he quickly changed his tone, looked me squarely in the face and added, "But I do know that the queen has not been sent for by Xerxes in over a month. Others are enjoying his evening company at present. So even if she were inclined to help, she faces the same risks as everyone else. And to be ever so indelicate about the matter, Xerxes has not always dealt kindly with his queens, especially if they should happen to question his judgement."

I snorted. "Do not feel too sorry for my fall from grace. My nights are much more tranquil as a result, I assure you. For every hardship there is a comfort. What I want to know," I peered at him intently and softened my voice invitingly, "is why would a senior clerk of the Exchequer keep track of when the queen has last slept with the king?"

"Please," he began, his voice as soft as mine, "I have not yet lied to you. Let me at least go to my grave with my probity intact. I have brought trouble down on enough people. Guess what you will, but do not press me. You helped Esther once before. Surely you still hold some kindness towards her. I am responsible for enough blood already."

It was my turn to smile sadly. "It's true," I said, "you are well informed. I did help Esther once." And in that instant I made up my mind. "There are ways to have the royal sceptre extended — to the queen, that is. It is all in how Esther presents herself. Xerxes has his vulnerabilities, like any man. Should she ever have an interest in knowing how to go about it, I am easily found."

And without waiting for an answer, I left him.

* * *

For the rich and powerful, dressing for a function is not trivial. We say as much to each other by what we wear as we do by speaking. At least, we women do. In nature it is usually the male who preens and struts his plumage or horns in clown-like courtship. In humans, both sexes have acquired the custom, except that we women are more creative in putting it to use. Most often it is a way of establishing a social pecking order. It took me an hour to decide what I would wear on the day I received Esther. Ten years had passed since we had last seen each other, and time was more her friend than mine. Still, I was not without some artful deceptions. As the day approached I found myself less wanting to help. The feeling surprised me. The hurt of rejection, thought to have long since atrophied, was not dead after all, only dormant, waiting its chance to wound all over again. But I would not yield to its ambush, although I did choose the wrong clothes because of it. I wore my most regal gown, with enough jewelry to buy a small province. Esther appeared in the plainest of tunics and wore only the slimmest gold orb on her head as proof of her status. Never had I been so thoroughly bested in a competition. Ten years, and Esther's frank innocence only shone brighter so that no other adornment was needed. It surrounded her with a kind of luster that made my whole person feel like a cheap brass trinket.

The muck of intrigue has not even touched the hem of her dress, I thought. How she had escaped it, I did not know, for it had swallowed whole the rest of us. For all my worldly wisdom, I felt dirty standing in my own house. I wondered if Xerxes felt the same way in her presence, or if he found comfort that such goodness of spirit did not despise him as it should. Probably a mixture of both, for he avoided her for long periods. I waited for her to speak first.

"I have need to see the king and he does not call for me," she began without preamble. "Mordecai said you would help me — again," she added.

I had rehearsed my lines a thousand times, perfecting my best imperial tone that would lay bare her vulnerability, her impoverished, desperate need for my help. She would have to grovel. Seeing her reduced, if only for a brief moment, would be my compensation. But in her first short sentence she had given me what I wanted: '*He does not call for me*', was what she said. *I too have been rejected*, was what she meant. Rejection is a shame like no other, so penetrating, so permanent, that even a violation is preferable to being passed over. She had already been hurt beyond anything I might inflict. We both had. And having been so freely given the one thing I craved, I no longer wanted it. This was the one woman in the world who actually knew my pain. On that we would form, if not a friendship, then at least an alliance.

"He's not here," I replied brightly, striving for light wit. "But Xerxes did always have a short attention span. You still look like you have what it takes, I must say." I added an inviting smile to my cheery tone. "Perhaps you intimidate the poor man. Sagging performance is hard for a man to hide." My joke had the desired effect and we both laughed a little. Pain was, once again, safely buried.

"The harem girls are getting younger," Esther admitted. "Hegai is retired and the new ones seem to be taught more . . ." She paused.

"Tricks?" I offered.

"I was going to say skills," Esther said, blushing. "But you could always speak more plainly than I."

"But nothing replaces a queen for comfort," I said. "We lose in the sprints but make it up in the marathons. Xerxes will come to his senses eventually and remember that to you alone can he unburden himself. Give him time."

"Time is in short supply," she said.

"Oh, then your matter is urgent?"

"It is. My only opportunity to approach him is in public, in the throne room while he conducts official business. Yet to do so without invitation courts death." She stopped and then, looking straight into my eyes, added, "And we both know death is not out of the question. On the wrong day, or even the wrong time of day, Xerxes can feel challenged. He remains sensitive — grows more so, if that were possible."

"Another upstart queen," I said. "I see what you mean. I have not exactly helped your cause."

Esther smiled by way of reply. Then, "I was hoping you might know something, some special technique, or dress, or gesture that would help reduce my risk."

"You are determined to try? You could perish."

"Yes," she said. "I am determined to try. And if I perish, I perish."[23]

You are a brave one, I thought. Against my will I warmed to her, and to the plight of her helpless kinsmen. The feeling did not often present itself, and I was not sure I liked it. Certainly I did not trust it; sympathy made for bad decisions. Compassion had no place in politics.

"I know of no sure way," I began. "So do not be lulled into thinking whatever I might say is a guarantee of anything."

"I understand," she answered. "The risk is mine." And then she laughed, as if refusing to be morbid. "But look on the brighter side. If what you suggest is not successful, it's not as if I will come back to complain. So what's to be done?"

"To the details, then," I said. "On certain occasions, when Xerxes holds court, it is important to him that he feels omnipotent. He plays at being a god, meting out great favours or cruel punishments almost at random. I've seen him give away whole estates to one petitioner and hang the next with hardly a thought. Watching the faces of those whose life he holds, their looks of terror, desperation or relief — it is his most dangerous source of solace." I paused, considering whether to tell her the whole truth but judged that she might already have guessed it. I continued. "He also becomes aroused. Holding a man's life in his hands, knowing that a single word or gesture from him, and the man is instantly dead, or wealthy — it is erotic for him in a way that his harem girls are not, and I think, more satisfying."

"Ah. That explains some things. I've heard about this . . . mood," Esther replied, "but only in its private manifestation. He broke a girl's hand once for stroking him the wrong way. As it was told to me, he took as much pleasure in doing it as if the girl had satisfied him in the usual fashion."

"If you are to succeed in your request," I said, "that is the kind of day you must wait for."

"But how can I judge which day that will be?"

'By the clothes he chooses," I replied. "The days on which he wears his most elaborate robes of office are the days on which he most wants to taste power. It is on the days when he is more plainly dressed that he is more reasonable. Tell me, does he still have a cloak that is a weave of purple and gold?"

"He does," nodded Esther. "It closes around his neck with a brooch bearing the image of Ahura Mazda. He also has a stole, heavily decorated with jewels, that he wears at the same time."

"That will be the sign," I answered. "Have him watched. The day he enters the throne room in that attire is the day you have your best chance."

"You are suggesting I approach a lion when he is most hungry," Esther objected. "Surely it should be a day when he is more sedate."

I smiled at her. "Ah, but that's just it. You'll have brought food — the very thing he most craves on those days."

"Which is to feel all-powerful?"

"Exactly."

"And how might I do that? What do I say?"

"You don't say anything. You faint."

"Faint?"

"Faint, swoon, collapse to the floor, lie prostrate. Practice is essential. It must appear natural, without the least hint of contrivance or forethought. Just as you approach the throne, before his guards step forward, you look up at his face. It is stern and foreboding. You have entered unbidden into the presence of a god. You are overcome by his majesty. What else can a helpless woman do except expire under his stern omniscient gaze?"

A hint of understanding played across Esther's face as she grasped the essence of the stratagem. She spoke. "And having so publicly confirmed his absolute and total power over me, he can show mercy."

"Benevolence, even tenderness. After all, you are the public queen he always wanted, lying limp at his feet. To kill you at the moment when you have already yielded, gives no pleasure."

"And after I am revived," Esther followed with the next envisioned scene, "he extends the Royal sceptre and I make my request?"

"If you have been convincing, he will have leaped from the throne and picked you up himself, alarmed but still pleased at the effect of your even seeing him. And you will not mention your petition at all. You are still trembling at the sight of him, and all speech has abandoned you. He will press you, eager to show his generosity in front of all the assembled. But you will speak so weakly he has to bend his face close to yours. He will feel your comely flesh, through your oh so thin but unadorned tunic as you give yourself up to his strong embrace. He is your protector, and your body is limp at his power. The most you can do is to invite him, with great effort of speech, to an intimate dinner — in your quarters — that you have prepared."

Esther looked at me with amazement. "It will work. You are every bit as brilliant as people say you are. I can see it all happening just that way. And at dinner, when we are alone, I will talk to him."

"Except that you will not be alone," I replied.

"What?"

"You will have invited Haman to come with the king to dine in your private chambers."

Esther's face froze into a mask of polished ivory. "And why would I want to do that?" she asked stiffly.

"Because Haman is the reason you must speak to Xerxes." I waved away her beginning protest. "Don't take me for a fool," I continued. "Haman is your enemy. It is his destruction or yours. There is no third way."

Welcome to the game, I thought. Welcome to the loss of innocence. Esther sat quietly, taking in what I had so bluntly voiced. Watching her, it occurred to me that until that moment she hadn't thought much past just getting an audience with Xerxes. Up until then she could still pretend that it was all just harmless manipulation of a husband-king. But the bald truth was that for her to be successful, Haman would have to die, and she would be the cause.

She spoke, finally, only slightly more open. "But even if what you say is true, why would I want to invite Haman?"

"So that when the king finally discovers that Haman is a threat to his weak but beautiful queen who has thrown herself at his feet for protection there is an outlet for the king's rage. At the height of his mood, there will be Haman, close at hand to receive the king's punishment. You know as well as I do, Xerxes would never order the death of his most trusted and senior advisor except in the heat of passion. If Xerxes has time to think about it, or if Haman has time to prepare a defense, you will never succeed. Haman's death will be swift, or not at all. Let the king regret all he wants after the fit has passed. The dead do not come back."

"And how am I to bring all this about?"

"That is for you to solve. You came asking only to know how to approach the king. I have told you that and more. But the ending is yours alone to make as you are able. Beyond what I have already told you, I can add nothing."

"You have given me more than I deserve. I am grateful." Esther paused, and a shrewd look crept into her eyes. "Is there some small thing I might do to show my thanks?"

I'd been waiting for the question, knowing it was in her nature to ask, if for no other reason than to clarify the extent of the obligation she had acquired. "There is," I answered.

"Name it."

"Some months back, Mordecai — an acquaintance of yours for some years, if my information is correct — came to you with news of a plot against the king's life."

"I remember it well. It was during a time when I had easier access to Xerxes. I went and told him about it and the men were caught. Artabanus arranged for their discovery."

"Why did Mordecai choose you?"

"I do not know." The question puzzled Esther. It was obvious she had never questioned the matter in her own mind. "I am the queen. Above all suspicion I suppose, and therefore to be trusted. I keep my station solely at Xerxes' pleasure. If he dies, I will be disposed of soon enough. It is your children who will take the throne. It is still as you said long ago. I am an interlude in the established order of things."

"Tell me. Think back to when Mordecai told you about Bigthana and Teresh. What did Mordecai say to you when he brought you the news?"

"Only that the king must learn of it quickly and directly. That I should trust no one else with the message. From my lips to his ears — that was the phrase he used, or something like it. But what is it you want from me? What service can I give you?"

"None after all. See to Haman's downfall and I am content." I had got what I wanted. Mordecai *did* suspect that others were involved in the plot against Xerxes, others who were probably still actively scheming. Esther had confirmed it without even knowing. '*Trust no one else with the message.*'

Trust no one period, I thought. Some things at court never change.

* * *

Usually a condemned man awaits his death sentence in the confines of some foul pit. His cries or curses are of no real consequence to anyone, for in his isolation he is already as good as dead to the rest of us. His long shadow of despair is carefully isolated so that it does not disturb those who still enjoy the sunlight.

But a condemned people is not so easily hidden. The Jews of our city retained their liberty. There was no fear of anyone running away. Haman's decree had been published in all three million square miles that was Persia. There was, quite literally, nowhere to run. Like Mordecai, the Jews did not retire from their trades. We still bought their merchandise in the markets and sent our goods on their caravans, provided of course they would reach their destinations before the thirteenth day of Adar.

It would have been easier on us if they had retired to their homes and simply faded from our collective memory. But we had *all* been conscripted somehow into a public theatre, with us now playing the ghoulish role of executioners while the condemned victims fixed their large despairing eyes on us, pleading for mercy whilst handing us back our change for our vegetables. Everyone knew who was Jewish. They all wore sackcloth and ashes, the universal signs of public mourning. It was as if they had begun the funeral dirge in advance of the body being lowered into the ground, knowing that there would be no one left afterwards to sing the laments or offer up the required prayers to their god. At night, from the Jewish quarter, a long low wail wafted in the air as people gathered to chant their Hebrew prayers of petition. It sounded like a wounded beast in its stall that even the most hardened farmer would have quickly dispatched.

There was no escaping their misery. It became ours, too, however much we resisted, for it was evident everywhere. By the end of the second month it was as if the stench of rotting flesh had already filled our city — a permanent whiff of accusation despite the fact that the corpses still walked among us. But we were victims too, or so we told each other, when we talked about it at all. Refusing to carry out a royal edict, however degrading, meant that we too would die. Our natural impulse toward mercy had been constrained by the higher authority of the realm. We could do nothing except obey, passive agents of the Imperial order. Sorrowful, yes, that sentiment was still permitted. But in the end, we would be obedient Persians. Others of course took a quicker road to a hardened conscience and embraced the public salve that all Jews were traitors. In the end we each chose whatever response best allowed us to sleep.

I, of course, waited with some eagerness, knowing that the last scene of the drama that engulfed us all had not been written, or at least was open to revisions. I moved about the city more, in search of indications that Esther had found her opportunity. It was on such a foray that I chanced to meet Mordecai again, although the circumstances could not have been more bizarre. Looking back, it was as if the author of our collective misfortune, sensing the agony of audience and actors alike, provided a comic interlude to ease the tension and give us all a respite from the grand tragedy.

It began when I was just about to turn a corner of a major street, my two pages having already disappeared in front of me.

"Make way for him whom the king honours," said a loud voice. "See the honour that falls on him whom the king loves."

We all met at the corner and I was blocked by a man leading a richly decorated charger on which sat another man wrapped in an equally ornate cloak. It was the cloak I recognized first, and gasped. It was the very same cloak that I had described to Esther, one of Xerxes' personal favourites. But my surprise was not complete. The man leading the horse was none other than Haman and the man sitting astride the horse was Mordecai. None of us knew quite what to say. Haman's usually neat and oiled hair clung to his forehead from the sweat of his efforts, and the horse had managed to deposit large dollops of drool on his sleeve that held the bridle. Worse, I could see that he'd stepped in something mucky that still oozed from between his toes of one foot. I knew the man only slightly, but his fastidious attention to his appearance was a palace legend. It was well known that he spent more time on his daily toilet than did a lot of women, and rumour was that he actually blackened his hair to appear more youthful than his age. Never would I have thought he would appear in public in such a humiliated state. I wasn't sure I should recognize him to spare him at least that additional insult, but it was too late.

"Vashti, daughter of Ortanes," he said limply. "By order of Xerxes himself I am enjoined to show the king's affection for one who has so earnestly served him." He nodded backward toward Mordecai but refused to turn his head. I glanced up.

"My lady," Mordecai said, nodding solemnly but obviously unable to hide his grin at Haman's increased discomfiture.

"Mordecai?" I peered up over Haman's short body and peered at the figure sitting on the horse.

"Your servant," he said. "You are already acquainted with my squire."

"You seem to have come up in the world," I replied. Humour seemed the best course for everyone.

"Only for a day," Haman blurted out, "and it is almost over."

I kept talking to Mordecai. "But is that not a robe of mourning that I see beneath what I know to be the king's favourite cloak of office? And that chain around your neck — it belongs to the Grand Vizier, if memory serves me right."

"The emblems of the king's affection and honour," confirmed Mordecai, "but Haman is right. We are just now proceeding back to my usual place at the gate where I shall be relieved of my finery."

"But what is the cause of this?" I asked the question of Haman. I was curious to hear his explanation and only hoped I would not smile as I listened.

"Some months back Mordecai provided a trifling service to the king and Xerxes, out of his generous heart, wished to show the citizens of Susa the manner in which he rewards all those who render him aid. He consulted me in the matter, of course. I am his closest advisor."[24]

"It is a creative and generous honour that you suggested," I replied. "Is that not one of the king's own horses as well?"

"It is, a fine spirited beast," said Haman in a tone that suggested he would gladly kill it if it were possible.

"And may I ask what trifling service a clerk of the Treasury might have done to be recompensed in this elaborate manner?"

"There was an attempted conspiracy," answered Haman again. "Two junior butlers who sought to poison the king's cup. Artabanus was already well on his way to discover it but Mordecai is thought to have uncovered it first. At least that is what the Palace scribes recorded."

"That was some time ago," I answered. "The king has deliberated at some length before showing his gratitude."

Haman spotted his chance and took it. "That matter was so ordinary that the king was not even aware that Mordecai played some modest role. But by chance, last night he called for the Palace logbook to be read to him — he could not sleep it seems, and by chance this was the entry that was chosen."

"By chance," I repeated, glancing up at Mordecai, who was by this time grinning like a man half his age.

"He could not sleep," continued Haman, "because he had just returned from an intimate dinner with the queen."

"Oh?" I said.

"To which I too was invited. No one else."

"Just the three of you. It simply confirms the esteem with which Xerxes regards you. Indeed, your influence is oft remarked on."

So Esther had approached the king and had not had her head removed for her temerity. But here Haman stood before me, still alive. Something had gone awry.

I continued. "I trust the queen has not suffered from a similar insomnia." I gave Haman my most honeyed of smiles before I added, "Or perhaps we should expect her to be even more disturbed considering that the two greatest men in the kingdom visited her chambers. Not even I can boast of such an accomplishment."

Haman brightened even as I spoke. You are *such* a fool, I thought.

"The queen, it seems, cannot get enough of our company. For this very evening we are returning to dine with her again."

"Just the three of you — as before?"

"The king and I are inseparable," was Haman's proud reply. "And the queen, I must tell you, shows me considerable favour of late. There is some small concern troubling the queen. No doubt she needs the king's help, or thinks she does to overcome whatever vexes her. A domestic disturbance, no doubt, or perhaps one of the harem girls has offended her. Women build the least little irritant into dragons that ravage their imaginations and will not leave."

I smiled again. "It is why we need men such as you."

Haman gulped down the compliment without reflection. "No doubt she will tell us this evening what is troubling her and by morning, whatever petty petition that burns in her bosom will be granted. Would that all affairs of state that burden me were so easily solved as a woman's troubles."

"I am keeping you," I replied, afraid that if I prolonged the conversation any longer I would start to laugh.

Haman, having momentarily forgotten his present humiliation, afforded me a regal nod before pushing past me. "Come honour the man whom the king loves," I heard his retreating voice ring out. All shame had left his tone, replaced with conceited confidence. Mordecai was a mere mid-day irritant. Tonight, Haman would dine with the king and queen.

I smiled to myself. Be careful what you wish for, Haman. Things are not always what they seem.

No one knows for sure what happened that night in Esther's chambers. The Jewish version, published years later, of course, stops just short of suggesting that Haman was caught in the act of forcing himself on Esther. They claim[25] that Xerxes, on hearing both that his queen was Jewish and that Haman had hatched a heinous scheme for wholesale slaughter of her people, left the room where the three of them were eating, in 'heavy anger'. Knowing him so well, I figured that 'drunken rage' was probably a more accurate description but the Jewish writers were always discreet in describing the king's moods. Returning a short while later, the king found Haman on his knees before Esther, pleading for his life. Whatever his posture or intent, what the king saw through his drunken haze was the head of his closest friend now pressed up tight against the queen's breasts.

To use a Jewish understatement, it did not end well for Haman. Early next morning my palace friends sent word that Haman had been hung about midnight. Xerxes was said to have personally stood and watched the proceedings. The irony, or so the rumours went, was that the very gallows

57

from which his body still dangled, he'd built himself hoping to place Mordecai in the noose.

Perhaps that is the whole story. But I will always wonder what exactly Esther said to Haman when they were alone. Something she said must have enticed him to press his flesh so closely to her own, and in a pose that would so easily be mistaken for a sexual advance. A man pleading for his very life in stark terror is not usually mistaken for a man engaged in bedroom conquests. Either way, Esther had earned my respect. When it came to Xerxes, she was my equal. And in a strange sort of way I was relieved. Xerxes would get the watchful care he needed.

Other events tumbled into place. Haman's estates were given to Esther, who in turn asked Mordecai to manage them. Mordecai, having been properly introduced to the king, was next seen wearing the Grand Vizier's chain of office together with the Imperial signet ring that only recently had been on Haman's finger. It turned out that Mordecai was Esther's uncle, having been raised by him after her own parents had died. In hindsight, it should have been obvious to everyone, but then a lot of things should have been. Xerxes made Mordecai his most senior advisor, who quickly reminded the king with utmost tact that the Council of Seven were also good and loyal nobles and the source of great wisdom. I hoped that Mordecai would keep his job. At least, he'd proved his loyalty.

It was all a stellar end to a spectacular drama, except for one small detail. Haman's decree could not be rescinded. The Day of Purim still awaited the Jews. The problem was a classic crisis of state, at least while Xerxes ruled. Father Haman, first among the Persians, was now dead and rotting outside the city walls. But it was not Haman who had issued the royal proclamation. It was *Xerxes'* wish that the Jews be destroyed. And the king is never wrong. That is the first principle of court policy. It fell to Mordecai, as the newly minted Grand Vizier, to reverse a royal decree without the king actually having changed his mind. Mordecai proved quite capable of revising history.

Our king, it turned out, had not been wrong in his first dispatch; rather, he had been deceived by none other than the man he had most loved and trusted! Only the diligent investigation of the king, carried out personally, combined with his astute wisdom, enabled him to uncover the truth both about Haman's treachery and the Jews' loyalty. The earlier edict, alas, must still stand. On the thirteenth day of Adar people might still kill Jews. Only now, the Jews could retaliate, with total impunity.

On the twenty-third day of the month of Sivan, seventy days after Haman's edict, Mordecai displayed his political brilliance. Issued with all the same pomp and urgency as Haman's, and sent out in as many languages, a new decree was dispatched to all one hundred and twenty-seven provinces.

Xerxes, the great king, to all those who are his faithful subjects.

Know this: Many are the men who on receiving kind and generous benefits together with high honours solely from the kindness of a sovereign heart are not only injurious to their inferiors but do evil to those who have been their benefactors. They steal the air of gratitude and by their insolent abuse of what they have received, turn against those who are the authors of it. And this they do, not fearing either man or God, thinking their deceit is hidden. Some of these men, having been placed in high position for the management of the public weal, harbour private malice against some others, and think naught of using the trust they have been given, to persuade those who have absolute power to heap anger on those who have done no harm, until those who have been so falsely accused by lies and slander are in danger of perishing.

Such men are not discovered from ancient tales, or dwell in distant lands only. Under our own eyes may we find examples of this perfidy, so that it is no longer fit to attend the persuasions that reach mine ears without the certitude of my own determinations. Then may I be sure that the truly wicked will be punished and favour may be shown to the innocents.

This was the case of Haman, son of Hammedatha and by birth an Amalekite whose first deceit was to claim Persia as his native home. Once safely taken into our bosom and partaking of our kindness to so great a degree as to be called "Father," and rising to greatness second only to mine own, the magnitude of his bounty deluded his sound reason. For gratitude he chose instead to conspire against me, the source of his authority, trying to take away my wise counselor Mordecai, scheming to have both him and Esther, the partner of my life, brought to destruction. He contrived thus to deprive me of my friends and transfer the government to other knavish brigands of the same ilk.

But having perceived the scope of his treachery, I ascertained with my own sight that these Jews were not wicked but rather conducted their lives in quietness and in the fear of both their god and of their king, whose welfare they have advanced since the days of my father's father.

Therefore, I do not only free them from the punishments to which you have been instructed in an earlier epistle sent by Haman, but I order that all honour be paid them as befits their special fealty. I give you charge that the Jews may be permitted to follow their own laws as are peculiar to them, and that on the thirteenth day of Adar they be granted the right to take up arms and defend themselves from any unjust violence as may beset them. For God has made this day a day of their salvation instead of a day of destruction.

And therefore do I also urge them that, having prepared themselves for the aforementioned day, they are at liberty to avenge themselves on their enemies and that no magistrate or militia will frustrate this right conferred on them this day, neither offer sanctuary to any of those on whom the judgement of the Jews may settle.[26]

This time the city did laugh, but with relief that a terrible abomination had been averted. Haman's decree would remain in effect. But now the Jews had been authorized to arm themselves and attack their enemies with impunity. On balance, the Jews showed great restraint. Haman's ten sons were hung, of course. But only about eight hundred others were killed in our city. Elsewhere in the provinces the butcher's bill was thought to have been about seventy-five thousand. Remarkably, the Jews did not touch the property of those they killed. It was a forceful gesture that garnered much respect for the Jews. Avarice runs deep in the heart of every man. No one could say that the Jews had exploited their preferred status for economic gain. Their revenge, therefore, acquired an aura of righteousness. Those they killed must have deserved their fate. At least that's how we Persians saw it.

* * *

In *Esther* the tale stops here. I don't blame the author for having closed on a high note. Peace in the realm, a loyal Jew chief-of-state, Xerxes secure on his throne with a beautiful, brave, and Jewish queen at his side. The ending is irresistible. But there are three score years between where Esther leaves off and Nehemiah picks up the tale of Jewish destiny.

Jewish destiny. Persian interests. Maybe they are the same story, but I can only speak to one of them. The opening of Nehemiah's book is simple. Nehemiah prays to that god of his, and his god answers Nehemiah's petition — that's what Nehemiah wants you to believe. Oh that life was really that straightforward.

* * *

For several years after the Purim life was good. My two youngest sons grew quickly into strapping adolescents that any mother would be proud of. Darius kept to himself, but Artaxerxes and Hystaspes only seemed to increase in their affection for me. Artabanus continued his watchful care and ensured their education was complete as befitting their station.

To the north, the Greeks showed no signs of mounting a counter offensive and invading our established territory. At the other end of our Empire, the Egyptians seemed content with our rule. I credit my brother Achaemenes for that. He was their satrap and did not antagonize them needlessly, insisting on our taxes but otherwise ruling with great tolerance. Mordecai was an astute Grand Vizier, and we all benefited from his unswerving dedication to Xerxes' welfare. As for our king, Xerxes busied himself with his building project at Persepolis and consequently was absent from court for long periods. This meant that much of the State business fell to people like Mordecai, Artabanus and the Council of Seven. But frankly, we were all better served as a result. Xerxes was about as good an administrator as he was a military man.[27]

The first inkling I got of trouble was through the most trivial of details. My son Artaxerxes visited me one day with a complaint, seeking my advice, and perhaps approval, for what he wanted to do.

"I've been given a new cupbearer," he said. "A Jew," he added.

"Oh? And does this Jew not please you?" I asked. It was not just an idle question. One's cupbearer, in addition to testing any food or drink lest they be poisoned, was by far the most confidential of one's servants. The good ones were rarely out of sight and it took considerable skill for them to be both constantly vigilant but also invisible at the appropriate times. Artaxerxes was fast on his way to adulthood and would resent this constant intrusion on his privacy.

"He does not," my son answered emphatically. Something about the way he said it reminded me of his father. You can never completely escape your parents, I thought.

"Is he lax in his duties?" I probed. "Perhaps he is shy about testing your food and drink."

"He is neither shy nor lax. On the contrary, he tests everything. Every time I turn around he is there, like a second shadow. He all but sleeps in my bed, and I think he would if I suggested it. As it is, I'm sure he searches those that do before they enter." Artaxerxes looked at me obliquely to see if I would comment, but there are some things a mother simply pretends not to understand.

I smiled. "And does this Jew who seems to sleep outside your door like a faithful dog have a name?"

"Nehemiah. We are about the same age, but apart from that we share nothing. And he is ugly. There are pock-marks on his cheeks which I think are left over from some youthful ailment. He lets the hair grow long down his temples and defends this grotesque habit in the name of his religious obligations. He has too much fat on him, and tries to hide this disfigurement by wearing too many clothes. As a result his forehead is always in a sweat. He is both short and short-tempered with everyone but me. He hovers and darts around like a mad hummingbird. He sees conspiracies everywhere — he went so far as to drink some of my bathwater the other day. My bathwater!"

"Like having your wet nurse continually in your presence," I laughed. "Yes, I can see why this would upset you. So send him back to Uncle Artabanus and tell him that this Nehemiah does not please you. It's not as if the palace has a shortage of servants."

Artaxerxes paused and lowered his head slightly so that his eyes focused somewhere close to my ankles. "Artabanus did not select him."

My stomach tightened ever so slightly. "But your personal attendants, anyone who works anywhere at court — they all serve by his command. Not that you are not entirely free to choose for yourself," I added. "Chamberlains — those who see to your most intimate needs — only you can judge their fit. But tell me, if Artabanus did not send him to you, who did?"

"Mordecai," was his reply.

The Grand Vizier, now selecting cupbearers, I thought. Why would he bother, especially since he knows it will only irritate Artabanus?

"Strange for so senior an advisor to interest himself in your domestic arrangements, " I said slowly. "Perhaps Nehemiah is his friend, or a distant kinsman of Esther's family whom he seeks to advance at court?"

"Mordecai did not say. He only said that he had found someone 'in whom there was no guile'. An odd, cryptic phrase, which is why I remember it exactly. He asked me to accept this Nehemiah fellow and that if Artabanus objected, I should stand on my royal prerogative to select those who serve closest to me."

"And did Artabanus comment on your new cupbearer?"

"He did. I replied as Mordecai suggested, but all the same, Artabanus was clearly hurt. He is my friend much more than Mordecai is and I hate to offend."

"Except that now you find this Nehemiah an irritant. So send him back to Mordecai," I answered. "Tell Mordecai it is your decision." My son was obviously caught in a game between two powerful men and lacked the experience to know what to do. It irked me that Mordecai appeared to have taken advantage of my son.

"I did send Nehemiah back to Mordecai," Artaxerxes said, "and the Grand Vizier's reply was that I should first come to you to discuss the matter."

"Oh," I said for the second time, much more slowly. It seemed that Mordecai was sending me a message somehow. There was trouble brewing somewhere, old conspiracies revived. The scorpion had grown a new tail.

"Was Hystaspes also assigned a cupbearer by Mordecai?" I asked, stalling for time before committing myself.

"Yes, and his is Jewish too, although not nearly the prickly fanatic that I have been saddled with. Hystaspes waits for my lead and will do what I tell him."

"You must have a little sympathy for the Jews," I said. "To avoid complete destruction by so slender a thread of chance leaves deep marks on a man's mind. We cannot fault the Jews for imagining danger where none exists. Who knows when another Haman might arise — at least I'm sure that is what they must feel. And they are a scattered people — no homeland for safety."

"Yes, I know all about that already," Artaxerxes sighed. "I already know more about Jews than I wish to. I know about how the Babylonians destroyed their precious Jerusalem, how my grandfather Darius was generous in his permission to allow some to return and begin a reconstruction but how Xerxes stopped it. I know that their temple is finished but that it lies amidst a ruined city. Nehemiah would talk of nothing else if I allowed it."

64

"And Darius your brother?" I asked, totally ignoring my son's rant. "Did Darius receive a Jewish cupbearer as well?"

"Darius is master of his own affairs," Artaxerxes said flatly. " I would not know of his domestic arrangements." My sons grow even more distant from each other, I thought.

"Artaxerxes," I began, "Nehemiah should remain your closest and most trusted servant. That is my advice — no, more than my advice. That is my wish. Learn to tolerate his constant prattle about his precious homeland. He is not any different from other displaced people who have not yet intermarried enough to forget tribal roots. And learn how to put servants in their place! It's time you stiffened your back a bit, and gaining mastery of this Nehemiah will be good practice for you. Mordecai does not meddle in your affairs without good cause and while I do not understand his actions, I would trust Mordecai with my life, as should you. He has not thrust this prickly hedgehog at you just to be difficult. I will make enquiries. But until then, keep this Jewish zealot close to you."

* * *

The Grand Vizier does not attend the private home of the Queen Mother. The Queen Mother attends the Grand Vizier at his official quarters, constructed in smaller scale, of course, quite like the royal state receiving hall. Furthermore, the Queen Mother makes an appointment and gracefully writes a note of gratitude that such an important advisor would find time amidst the pressing affairs of state to grant her an audience. But the stricture of social conventions did not diminish either our friendship or the clarity of conversations. Mordecai received me promptly, rising from his chair and walking towards me so that we met in the middle of the cavernous room. Since the desk from which he worked sat on a raised dais at one end, it was an overtly gracious signal. His secretaries exited quietly through a side door as if by prior arrangement. What we said would not be overheard.

THE LEFT HAND OF GOD

"Your wardrobe has improved considerably since we last met," I began lightly.

"I fired my tailor and found a better one." He grinned. Despite his keen intelligence, advancing age, and now his high office, Mordecai took a childlike glee at life's simple pleasures that came his way. It was quite endearing.

"You have come up in the world!" I answered. "And I am genuinely happy at your good fortune. Clearly the God you serve is powerful. Perhaps I should forsake mine, and follow yours — if he would have a lowly Persian as an acolyte."

"You joke," he said. "But I did hear a report of two cities — in the province of Partha — where on the Day of Purim the men circumcised themselves so as to become Jews."[28]

"Now you are the one who jokes," I replied. "But if it's even half true it's a tribute to your skill at persuasion."

"No," he said, "it is as you said before. We serve a powerful God, who in his great mercy saved his people from extinction. And you had no small part in it. Perhaps you serve our God after all."

"If Esther had lost her head, I was afraid that Xerxes might ask for me again," I answered. "And I have already served my sentence. Besides, Haman was a smarmy piece of work if ever there was one — pompous little upstart."

"So tell me," Mordecai began as we strolled back towards his escritoire, "how can I render aid to someone who stood by us when things were darkest?"

"Artaxerxes came to see me," I said.

"And Nehemiah is annoying him beyond words," supplied Mordecai. "And you've come either to have Nehemiah sent back to me, or find the reason that I torment the king's son so brazenly."

"Your prescience is surpassed only by your candour," I said. "But leave aside your meddling in Artabanus' domain. This Nehemiah sounds like an unusual choice for a servant."

"He is, I agree. The Day of Purim affected him deeply. It did for many of us, but especially on our youth. They felt so vulnerable, I suppose. There was no safe haven anywhere. And that, they are determined to change. There is much talk among them of going home."

"Home?" I said. "Susa is your home."

"They mean Jerusalem."

"I trust the elders among you are a voice of moderation and caution," I replied in a measured tone. The conversation was straying into dangerous areas.

"Xerxes has let you all live. But what he means is that you should live among us, as Persians. He stopped the rebuilding of Jerusalem's walls once before, and he will do it again. As he should." I peered closely at Mordecai, making sure that he had heard my last sentence. Then a little more gently, "Jerusalem is too close to Egypt, and Egypt is too dangerous to us all. I get reports from my brother. Peace in the Nile delta is precarious despite the autonomy he grants them."

"And I agree with all you say," Mordecai replied. "Still, one good thing has come of Haman's perfidy. We are rediscovering our traditions, our history."

"Nothing like a Day of Purim to focus the mind," I said, glad to have heard his agreement.

"Did you know we were once slaves in Egypt?" he said. "For four hundred years we waited, until our God gave us our freedom and a homeland."

"Mordecai, if I did not know you better, I'd suspect you of fomenting a rebellion. Persia is your homeland, and Xerxes gives you freedom. Tell your youth to be content with what they have. Your words surprise me — more than surprise. They shock and unsettle. Nehemiah will be returned to you." I rose to go.

Springing to his feet with me, he reached for my sleeve. "Please, Vashti, Queen Mother and most loyal of Persians, forgive me. Our conversation has started at the wrong end of things."

I allowed him to steer me back into my chair and he sat as well. "There is another plot against the king," he said quietly. "That is where I should have started. Worse, it may not only be against the king. Some of what we know suggests your sons may be targets as well. Nehemiah — and I have recruited a score more of his temperament — is in my service."

"Who is behind it?" I asked with equal quiet.

"We do not know as yet, nor have we any knowledge of how the plot is to be carried out."

"My sons," I whispered.

Mordecai reached for my sleeve again, and laid his hand ever so gently on my arm. "I am most, most sorry. We do everything that we can."

"Who are your sources?" I asked.

"I would prefer to say only that I've had my suspicions for some time."

"Ever since Bigthana and Teresh?"

He nodded. "I always thought they were part of a bigger conspiracy. It has been over a decade, and I hoped that the plan had been abandoned. Alas, my sources tell me otherwise."

"But if my sons are also at risk, this is not just about Xerxes. They mean to extinguish *all* claimants to the throne. It is not murder you speak of; it's a coup. Some other family seeks to supplant us entirely."

Mordecai said nothing, apparently waiting to see where my line of thought would take me. It did not take me long.

"The Council of Seven. They are the only families who would dare such cupidity. But that's impossible. My family would have heard something. My father is a member."

Mordecai waited a moment, then nudged me toward the final conclusion.

"Unless . . ." he said.

"Unless they are involved." I was not sure if I had said the words aloud or only thought them in my head. Obviously I had spoken them.

"And if they are," Mordecai said, "they would have been careful to keep it from you."

"Unthinkable."

"I agree. But until I know more, everyone is a suspect and no theory can be summarily discarded."

"Has Xerxes been informed?"

Mordecai did not answer immediately. "I am not sure," he said finally. "A private word with him is impossible and even if I had the chance, what would I tell him? Unlike the last time, I can point to no one. What am I to say: 'Be on your guard against everyone?'"

"Send a message, a warning at least, through Esther. She has ample opportunity to speak to Xerxes."

"The king's interests are elsewhere," Mordecai began delicately, "and have been for quite some time."

"He always had a short attention span, among other things. Esther should not be surprised. Still, it's too bad." I didn't really mean it. If Esther was no longer sleeping with the king, at least I didn't have to worry about competing heirs. Popular though she might be, from what Mordecai was suggesting, she wasn't either useful or dangerous. I returned to the more urgent matter and asked, "So, what steps have you taken?"

"I have taken Artabanus into my confidence. He said that Xerxes would be informed. Said also that he too had suspicions. Beyond that we did not talk about our sources. But he thanked me for having warned him."

"It's not the first time."

Mordecai paused. "So now you have the whole story, such as it is."

"Not quite," I answered. "Nehemiah and your band of zealots: why should they be trusted? After all, it was Xerxes who nearly had them all killed."

"No, for that they blame Haman. I'm sorry to have to say it so plainly to you, but Xerxes is regarded as dissolute, and easily manipulated. Their great ambition is to save his life again and be rewarded for it."

"In what manner?" I already suspected the answer.

"To be granted permission to rebuild Jerusalem."

"And you encourage this?"

"Only by a Persian proclamation can we Jews ever hope for a homeland again. We are not fools, nor are we insurgents."

"You did not answer my question. Do you encourage this wild hope?"

Mordecai sighed deeply. "All my life I have looked to the welfare of your family. Susa is where I will be buried, hopefully with honour. Jerusalem will remain only a story for me, and I have made my peace with that. But for others, younger than myself, the Purim has stirred a great longing. And if their motivations can be bent to the service of the king whom I have sworn to protect, then I will exploit it shamelessly."

"So you do support this quest for a homeland."

"Yes!" Mordecai said loudly into my face. All his usual restraint had left him. "Yes, I encourage these hopes. For it means that Nehemiah and his friends cannot be subverted. Money or position mean nothing to them. They simply want to leave. And if saving your former husband's neck will accomplish that, I think they would give their lives to achieve it."[29]

I could not disagree with him. Those whom he'd recruited and deployed throughout the palace would not be corrupted. "Thank you," I said simply. "I will have a word with Artaxerxes. Nehemiah will remain in his retinue, you may be assured of that."

Mordecai nodded his appreciation.

"But what of Darius?" I asked. "Artaxerxes says that only he and Hystaspes have received cupbearers on your initiative. Do you not fear most for my eldest?"

Mordecai smiled quizzically. "I have confided in people only to the extent that they need to know," he said. "But since he is your son, I will tell you. There is one servant within his household that keeps me informed — Bacabasus is his name.[30] He attends your son's wardrobe and therefore has frequent reason to be in Darius' presence." Mordecai smiled again, clearly pleased to show off his far-sighted ingenuity. "He has served your son now for over five years. Bacabasus was among the first I recruited to my service. Darius is unaware of my interests."

"You've been suspicious for that long?"

Mordecai smiled again. "Prudence and Patience. They are a counselor's best friends."

I rose to leave. "Keep me informed," I said. "And should my own spies discover anything, I will likewise send you word."

"Agreed," he answered.

* * *

When my servant roused me from sleep without even an apology and told me that the king commanded my presence, I knew the viper had struck. It was not many days after I'd spoken with Mordecai, and even in my half-waking state, I immediately wondered if our conversation had set something in motion. Impossible, I concluded. Still, I felt uneasy.

I dressed and by the time I reached the courtyard, a small carriage was already waiting. In less than half an hour since being wakened, I stood in the palace foyer. I had already been stopped twice, once on stepping down out of my carriage at the bottom of the steps leading up to the palace entrance and a second time just before the doors to the palace were opened for me. Had I not been so well known I'm not sure I would have gained admittance, despite having been summoned. The king's personal guard were everywhere, and in full battle readiness. Servants dotted the hallways holding extra torches high over their heads so that there were no shadows. I stated my business curtly for the third time to the officer in charge of the palace entrance. The doors to the throne room were scarcely one hundred paces from where we stood. Still, it took four men to escort me, crowding me on all sides.

I entered the cavernous chamber where Xerxes held forth on state business. It was here that Esther had risked her life, approaching through the same doors I had just passed, making her way to the far end and fainting at the bottom of the eight broad steps leading up to Xerxes' elaborate, high-backed throne. But tonight there was no Xerxes. Instead, standing in front of the throne stood Artaxerxes and beside him Artabanus and two of his sons.[31] On the first step, fanned out in precise military pattern, were a score of guards, swords held horizontally out in front of them, barring anyone's approach. I strode half the distance toward the raised dais on which my son stood so that we could clearly see each other. My son held a short sword in one hand. His face was flushed and his eyes were bright and watchful. They held excitement, but no fear. Artabanus too was armed.

"I have been summoned." I raised my voice. "Where is Xerxes?"

"Dead," my son's voice came back to me.

"By whose hand?" My voice was hard and flat, for I had had banished all feelings.

"Darius, your son," Artaxerxes continued, "who has already been recompensed for his treachery."

"Dead as well?" I asked. Calamitous news did not diminish my awareness of his subtle meaning. So already the culprit was 'my son' and not Artaxerxes' brother. And was I to blame for being his mother?

This time it was Artabanus who answered. "Killed in his bed while feigning sleep. Artaxerxes, your son, avenged the murder of his father and now claims the throne, as is his right and duty. I have summoned the Council of Seven and we wait for them here so that they can pledge their fealty without delay. There will be time later for a more formal installation. At present all we need is to know that they will support their new king. Let us hope that Darius acted alone and that none of the noble families harbour like-minded insurgents. But please, approach and join us. Much has occurred here tonight and you should know all."

The guards made a space for me and I made my way to the top of the steps. Ignoring Artabanus, I studied my son's face carefully, looking for some sign of remorse or guilt. If I'd understood what I'd just been told, then he had probably killed his older brother less than an hour ago. It was the first time he had actually plunged his sword into living flesh, at least as far as I knew. I could only guess at what he was feeling. But although his face remained flush with the aftershocks he returned my gaze openly.

"Xerxes summoned me," I began. "How long ago did he die?"

"I summoned you," said Artaxerxes. "I did not want you to hear the news from anyone other than me."

"You are certain Darius slew Xerxes?" I asked.

"Quite." But again it was Artabanus who had answered a question that I had put to my son. He continued. "It was my fate to have discovered the deed. Some urgent dispatches had arrived from one of the provinces, serious enough to disturb the king. I am one of the few with privilege to do so. He had retired in the company of a young girl from the harem so I was discreet when making my entrance."

"The girl?" I asked.

"Bleeding badly and lying beside the king. I asked her who had done this and she named Darius."

"Where is the girl now?"

"She did not survive her wounds."

"And you are certain she named Darius?"

"Yes," Artabanus answered, "but Darius was also seen entering Xerxes' sleeping quarters by the two chamberlains on duty outside his door. They thought nothing of it, and had no cause to challenge him. They are both men I chose myself to serve the king, beyond suspicion."

"I see," was all I said.

Artaxerxes took up telling me the details of what had happened. "Artabanus came directly to me. Darius no doubt would want both me and Hystaspes out of the way so that no one could challenge his claim to the throne. As Artabanus made clear, if not confronted immediately, by morning Darius would well have rallied the court officials and established his claim."

Except that it is you now standing in his place, I thought.

"I suggested we go to Darius at once," Artabanus resumed. "Two of my sons had come to me by this time. With four of us, Darius could not escape, nor could he harm his brother."

"Yet when you entered his quarters, he was asleep on his couch," I said.

"Only pretending," Artaxerxes cut in. "He cried out quickly enough when I thrust my sword into him."

"Mine too." I turned at the voice. It was a son of Artabanus who spoke.

"But in either case, whether asleep or merely pretending, he was not on his way to dispatch his brothers," I replied.

A momentary, sullen silence ensued. Artaxerxes had not expected me to cross-examine him on the night's proceedings. He had accepted what had been told him — nay, had acted on it with the same impulsive haste that I had seen so often in his father. The story leaked badly, but I concluded quickly that little was gained by my continued probing. Xerxes and Darius were dead, justly or unjustly. Artaxerxes was the next legitimate heir and the throne could not remain empty. The least sign of weakness in Artaxerxes, and some other family would quickly mount a challenge. The consequences would be catastrophic to us all. Civil war was a given. And while Persian was busy killing Persian, Egypt would rebel, knowing that our armies would be in disarray. The Empire would be in tatters within a year.

Artaxerxes stood before me, demanding my allegiance. My summons had come 'from the king'. The phrasing had been deliberate. Whatever the truth of the night's events were, Artabanus had thrown his support behind

Artaxerxes. The palace staff, which included the Imperial Guard, would not protest so long as Artabanus did not. Already he was showing himself an able mentor, discreetly in the background. The truth of the night's events was already irrelevant. Power goes to those who act quickly, not to those who seek truth. And somewhere in this chaos was an opportunity for me.

"You have done what best protects the realm," I said finally, attempting a formal and more conciliatory tone. "You have shown that you will bring traitors to account for the deeds and that family is not above your wise justice, however much it is in your heart to show mercy. In everything you have shown yourself worthy to sit on the throne — and be my king." I inclined my head ever so slightly toward my son. It was the most I could bring myself to do. Scarcely a week ago, I thought, and your worst problem was that your cupbearer did not please you. You will need him now more than ever for truly, you have no idea what snares await you.

Having shown that I accepted their version of the evening's events without protest, I thought it safe to ask the one question that was most troubling me. "What drove Darius to such violence?" I ventured. "He would have come to the throne in the natural course of events. No one has ever disputed his rights."

Artabanus replied with a speed that showed he'd already anticipated the question, if not from me, then from others. "Alas, it seems he could never get over his wife having visited Xerxes' bed. You remember the incident, I'm sure, for you were not exactly kind to the girl's mother. Two men are never content to share one woman. Darius was simply biding his time to exact his own vengeance."

"Ah," I said. "Of course."

I took my leave as quickly as I could. Artaxerxes was not the only one who needed to consolidate his power. With Xerxes dead, and my favourite, more compliant son on the throne, my own fortunes had changed. Artabanus would not be the only voice behind Artaxerxes' throne. To begin with, it was time to send Esther packing. A queen widow is not without status, and entitled to sympathy. And it *was* my son who had killed her husband. She was much too well liked at court. Sooner or later, she was bound to get in my way.

* * *

She saw me in a small alcove that jutted out from the hallway just opposite the room where she slept. Only the usual number of servants were at hand, and none of the Imperial Regiment. I was still in advance of the news; there was still time.

Even half-dressed and with her hair still cloyed with sleep, Esther was beautiful. I was surprised that I even thought of such a thing, and pushed my momentary jealousy back inside.

"Xerxes is dead," I began. "Murdered by my eldest son who has in turn been killed by Artaxerxes. At least that is the public story. Who knows who really killed whom. For the moment the killing has stopped and Artaxerxes is marshalling his supporters in the throne room."

Esther took in my news quietly, then asked, "Was he alone — Xerxes, I mean — when he died?"

"No. But count yourself lucky that you had not been sent for. The girl was killed along with him."

"I'm sorry."

I wasn't sure to what specific portion of my news she was referring.

"I have not enjoyed Xerxes' company for some time now." There was something wistful about the way she said it, as if now, on news of his death, she was actually going to miss him. That was the difference between her and me, I thought, she actually had feelings for people.

But aloud, I only snorted. "Most women would be relieved. But none of that matters now. What matters is that by morning, Persians will have a new king, backed by the Council of Seven and the families they represent.

And what matters most to *you* is that Xerxes' women will no longer serve any useful purpose. They are one of the few possessions that are not passed along. In short, they are taking up valuable space that will soon be occupied by others. They will be cleared out like so much palace dreck. The ones from good families will be sent home. The others," — I stopped and shrugged — "Xerxes' horses will receive more attentive consideration."

"Including the queen?" Esther asked.

"Especially the queen," I replied. "Why do you think I've come to you so urgently? By morning, I would not even vouch for your liberty."

"You mean I would be imprisoned?"

"Or something worse. If you had family or children, it might be different."

"You mean, if I was one of you," said Esther.

"Yes, to put it bluntly. But you are not."

"No. As you told me so long ago, I am but an amusement." A soft smile played over Esther's face. "And now the entertainment has ended."

"I have always spoken plainly to you and will again, especially at this hour. You are simply the late king's most visible bedroom bauble and of no use to anyone. And now something of an embarrassment. Nobody wants the king's widow hanging on at court."

"And you have come not only to warn me, but also to give advice, no doubt," said Esther. "I have always admired the speed with which you grasp the essence of things. So tell me, what do you suggest?"

"Disappear."

"Tonight?"

"Now. Get out of Susa. Go somewhere far, far away and live out your days under some other name. You have saved your people. Now it is their turn to save you. Disappear so that you cannot be found. Go back to being the orphan girl you were before all this."

"Hadassah."

"What?"

"Hadassah.[32] That was my name before Mordecai made me change it."

"Then go and be that woman again."

"But I've done nothing wrong."

"You had the king's confidence. Who knows what secrets he told you over the years. What's wrong is that you are a queen without a king to protect her. Artaxerxes will be married within a year, the Council of Seven will see to that. And whoever he marries had best deliver an heir in short order.[33] How long would you last under the new regime? Every memory of Xerxes will be extinguished, and that includes you."

"But how can I leave tonight?"

"Go back inside your room. Gather together a few clothes — and your jewelry, of course. But put on a long cloak with a cowl that covers your face. Then come with me as my servant. My carriage is outside the main entrance. After I have returned home it will take you wherever you wish to go. Travel in it for weeks if you need to. Only when you are safely hidden away should you send word to Mordecai. If asked about your disappearance, he must be able to say truthfully that he has knows nothing of how you left, nor of your whereabouts. Many a jackal will be drooling after his job, looking for a chance to catch him out in some deceit."

"You are certain that Darius was the cause of Xerxes' death? That he acted alone and there is no bigger conspiracy?"

"Yes," I answered. "And Artaxerxes has already killed him. But why do you care about that?"

"My hasty disappearance will attract rumours. I would rather die than risk having my people suffer for another 'Jewish conspiracy.' One thing Haman's actions have taught us all is that we make convenient scapegoats."

"Persian has betrayed Persian. This night's violence is of our own doing."

"Then I will come with you and do as you suggest. Once again you have shown me great kindness." She looked pointedly into my face. "And you of course gain nothing in return."

"Be quick," I replied. "I will wait here for you."

* * *

So Esther disappeared and was never heard from again.[34] When my carriage arrived back home some two weeks afterwards, I asked no questions of the driver. Whether Mordecai ever got news from her I do not know for we never spoke of Esther again. It was as if she had never existed.

Had I told Esther the truth about the danger she faced by staying at court? No, of course not. And given a day or two to think about it, she probably would have seen through my urgent sophistry. But I have absolutely no regret about having lied to her. People hear what they want to hear, and seek a version of the truth that justifies their desires. I was just giving Esther a reason and the means to do what she had always wanted to do — leave the court. She had always wanted freedom. In the end, I gave her what she most wanted.

Within two weeks of Xerxes' death, I had returned to court. Artaxerxes genuinely welcomed me and provided me quarters in keeping with my station. Old "uncle" Artabanus would not be the only dulcet voice whispering wise counsel from behind the throne. He was about to be joined by the Queen Mother. Artaxerxes and I would make good rulers. The familiar scent of power had never smelled so sweet. And now it was mine to wear again.

* * *

Less than a month after his formal installation, Artaxerxes arrived without notice at my quarters while I was still having breakfast. He came with only one servant, whom he left standing just outside my doors. Trouble was writ large on his open face.

It's hard on you, I thought. Here you are, the most powerful man alive, looking like a frightened boy who has done something dreadful. We have asked you to grow up faster than is possible. You are not yet even twenty.[35] Our kings do not wander the halls, visiting their subjects like a tremulous suitor. They sit on the great throne, as avatars, caparisoned in splendour, striking fear into all who dare approach. But at this present moment you look for all the world like a boy in search of his mother's comfort.

"I have been betrayed," he said, "so much so that, apart from you I do not know who my real friends are."[36]

"You are our king, now," I said gently. "And as such you have no friends; only officials whose momentary interests are aligned with yours. So who was the first to disappoint you. Tell me it is not Nehemiah. After the fuss I made to make you keep him, I would be shamefaced if he proved unworthy." I gave my son an encouraging smile.

"No," Artaxerxes said with wood-like seriousness. "Nehemiah sticks to me still like a burr on my sandal. I cannot get rid of him and at present I am glad of it. It's he who waits outside. And it's from him that I learned of the treachery that still stalks us all."

"Tell me everything," I said, as gently as before. My son is in shock, I thought. What new disaster has struck?

"The night Xerxes was killed, my brother Darius never left his apartments. So says his wardrobe chamberlain. He came to Nehemiah — they are both Jews. Nehemiah, in turn, told me.

And Mordecai as well, no doubt, I thought.

"Go on," I said.

"If true," continued Artaxerxes, "then Artabanus has misled us all and I — " he stopped and for a minute I wondered if he was going to cry " — and I have killed my brother without cause. Artabanus is the only other person who had opportunity to kill the king. By his own admission he was there.

He woke me personally with the news. And we have only his version of the night's events. The harem girl is dead."

"Killed by Artabanus just as easily as by Darius," I cut in. "But what of the attendants who claim to have seen Darius enter Xerxes' rooms?"

"I cannot find them," answered Artaxerxes. "My enquiries were covert, I assure you, but they were thorough. They are no longer at court and no one seems to know where they went."

"Handpicked by Artabanus himself to attend the king," I replied. "Convenient."

Artaxerxes looked desperately up at me, as if hoping that at any moment I might pull some magic salve from beneath my sleeve to soothe his distress. He did not speak, only kept staring at me.

"So," I continued, "it seems we have two possibilities. Either things happened just as Artabanus says they did, or this servant — what is his name?"

"Bacabasus."[37]

"Or this Bacabasus speaks the truth and you indeed have shed the innocent blood of your brother, while the true murderer remains your closest counselor. They cannot both be right. And if Artabanus is the viper you now think he is, how long do you think it will be before *you* meet with some tragic mishap?"

Artaxerxes did not answer. Instead he said, "Mother, what should I do?"

It was the question I'd been waiting for.

"Whom do you believe?"

"The servant. If Darius had truly killed my father, returning to bed and feigning sleep is the last thing he would do. I acted hastily when Artabanus first came to me."

No, I thought. You believed what you wanted to believe. It let you kill your brother and take the throne for yourself under the guise of justice.

Except now, you realize that your own position is tenuous and that the man who helped you gain the crown now means to take it from you.

"There is another reason I believe that Darius did not kill Xerxes," my son continued. "These Jews who serve us gain nothing by lying. Artabanus, on the other hand, commands enough respect to wear my crown himself if he could seize it. Already I see that some of the noble families treat him as if he were the true king and I am a kind of figurehead. You are right about his influence over me. I am much too easily led."

"It is only because of your age," I assured him. "Do not question your courage. You shall soon have a chance to show the world your fortitude."

"So what's to be done?" Artaxerxes repeated his question.

"Kill Artabanus, of course. Kill him publicly and as brutally as you can. Assemble the Imperial Regiment as if for an inspection. Artabanus will be there. Then, while everyone is looking, cut him down with your own sword. Do not give him time to speak. You are king. Stand before your troops with bloodied hands and tell them that this is the fate of all traitors who dare to defy your power. Shout it out. Recount the foul deeds of the savage and how he abused the trust he had been given. Accuse him of all manner of atrocities. Cut off his head if you like, and mount it on a pike pole. Parade it in front of your guardsmen. Let his body rot in a fetid memorial to your retribution. Dispatch troops and round up his sons. Make sure that they too are dead before the day is out. If you want people to follow you, first, make them fear you. There is time afterwards for beneficence."[38]

"But what of his supporters?" Artaxerxes asked.

"Once Artabanus is dead," I replied, "who is there to support?"

"You speak as if I were a thespian, about to deliver my lines in some epic drama; not planning to disembowel a man who has cared for me like a father."

"Do not scorn the power of theatre," I retorted. "It is a time-honoured art of kings. And you recoil from killing an old friend? You find it abhorrent?"

I drew him close to me, held both his arms until our faces were only inches away. "My son, if you would be king, then show yourself worthy — not to me, not even to the courtiers and officers however much you need their good opinion. Show yourself worthy to yourself. Reach deep within and find the strength to do this wretched piece of justice. Avenge the memory of your father and the blood of your brother. It is the only way you will sit on the throne with any kind of peace."

"I shall do it," he answered. I watched him leave, walking taller.

I wasn't worried that he might not succeed. We are all mixtures of good and bad, ambition and humility. Artaxerxes, despite his gentleness, was still my son. Deep down, he coveted the throne and would do what it took to secure it. Deep down, I knew that through him, my own influence would increase. Neither one of us had expressed regret about what he'd done to his brother. It served us both that Darius was dead. More than each other, our family loved power.

Artaxerxes and I would rule Persia well.

* * *

My son killed Artabanus and no one objected. He did it publicly and I was told that he did a clean job of it. Mordecai retired full of years and honour from Persian and Jew alike. He never lived to see Jerusalem. The memorial over his grave reads, "He worked for the advancement of his people and the welfare of Jews everywhere."[39] Nehemiah remained irritatingly vigilant and, yes, strangely enough, he and Artaxerxes developed an odd affection for each other. No one ever tried to poison my son![40]

But not before twenty years had passed would Artaxerxes send the Jews to go restore their beloved city. For most of that time, my son was adamantly opposed to the idea. [41] To hear Nehemiah tell the tale[42] — his memoirs are widely published — you'd think that permission was granted *solely* out of the great love my son had for his cupbearer. Be careful when you read

Nehemiah's version of things. It's a hero's account of himself. His enemies are large and legion, and success is impossible were it not for the power of his sovereign God, Yahweh — oh, and Nehemiah's brilliant leadership and commanding personality.

Were the Jews allowed to go? Or were they sent?

Truth is a murky business. The Persian truth is that Artaxerxes and I needed to populate our southern flank with loyal subjects, people who would be especially indebted to my son and not swayed by the winds of independence that blew so constantly in the area. Who better to watch over our backside than the Jews, especially with Nehemiah in charge? By the end of their exodus, fifty thousand Jews went back to their precious homeland.

In the end, everybody got what they wanted.

* * *

So that is my story, of how the Jews were not annihilated by Haman, of how Esther was our queen for a time, and how Nehemiah went to rebuild the walls of Jerusalem. Think of me when you read the Jewish versions. Did Yahweh steer the events of Persia — steer my life — all in accordance with some grand salvation history? If so, he is a busy God — some would say overly involved in the affairs of men.

Perhaps he had a hand in it.

For certain, I did.

* * *

The name of God does not appear in the book of Esther.

ENDNOTES

1. The wife of King Xerxes is called Vashti only in the book of *Esther*. All other historical sources identify one Amëstris, from one of the seven noble families, as his only wife. She was the birth mother of his three children, and there is no record of a divorce. Furthermore, Amëstris accompanied Xerxes on the Greek campaign in 480 BC, three years after the date that *Esther* says she was divorced.

Scholars have made much of the various inconsistencies between the details of *Esther* and other historical accounts of the same history. Those who insist on the historical accuracy of *Esther* for the sake of dogma go to great lengths seeking a synthesis in the facts. Clear resolution on scholarly, textual, or archeological evidence is just not possible.

Since this is a work of literature, however, I have deliberately constructed a story that draws on all sources of information. My starting point was to treat Vashti and Amëstris as the same person and that the biblical story of *Esther* should be taken at face value. Vashti's cruelty, her influence over her sons, and her meddling in foreign affairs are all based on historical accounts from Amëstris's life. Similarly, the drama of Purim as described in *Esther* is assumed to be equally valid history. To arbitrarily assume that Herodotus is a more honest or accurate historian than the Jewish writer of *Esther* borders on either philosophical presumption, or, worse, secular bigotry. To those scholars who cringe at my temerity in resolving historical conflicts with such simplicity, I humbly point out that "the absence of evidence is not the evidence of absence." I encourage you to read the biblical book of *Esther* and judge for yourself whether this interpretation of the events is within the realm of the possible.

2. In some versions of Esther's story, Purim is referred to as the *"Day of Mordecai."* It suggests that the conflict between Haman and Mordecai was considered the essence of the story and that Esther played a subordinate role in saving her people.

3. Louis Ginzberg (*Legend of the Jews*, Volume IV, Chapter 12) records an elaborate version of the Esther story that closely resembles a fairy tale. A second version was written by Josephus, a first-century historian. In the details, his account follows the biblical version. There is one glaring inconsistency to this section of his work: he confuses Xerxes with his son Artaxerxes and therefore places the whole story somewhat later in history.

4. This ancient India fable was made popular by the American poet John Godfrey Saxe, 1816–1867.

5. Amëstris died in 422 BC at the age of 83, the same year her son Artax-

erxes also died. Conceivably, she would have lived to see three Persian kings die — her uncle Darius (522–486), her husband Xerxes (486–465) and her son Artaxerxes (465–422).

6. So says Louis Ginzberg, page 8.

7. Herodotus, in *The Histories*, Bk IX, Sections 108-113.

8. If we use the dates provided in *Esther*, Vashti's divorce took place in 483, Esther's coronation in January of 478 and Purim in 473. However, from other sources we know that Xerxes was campaigning in Europe from about 482 to 479. To correlate the story of Esther with other historical documents, the search for a new queen took almost five years during which Xerxes was largely absent.

9. Vashti's concern that her sons remain the uncontested heirs to the throne was not at all theoretical. Darius, Xerxes' father, had three sons by one wife, and four more by another. The two eldest sons each claimed to be the legitimate heir to the throne. The issue was resolved peaceably but not without fierce arguments from both sons. The stakes were obviously high and, as we have already seen in the story, fratricide was not uncommon.

10. The actual size of Xerxes' army is hotly contested among the historians with no resolution possible. In keeping with Xerxes' character, I have chosen a figure of appropriate priapic proportions.

11. Artaxerxes retained this nickname until he assumed the throne in 465BC.

12. The first confrontation between the ancestors of Mordecai and Haman took place about one thousand years before the time of this story. In about 1500 BC, the tribe of Amalek (Amalekites) attacked the Israelites while they were traveling from Egypt to the Promised Land. While Moses observed from a high hill, Joshua decisively defeated the Amalekites. At the end, God (speaking through Moses) declared a solemn oath that He would completely blot out the memory of the Amalekites and 'The LORD will be at war against the Amalekites from generation to generation.' This first encounter is described in Exodus 17: 8–16 and makes interesting reading.

Five hundred years later (1000 BC), King Saul, from the tribe of Benjamin, Israel's first king, is instructed by the prophet Samuel to engage the Amalekites and totally destroy them. On gaining victory, however, Saul chooses to spare the life of their king (Agag) along with the better specimens of livestock. Samuel confronts Saul with his deceit and kills Agag himself. For this act of disobedience, the kingdom is taken from Saul and it is King David who is anointed king in Saul's place.

By linking Haman to the Amalekites, the author of *Esther* cleverly brings forward this ancient feud and invokes the original oath of God that all Amalekites will be destroyed. Mordecai is also from the tribe of Benjamin, and will complete the job originally given to his ancestor Saul. Haman's death is therefore seen as fulfillment of an ancient prophecy dating back to the days of Moses.

Some fictional re-writers of *Esther* have made much of these literary clues on which to formulate plot and motive, even suggesting that it was Haman's family that killed Esther's parents, leaving her an orphan in the care of Mordecai. Whatever one may conjecture, these literary allusions to Israel's ancient history show remarkable skill of the original storyteller.

13. A cuneiform tablet, discovered near Babylon, mentions a certain Mardukaya who was a senior accountant or minister of finance for King Xerxes. The names are sufficiently close that some scholars have equated this person with Mordecai. The book of *Esther* does not specify Mordecai's occupation.

14. Louis Ginzberg's *Legend of the Jews* explains Mordecai's refusal to "bend the knee" was because Haman had fastened an idol to his cloak, which Mordecai in good Jewish conscience refused to honour. However, the legend goes on to explain that the entrenched enmity between the two men stemmed from a time when they were both generals in Xerxes' army, sent to subdue an uprising in India. Haman foolishly squandered his supplies very quickly and, when his troops threatened to mutiny, sought aid from Mordecai. The terms of Mordecai's help were somewhat severe: Haman was to be the slave of Mordecai in perpetuity. The contract was inscribed on Mordecai's knee. Rather than "bend the knee" to Haman, it had been Mordecai's habit to flex his own knee whenever the two men met so as to remind Haman of his obligation. Haman was constantly apprehensive that Mordecai would make public his indebtedness, causing Haman great embarrassment.

15. Named in Esther 2:21.

16. In one variant legend of Esther, Mordecai is said to have uncovered the plot because of his linguistic skills. Bigthan and Teresh were said to be conspiring together in their native tongue, Tarsian, thinking that no one would understand them. Mordecai, however, being a member of the Sanhedrin, ". . . knew all the seventy languages of the world. Thus their own tongue betrayed them" (Ginsberg, *Legend of the Jews*).

17. Named in Esther 4:4 ff. This eunuch, assigned to Esther, was the courier between Mordecai and Esther. He would meet Mordecai in some public place and often take back written instructions or documents for Esther to read.

18. April 14th, 474 BC, according to the Roman calendar.

19. Esther 3:15.

20. March 7th 473 BC, almost one year from the publication date.

21. This particular version was taken from the writings of Josephus, a first

century Jewish historian, whose twenty-volume history of the Jews is entitled *Jewish Antiquities* (Bk II, chapter 6).

22. See Ezra 4:6ff. Xerxes did in fact stop Jerusalem's reconstruction in 486BC, the year he assumed the throne. It is not clear that he knew of his father's previous support and sympathy. However, it is clear that relations with Egypt were strained and in 484 BC Xerxes was forced to put down a serious revolt by Egyptian insurgents. It is understandable that he would be wary of allowing any walled city that could be used against him in some future campaign. It was Xerxes' son, Artaxerxes, who in 445 BC eventually permitted reconstruction to resume. Nehemiah, his Jewish cupbearer, was given leave to complete the restoration.

23. Esther 4:16 contains Esther's classic line *"If I perish, I perish."* In the canonical version, she sends it in a written communication to Mordecai telling him of her resolve to go and plead for the Jews, asking that he gather up the Jews of Susa to pray for her while she makes her attempt. It is the last communiqué she has with Mordecai until the drama is complete.

24. Haman was consulted, but was under the mistaken impression that he was the man whom Xerxes wished to honour. What he hoped would be a hugely public aggrandizement became instead a humiliation.

25. Esther chapter 7 contains the details of this last banquet, abruptly ending in Haman's death.

26. Based on a version written by Josephus, in his *Jewish Antiquities* (Bk II, Ch. 6).

27. The Roman historian Justin, writing in AD 300, states that Xerxes had become "an object of contempt even to his own subjects." Whether because of his bungled war with the Greeks or his extravagant hedonism, some historians suggest that his murder was motivated by a general disgust for his leadership and a desire to replace the family with one who would restore Persian glory.

28. As reported by Josephus in his account of this story.

29. The idea that highly placed Jews deliberately sought to curry royal Persian favour in the hopes of being able to return to their homeland is not simply an arbitrary literary device. While there is no direct historical evidence, no fewer than three successive Persian kings received exceptionally loyal service from highly placed Jewish courtiers. The tradition began with Daniel, who served King Darius, was continued by Mordecai who saved the life of Xerxes, and completed by Nehemiah who was the cupbearer to Artaxerxes. Each Persian king in turn showed some special dispensation to the Jewish community. Darius authorized the rebuilding of the Jerusalem temple, going so far as to advance royal funds to the cause. Xerxes revoked Haman's decree and promoted

Mordecai to the rank of Grand Vizier. Artaxerxes not only granted Nehemiah an eleven-year leave of absence to rebuild Jerusalem, he also appointed Ezra as a kind of Minister of Jewish affairs, granting him authority to reinstate Jewish ritual law within the province of Judah (Yehud).

Assuming that the story of Esther with its Day of Purim has historical validity, it is logical to think that in its aftermath the desire for some kind of permanent sanctuary (i.e., Jerusalem) would have increased. Certainly Jewish piety grew in popularity, as witnessed by Ezra's influence in establishing a number of academies to research and practice Mosaic rituals. In fact, it was Persian Jews who compiled what is referred to as Torah — the words of Moses. Highly placed Jews would have been quite willing to pursue a political strategy at court that would secure the Jews' the right to return home.

Whatever Nehemiah's actual role was in helping Artaxerxes ascend the throne and avoid being murdered by treasonous elements seeking to establish a new Persian dynasty, one cannot deny the enormity of the boon he was granted when allowed to rebuild Jerusalem.

30. The name of the informant comes from one of the historical accounts. It is not clear exactly how Artaxerxes discovered Artabanus' perfidy.

31. In one version of Xerxes' murder, Artabanus is assisted by his "seven stout sons," one of whom thrust his sword into the sleeping Darius at the same time that Artaxerxes did. Whether to be doubly sure of the murder, or because the teenaged Artaxerxes who was "but a boy" might have been squeamish about killing his brother, the story does not say.

32. Esther 2:7: Mordecai did not explicitly tell her to change her name. But the etymology of Esther is Persian (meaning 'star'), while Hadassah is Hebrew (meaning 'myrtle').

33. Artaxerxes did in fact marry a woman named Damaspia, but she provided only one heir to the throne. When Artaxerxes died (425 BC) his one legitimate son reigned for only 45 days before being killed by a consortium of illegitimate half-brothers. Vashti's concern that Esther might provide competing progeny is not simply a literary device. Persian dynasties were inherently unstable.

34. There is no mention of Esther outside of the canonical story.

35. Artaxerxes was thought to be about eighteen years of age when he ascended to the throne. He died in 425 BC at about age 61.

36. There are four historical accounts of how Xerxes was murdered and his middle son, Artaxerxes, came to the throne. The three main ancient authors are: (a) Diodorus, a first-century Greek historian, (b) Justin, a third-century Roman historian, (c) Ctesias, who wrote in 400 BC and was a Greek physician serving

in the Persian court. Aristotle also makes passing reference to this intrigue. It is impossible to reconstruct the sources into a unified narrative. The writers are in agreement only that:

> 1. Xerxes was murdered;
>
> 2. someone named Artabanus, a senior court official (king's chief butler, chief of palace security, cupbearer, Grand Vizier or head magus depending on the source), was the murderer;
>
> 3. Artaxerxes was a pawn of Artabanus when he killed his older brother, but that,
>
> 4. on being informed of the treason, Artaxerxes quickly dispatched Artabanus and his sons.

37. This is the name of the butler in Justinus' (a third-century Roman historian) account who, on being taken into Artabanus' confidence, "was content that the government should remain in the present family and disclosed the whole matter to Artaxerxes, acquainting him by what means his father had been killed, and how his brother had been murdered on false suspicion of parricide; and, finally how a plot was being laid for himself (Artaxerxes). Artaxerxes, fearing the number of Artabanus' sons, gave orders for the troops to be ready under arms on the following day, as if he meant to ascertain their strength. Artabanus accordingly presented himself under arms among the rest: the king, pretending that his corslet was too short for him, desired Artabanus to make an exchange with him and, while he was disarming himself, and defenceless, ran him through with his sword, ordering his sons at the same time to be apprehended" (*Epitome of the Philippic History of Pompeius Trogus*, Book III, Paragraph 1, Marcus Junianus Justinus).

38. Artaxerxes was generally remembered for his gentleness, nobleness of spirit and reasonable administration.

39. Esther 10:3.

40. Artaxerxes was the only Persian king not to be murdered while in office.

41. See Ezra 4:7–24. This passage summarizes official correspondence between local Samarian functionaries, inimical to Jewish interests who wrote Artaxerxes, warning him that local Jewish citizens had begun to restore Jerusalem's walls without any royal authorization. Artaxerxes promptly ordered an injunction against the work. Assuming that the king is correctly named, then sometime within the first fifteen years of Artxerxes' rule, (465–450 BC), having a fortified city on the south-west flank of the empire was considered a threat. The most logical timing of what Ezra describes would be during the Egyptian uprising (460–454 BC).

42 The opening portions of the Old Testament book entitled *Nehemiah* describe how Artaxerxes gave Nehemiah permission to return to Jerusalem. The book is an autobiographical memoir of the restoration of Jerusalem under the stellar leadership of Nehemiah (the author), and the hardships he faced completing the task.

THE LEFT HAND OF GOD

Nehemiah Viewing Secretly the ruins of the Walls of Jerusalem.
Gustave Doré (1832–1883)

S anballat squatted over the low clay pot. Every muscle in his body strained in the same service. Blood flowed to his face and air backed up behind his tightly pursed lips. It was the third time he'd sought out the pot in as many hours. The day wasn't beginning well at all. He closed his eyes, tightened his abdomen, and pushed. It was as close as a man could get to being in labour. He closed his eyes and prayed:

Why do you visit such trials on me, O Lord? Nehemiah will leave nothing but trouble behind him, and I will have to clean it up. How many times must you punish your people with false hope?

The prayer came to him with the same honest urgency that seized his body. A quick series of sounds — the soft thuds of small wet clumps together with much liquid, hitting the bottom of the pot. Sanballat's body relaxed. He had never quite figured out why praying came so naturally to him while squatting on a commode. No doubt any priest who knew of his habits would be scandalized. But something about the lowly act of voiding his bowels created absolute honesty. There was no hiding anything from the great YHWH. Yahweh, the God of Abraham, Isaac and Jacob, maker of heaven and earth. And since nothing could be hidden, why not tell the God of his people what was really worrying him? Wasn't that the whole point of a prayer?

Sanballat reached for a strip of cloth from the pile laid out beside the pot and began to clean himself.

I spend more time sitting here than I do in my receiving room, he thought. It's the food they served me last night. It's always the same in these country outposts. Their governor arrives and immediately they kill their fattest sheep and serve her up in a year's worth of olive oil. What do they think will be the result to a man's bowels? Why can't they just give me porridge?

But even as he cursed the excess of last night's welcoming banquet he knew that it was not to blame. He was a worrier. It was no joke when they said that a man could feel things in his gut, although people were careful to avoid any such turn of phrase in his presence.

Sanballat held his province together through worry[1]. The particular worry that kept driving him back to the latrine was news that a Jew named Nehemiah had arrived in Jerusalem fresh from the king's throne room at Susa. On hearing the news, Sanballat had ridden down from his own headquarters of Samaria — thirty miles further north — to take up provisional command at Beth-Horan only five miles north of Jerusalem. He liked to be close to his problems. The local mayor hadn't been happy; Sanballat had arrived with a dozen militia, his daughter Nikaso, and a small retinue of servants, who had promptly taken over the mayor's house and office. He was still not clear in his own mind how Nikaso[2] had convinced him that she should tag along. But like any father, he found it hard to deny the gracious and sly petitions of his only daughter. Not until it was far too late to do anything about it would he find out the real reason she had connived to accompany him.

* * *

Nehemiah's days always started with prayer. For most of his life, he had found some palace window that faced west toward Jerusalem. It had to have a low sill. Otherwise when Nehemiah kneeled he sometimes couldn't see out. Height didn't run in his family. But today any low window would do. Nehemiah was *in* Jerusalem. He'd arrived a few weeks ago from the city of Susa, capital of the Persian Empire. Since he'd arrived his prayers had taken on both new fervour and focus. Nevertheless they retained the same stilted formality he'd used all his life

God of heaven, the great and awesome God who keeps his covenant of love with those who love him: Let your ear be attentive and your eyes open to the prayer of your servant. Grant me success for your sake. Let the walls of Jerusalem rise for your glory and for the protection of your people.

And while he could not quite bring himself to actually say the words that next came into his mind, he at least thought them before getting to his feet. *And may all who oppose me in this be sent to hell!*

He hurried to meet his brother. Nehemiah always hurried.

* * *

Sanballat straightened his tunic, tightened his belt around his mostly still-firm stomach — he always cinched it tighter on these state visits — and readied himself to reenter the room he'd left so hurriedly a few moments earlier. Sanballat, satrap of the Province of Samaria, appointed by the great King Artaxerxes, ruler of three million square miles of Persian soil; Sanballat, a loyal governor of an obscure province but whose district had never once been late in remitting its taxes and whose citizens had never rebelled. True, Sanballat had never actually met his Persian master. The closest he ever got to the throne was his immediate superior — a man named Megabyzus whose seat of office was three hundred miles away at Damascus. But insofar as the tiny town of Beth-Horan was concerned, *he* was Persia's might and majesty.

Except now, it would appear, so also was Nehemiah, not five miles away.

For all its size and sprawl, the Persian Empire was remarkably simple in its structure. There were one hundred and twenty-seven[3] "Sanballats" scattered throughout the Empire who were court-appointed provincial governors, but only about twenty "Megabyzuses" in whose territories the governors operated. The dual reporting was an excellent check against unbridled ambition at any level.

The rules were clear and easily remembered: loyalty above all else; collect the taxes, send them on time, and keep the regional peace. As for how a governor achieved these goals, well, local initiatives were expected and each regent, satrap, governor, town mayor or district overseer — the entire chain of command — was surprisingly original in how each official managed his allotted fiefdom.

He re-entered the room to be met by a servant announcing that Tobiah had just arrived in the town. Sanballat hurried to the open courtyard in time for Tobiah's bulk to lumber into sight. Tobiah wasn't just fat. He was huge. A solid, square mass of flesh encased in a billowing blue tunic. Though the heat of the day still lay before them, Tobiah's head — perched atop his body like an olive garnish — shone bright with sweat. Both he and his donkey gave loud sighs of relief when Tobiah finally dismounted.

"Sanballat! Ruler of all the lands that matter in the kingdom of Artaxerxes." The loud salubrious salutation rolled out of Tobiah's mouth. Sanballat's mood lifted just at seeing his friend.

"Tobiah! My most favoured underling whose fawning devotion is an example for all who seek advancement," Sanballat said. "Come close and I'll try to get my arms around you, though from the looks of you it's still an impossible task."

Sanballat did in fact try to embrace his friend and both laughed at the failed attempt. Tobiah made people happy. It was his magic, made all the more potent because he was sincere in his art.

"How goes it?" Sanballat asked.

"God is good." Tobiah chuckled at his own well-worn joke: his reply was also the meaning of his name. "But you, Sanballat, look even worse than when you last gave me the joy of your company. Tell me, how is it with your bowels? Did you try to eat the dried almonds I sent?" He was probably the only man who could ask such an intimate question — in a low tone, of course, so no one else could hear — but impertinent just the same. From the mouth of anyone else, Sanballat would have had the offending tongue cut out without hesitation. He might have been a worrier, but he wasn't weak-willed.

But that was the charm of Tobiah. He was genuinely concerned for his more senior official. Sanballat did not answer, instead asked, "Is it true? Has Nehemiah arrived, then?"

"It is, and has wasted not a minute."

"You've met him?"

"No. I especially avoided him once I heard you were coming down. Didn't have any idea what the official response was supposed to be. Embarrassing for us both if I'd sent the wrong kind of messages. Thought it best to leave the field unsullied, as it were."

"That was wise. Besides, my friend, you have totally lost the finer arts of how to be rude and intimidating."

"I just want to help my fellow man carry his burdens."

"So there's a chance he has arrived without authority then?"

"No. Sadly I must confirm that his writ is quite in order; bears the seal of King Artaxerxes. And clearly states that Jerusalem's walls can be rebuilt. Published in Elamite, Babylonian, Aramaic and Hebrew. Four languages! That was an impressive touch. Shecaniah, my father-in-law, asked to read it and came directly to me afterwards. I'd sent Eliashib along as well. Shecaniah is forgetting things. But Eliashib is still in good form."

"What kind of man is he?" Sanballat asked, referring to Nehemiah. He needed to give his latest worry a face and personality. They gave at least some boundaries to what otherwise remained a shadowy enigma.

"Short and arrogant, according to my father-in-law. And he spits when he speaks. Eliashib changed his clothes afterwards. Muttered something about Persian drool having contaminated his priestly vestments. What is it about short men that makes them so prickly?" Tobiah mused out loud. "They seem to be happiest when they are most disagreeable."

"It's not just his stature," Sanballat offered. "Even you might be full of tetch if the seed of Abraham no longer lay within you."

"All too true." Tobiah touched his groin instinctively as if to reassure himself that none of his more intimate parts was missing. "A short eunuch. Calamity twice over. Whatever was God thinking of?"

"What of Nehemiah's brother, the one who scouted your area a few years back? I remember getting a report of his tour. What was his name? — Henni-something."

"Hananiah. He's been seen wearing an Imperial regimental uniform. Has a small unit of cavalry with him. They're impressive, from what my friends have told me. Fine mounts, and their regimental standard shows them to be a corps of the *Immortals*.[4] But I don't think they're much more than ceremony; thirty men at most. I take that as a hopeful sign."

"In what way?" It was not in Sanballat's nature to receive even the smallest scrap of hope without sniffing it quite carefully.

"It means that Artaxerxes may not care whether Nehemiah succeeds or not. He may just be letting his cupbearer indulge in a little fun. If Jerusalem were really all that important to the empire Artaxerxes would have sent a corps each of troops and engineers."

Sanballat was not about to be comforted so easily. "But a royal writ — "

" — that makes him governor of a ruined and deserted city and an equally broken down province you can ride through in a day. You are better off without them. You know how hard it's been to collect taxes these past ten years. And no one has honoured you for your provisional care."

"Tobiah, you see the whole world as a banquet of optimism. Your brains are now as fat as the rest of you."

"Fat, loyal and happy," Tobiah chortled. "I am bewildered that you still find me fit to do your bidding."

"Only until I find better help."

"Or until Megabyzus promotes me over you!"

Sanballat's immediate superior, Megabyzus, was Viceroy for "The Lands Beyond the River," or functionally speaking, everything that lay to the southwest of the Euphrates but north of Egypt. In his dealings with him, Sanballat was both cordial and cautious. He didn't know all the details, only that there had been a serious confrontation with the king that had bordered on treason. It had lasted three years and there had been rumours of civil war. But whatever the reasons for his tiff with Artaxerxes, just at present, Megabyzus was something of a court favourite. Still, his political fortunes seemed unstable, and Sanballat had no wish to lose his head in the event Megabyzus lost his.

Tobiah was Sanballat's appointment and the two of them went back a long way. Fast approaching fifty, they had been close friends for thirty years. Both men had worked their way up within their respective territories. It was really just fate that made Sanballat the senior ranking official; Samaria was Sanballat's home base and not only was it the largest city in the region, it was closer to Damascus, where Megabyzus held court. But both men were content in their appointed stations. Once, a very long time ago it seemed now, when they did not know each other well, they had gotten horribly drunk together and discovered that they shared a common ambition: "to die of old age."

"It's the tallest stalk of corn that loses its head first," Tobiah blathered. And Sanballat had farted his agreement. Governance had somehow seemed more straightforward when they were younger.

Both he and Tobiah came from Jewish families that had somehow kept their lineage intact against considerable odds. If the nation of Israel was once a stout and lofty tree in the forest of nations, it was by this time reduced to a stump with only the slenderest of shoots still alive. It had taken two savage axe blows to fell it. The first and cruelest had been delivered by the Assyrians three hundred years earlier. Ten of Israel's twelve tribes were wiped out, either killed or deported without hope of ever returning to their homeland. Sanballat's family had been part of a small group that had by some miracle stayed in the land.[5] Abraham, they still maintained, was their father, Moses was their prophet, and Yahweh was their God.

The misfortunes heaped upon Tobiah's forebears were relatively more recent. It had only been one hundred and fifty years since Nebuchadnezzar, ruling from Babylon, had pulled down the walls of Jerusalem and carted away Israel's last king together with a few thousand of its brightest citizens.[6] The Babylonians were remarkably humane — or astute — and allowed these exiled Jews to live as a distinct group, transplanted seedlings forced to make a go of it in foreign soil. Many had done quite well for themselves. Tobiah's forebears, however, had not been exiled. Instead, they had been part of a small group of Jews that had escaped Nebuchadnezzar's army by fleeing to Ammonite territory nearby. His family was the most dominant and wealthiest in the region.[7]

"I bring to you an invitation from my father-in-law, Shecaniah," Tobiah said, jostling Sanballat back to the present. "He would be honoured if you would grace his poor table with your presence, etcetera, etcetera, etcetera."

"You know full well I cannot accept the invitation. It would risk a confrontation with Nehemiah on what is, for the moment, his ground. Send back the appropriate regrets, the press of state matters, but that I shall not forget his gesture of support and good intentions. Why on earth did you ever marry into that family? You could have done much better. The mud of

Babylon is still wet on their tunics. How long have they been back — only thirty years?"

"Prejudice does not become your office," Tobiah replied. "There is room enough for all Jews in the homeland. Besides, I married for love."

"You married because Shecaniah's daughter can cook, and because her father is a banker with connections all the way back to Susa. What is the news of Eliashib? Still running the temple? I'm surprised he hasn't invited me as well. My home was always open to him or his sons whenever they traveled north."

"He remains the presiding priest and senior magistrate within the city — or what passes for the city," Tobiah said. "But he wishes to see you — urgently — so much so that I bring his ardent desire that you grant him an audience this very evening."

"You mean here? For dinner?"

"There is still time to send a messenger and stop him before he sets out," Tobiah replied. "But I saw no harm in telling him he should come."

"No, let him come. Clearly there is something urgent on his mind. How is the old goat?" Sanballat asked, not without affection.

"There were eyewitness reports of him having smiled a fortnight ago. Heralds were dispatched throughout the land with the news." Tobiah continued more seriously. "Ageing, like the rest of us, and running the temple as well as can be expected. There's scant money to be squeezed from the locals. Were it not for the occasional beneficence of homesick, guilty and thankfully rich Jews in Susa, he could not keep the temple open. He keeps asking about you."

Sanballat was now in his fifteenth year as governor of the region. Shortly after his installation, Eliashib had ridden up to pay his respects and pledge his loyalty. The journey had not really been necessary, and Sanballat, young and vulnerable, had not forgotten the gesture.

The kings of Persia were tolerant of Yahweh worship and had even financed the rebuilding of the temple one hundred years earlier. But independent temples were a source of federal tax. Religious freedom was a slight oxymoron within the empire. For the last ten years, Eliashib had remitted these taxes to Sanballat for forwarding on to Susa.

Sanballat and Eliashib both collected old Hebrew manuscripts. Any scrap of Torah written by Moses, or the poetry of King David, were hoarded by the bibliophiles of the land. But for the patient collector with enough funds, copies of the more famous oracles could be secured. The two men were free in lending their acquisitions to each other.

Nabis — that's what prophets were called, strange, usually tormented men whose job it was to fill the people's ears with the thunderous judgments of Yahweh. It was not a job you went looking for; it came to you. The oracles of famous men like Amos, Hosea and Isaiah were now two hundred and seventy years old. But recently — if you counted a hundred years ago as recent — men like Haggai, Zechariah and Obadiah had added their thin strands to Yahweh's orchestral voice.

To Sanballat's mind the more recent voices of Yahweh felt like snippets of speech flung over the shoulder of someone striding quickly out of sight. Much as he valued them, he imagined that a faint whiff of melancholy clung to them. They gave him the sense that either God or his chosen people had failed horribly. Whatever grand designs had been dreamed or promised were now rags, tattered chevrons idly flapping in a bitter wind over a destitute land.

The starkest of these voices still hung in the air. Sanballat had heard that a nabi called Malachi was still alive, although he had not made a public appearance in over a decade. If his oracles were trustworthy, then God's people were as broken as the land in which they lived. One bleak phrase was so piercing that it now lodged as an engram in Sanballat's mind:

Thus says Yahweh: "Oh, that one of you would shut the temple doors, so that you would not light useless fires on my altar! I am not pleased with you, and I will accept no more offerings from your hands."[8]

Only by default was Sanballat involved in the affairs of Yehud, the new name for what had once been the kingdom of Judah. At the beginning, there had been huge hope. Persia's first king, Cyrus, had granted freedom to any Jews who chose to return to their homeland. *"Seventy years of captivity had ended"* — that's what the recruiters had trumpeted back in Babylon, where the first Jewish ghetto had been established. *"Cyrus himself is paying to have our temple rebuilt."* But the only ones who kept showing up in the homeland were people whose luck had run out in Babylon. They usually arrived broke, with wild claims to huge estates that the new owners had no intention of relinquishing.

Seventy years of anemic or absentee governors had ensured a citizenry who remained poor. Eliashib's authority was both a local and limited temple franchise. The temple imposed its own taxes, minted local coins and appointed village magistrates. Insofar as something was not contrary to Persian law, the Jews could do pretty much as they liked. The truth was, no one really cared.

There were no federal garrisons in Yehud. It fell to Sanballat, the closest governor with any resources, to keep roads safe and repaired. And since he was too far away, it was really Tobiah, his agent, who ran the territory in matters that touched the Imperial organization. It was all quite messy, but it was the best that could be cobbled together.

And now, with the coming of Nehemiah, it seemed to Sanballat that even this patchwork arrangement of governance was about to unravel. Whatever was going to happen, all his innards confirmed his apprehension. Change is rarely good for the people in charge, thought Sanballat.

Tobiah continued speaking. "Eliashib remains a reasonable man in all respects. Tragic about his son, of course. Joida.[9] Leprosy is a horrible way to die."

"I hadn't heard that detail. Has Eliashib appointed his successor yet? I'd heard there's friction among the grandsons."

"No, he has not and your information is accurate. Jonathon and Joshua in particular both seem intent on being the next high priest."

"Do you still worship there, at the temple?" Sanballat asked.

"Regularly. And Eliashib has allowed me a small room connected to the temple from which to conduct my business."

"Nice of him. Does he owe you money?"

Tobiah laughed. "So far he has failed to grasp the benefits of a loan. But I am a devoted patron of his temple and that has the same effect. You are more fortunate. Worshipping Yahweh is much less expensive up your way."

It was Sanballat's turn to laugh. Although he and Eliashib worshipped the same God, their customs could not be more different. Sanballat and others like him made pilgrimages to an open-air altar maintained at the base of Mount Gerizim,[10] in accordance with the law of Moses. Religion, at least in its outward forms, was more occasional and limited to a few special celebrations throughout the year. In contrast, Eliashib's temple sacrificed animals twice a day and retained a small staff. But money was always changing hands and to Sanballat's mind the temple operations had always struck him as something closer to a shady, second-rate tax booth where corruption could be smelled but never proved. It came, he had concluded long ago, from the rank practice of mixing religion and politics. He had never challenged Eliashib about how he ran the temple. All the same, the air at Mount Gerizim seemed purer than at Jerusalem.

"What about his third grandson, Manasseh?" Sanballat asked. "He always struck me as being more, well, zealous than his brothers."

"Yes, he is still something of a romantic. Should have been a poet or written canticles for worship. Seems to stay out of the competition between his brothers. At least for the moment. I'm sure Eliashib will bring at least one of them tonight."

* * *

Nehemiah was standing when Hananiah entered to make his regular report. It was still obvious that his brother was almost a foot taller. And despite genuine brotherly affection, Nehemiah was still faintly resentful. Command headquarters consisted of the only two habitable rooms of the governor's mansion that sat about a hundred yards from the temple square.

Work on the houses will have to wait until after the wall is finished, Nehemiah thought.

"Sanballat's ridden down from Samaria and is staying at Beth-Horan," Hananiah began.

Nehemiah received the news impassively, so Hananiah continued. "Brought only his daughter and a dozen armed escorts. He won't try and stop us with force, at least not now."

"He's watching," Nehemiah said finally. "Let us hope that is how things will stay."

"You don't actually believe that, do you?"

"No. They didn't want the walls built five years ago — and they won that round. They haven't changed."

And neither have you, Hananiah thought, watching his brother's jaw, hard and rigid.

"Is your intelligence reliable?"

"Do you mean, can my spies be trusted?" Hananiah said. "Yes. I'm even beginning to get news for which I've not had to pay. You've caused quite a sensation. People talk of little else except your arrival. They're ready for a change. You're exotic — a mystery of sorts."

"I just relieve the boredom. Wait until they've worked a week or two on the wall and their enthusiasm will get sweated out of them. That's the problem with volunteer labour; no sticking power. It's all sprint and no marathon."

"I'm not so sure this time. You've touched a nerve. Look how eagerly people have already pledged to work on the wall. And Eliashib was the first to step forward. If Moses himself had showed up with a trowel I would not have been more surprised."

"What's the story on him?" asked Nehemiah. "He makes no secret of being Tobiah's friend — "

" — and still is," finished Hananiah. "A friend of Sanballat's too."

"And now he's suddenly helping me build my wall."

"Maybe he's glad to have the burden of collecting taxes become your headache. It's not as if the temple is awash with ill-gotten gains. Even if he wanted to feather his own nest, I get the impression that most people who live here are already well plucked ducks."

"He must know there will be consequences if he supports me," Nehemiah responded. "He was here five years ago when Tobiah stopped the project.[11] Yet now he's first in line to build. Is he a fanatic, do you think? Does he think I'll restore the throne of David once the walls are upright again?"

"Who knows another man's hope for sure? But he's Jewish to the core, and whatever else people know or don't know about you, my brother, they know that you're for us Jews. You're paying attention. Walls make us a people again, not just a bunch of peasant serfs slowly being ground into oblivion. Sanballat's an able enough governor, but he's made one fatal mistake."

"Which is?"

"He's ignored us all. He did nothing to help us when he could. People know when they're last in line."

"What's he like?" asked Nehemiah.

"Taller than you are, I'm afraid," Hananiah laughed. "And not nearly as . . . "

He searched for the right word trying to find a replacement for what had immediately come to mind. Explosive — that was his brother; a small tiny bundle of passion that threatened to burst into a thousand pieces without warning.

". . . energetic," Hananiah finally said. "Sanballat is methodical, cautious but tough when it's called for. It's not an easy thing running a province this far from the Imperial palace. Don't forget, it's the taxes that he's raised that have kept you and Artaxerxes swilling all that fine wine in Susa." Hananiah was perhaps the only person alive who could talk that way to Nehemiah and get away with it.

"Do you think he'll try and kill me?" There was a hint of eagerness about the way he asked the question.

"It's their prophets the Jews kill, not their engineers."

"Sanballat's not Jewish." Nehemiah spat out the words.

"He thinks he is," his brother answered. "Worships Yahweh; rumoured to be quite devout, actually. But he'll think long and hard before trying to murder the personal cupbearer to King Artaxerxes and who, so it is rumoured, attends the king while he is *with* the queen."

Hananiah allowed a salacious gleam to cross his face. "But of course, everyone knows my brother has been made safe."

"So that bit of gossip is still circulating then; good."

"And don't forget," Hananiah continued, "you are also a fellow governor."

"Not exactly," Nehemiah admitted. "And that's the problem. I'm not exactly sure what I am. Sanballat's had a free hand in this province of Yehud for over a decade. The territory is so small and poor it doesn't warrant provincial status. That's obvious to everyone with eyes. Only by the providence of Yahweh did I receive the King's warrant. Less than five years ago he'd ordered that Jerusalem be left in ruins. So whatever I am, it's strictly pro tem. Artaxerxes wants me back. He made that quite clear."

"But right now, my brother, you are a wall builder. And public opinion is with you."

* * *

It had been a full half hour since Sanballat had sent for his daughter and by the time she arrived, she could tell he was irritated. "Nikaso, Eliashib and perhaps some of his family will dine with us this evening. I want you to join us."

"Of course, father," was Nikaso's meek and immediate reply. Then seeing his continued frown added, "and I shall be dressed quite in keeping with my station, have no fears. I brought all the right clothes for state functions."

"Good," Sanballat grunted, and turned away. I can never stay angry with her, thought Sanballat. But why can't she dress like the other girls her age?

Nikaso was, at that moment, dressed in a short tunic she wore when riding and its dark sweat patches proved she had already been out. She could not imagine a day that did not include going somewhere on horseback, which was partly why she had wanted to come with her father. She was not what men called beautiful; she had a solid body and a plain-featured face surrounded by hair that she kept scandalously short, well above her shoulders but it did not get in the way when she rode. Her black eyes, set just too wide apart to be sensuous, looked out on the world utterly without pretense. The world had not yet betrayed her; she would not make the first move. She could not sew and had almost set the kitchen on fire the one time she tried to bake bread. But atop a horse, her whole body became filled with a regal ease and confidence that was enviable. She liked who she was, and as a consequence so did others.

Especially Manasseh. She did not tell her father that she already knew Eliashib was coming and that it would be his youngest grandson Manasseh who would accompany him. That morning she had found a note tied to the halter of her horse. It was unsigned and said only, "*I will see you before the day is out and pray that just this once the sun will race across the sky and cut short my agony of waiting.*" And of course, as soon as she read it, the sun seemed to stubbornly stop its ascent, as if to mock them both. But at least she could keep busy now. There were the details of the meal she would investigate — now technically her obligation as Sanballat's daughter — and her own preparations would take extra time.

Eliashib and Manasseh arrived just before sunset and Sanballat was on hand to help Eliashib dismount.

"Greetings, my old friend. It's been too long."

Eliashib showed his teeth in response and his eyes bulged wider than usual. It was the closest thing to a smile that his face would allow. There was absolutely nothing pleasing about Eliashib. He was tall, thin, and so bony that his cheekbones stuck out almost as far as his nose. His beard was stringy and sparse. His eyes protruded from sunken sockets so that he looked like a sun-dried eel for sale in the market. Sanballat offered a gentle embrace. He was always afraid of cracking the poor man like so much dry kindling. But he knew that within the frail and ugly form was a will made of iron, and probity beyond reach. Eliashib's loyalty was not for sale, nor was he easily moved from his opinions. And for that, Sanballat respected him a great deal.

"It's good of you to receive us," Eliashib replied. "You remember my grandson, Manasseh." Manasseh nodded and stammered something deferential as he gathered the reigns of their two horses.

"I'll show you to the stables." Nikaso was suddenly at hand looking fresh and regally demure. "I don't trust these servants to rub horses down properly unless I stand over them." The ride had been all of five miles and the animals showed no signs of sweat.

Her father raised an eyebrow ever so slightly when the two of them finally arrived back and settled themselves at the end of the low table.

"A thousand pardons, father," Nikaso said quickly. "The stable boy was not on hand." She hoped the low light from the oil lamps hid her face, for she could still feel it flush. Tobiah, who was considerably closer to her than her father, looked carefully at her, then at Manasseh. The thinnest hint of a smile flitted over his face and was gone almost at once.

Well, well, well, he thought. But he was quick to offer a necessary diversion. "You missed nothing except the boring talk of taxes, rumours of insurrections and the calamity of yet another poor harvest."

The dishes were passed around and news exchanged. The rebellion in Egypt was now definitely over thanks to the brilliant leadership of Megabyzus, who had led a federal regiment to deal with it. The outcome had not been at all certain and had taken five years to resolve.

"I remember the day when they all passed by," said Eliashib. "It was about the time when we'd been trying to rebuild Jerusalem's walls."

Tobiah laughed easily. "Eliashib, you are much too noble a man to harbour a grudge against me forever. The walls should not have gone up — not then and not now." He threw the last phrase casually into play while shoving his bulk towards a plate of spiced turnips. Sanballat matched his stealth.

"Bad for the region — walls that is," he said with his mouth half full of food. "With Egypt in turmoil the last thing Artaxerxes needs is a walled city full of us Jews pining for a son of David to be their king again. It took Nebuchadnezzar three years to destroy it when last we rebelled. I hate to think what carnage our lands would suffer if it ever came to that again. No, walls and Jews just don't mix. Temples and Jews, now that's a fine thing. But walls? They just give rebels something to hide behind." He took a huge draught of wine and wiped his mouth noisily on his sleeve.

But Eliashib was too old for conversational subtleties. Instead he just stared hard at Sanballat and said, "You are wrong in this matter, Governor. And my friendship with you compels me to tell you directly. Nehemiah has already begun the rebuilding. Every family of note has taken charge over a small section and will see to its completion. And I would rather you hear this from my lips, Sanballat. I was the first to volunteer."

Sanballat eyed Eliashib steadily but kept his tone relaxed. "I have a hard time picturing you on a scaffold, my friend, but since you are no longer my subject at law, I cannot compel you to cease your vain pursuits." And then, looking further along the table he continued, "Manasseh, I look to you to make sure your grandfather does not hurt himself or others." And finding Eliashib's face again he said, "I only hope this Nehemiah will stay long enough to deal with the trouble that will surely follow afterwards."

"I'm glad you will honour Nehemiah's right of office," Eliashib said. It was the wrong selection of words.

"Eliashib," Sanballat began with ice-filled tones, "the interpretation and enforcement of Imperial appointments is a civil and, I might add, Persian matter. You would do well to remember where your own jurisdiction ends, which is on the last step of the temple terrace, as I recall."

But Eliashib had committed himself. "I am glad you remind me of my limitations," he replied, sending the icy tone back up the table, "for you will be first to understand that the meagre taxes I collect in the name of the King must be remitted to the Persian governor in whose province sits my temple. And since our small province of Yehud now once again enjoys direct Imperial supervision, Nehemiah must receive what formerly I brought to you."

All sound had fled the room. No one even chewed what food still lay in their mouths. Every eye was on Sanballat, waiting for some kind of violent response to such a direct challenge. It came in the form of a long, belligerent belch, and on hearing it, the whole room exhaled as well.

"Your diligence in remaining a loyal Persian subject becomes you, as does your courage. I shall expect no less of you once Nehemiah is recalled to court and Yehud becomes my problem once again." Then he added, "Eliashib, we are both too old to do little more than bray at each other — wild donkeys without teeth, that's what we are. And since you are the only man in the whole region whose library I covet, I shall overlook your current stubbornness and still seek your friendship. But you will regret your part in this mad adventure, remember it." Sanballat finished his speech with a smile, both genuine and sad. And then so as to signal the conversation had ended, he addressed the table.

"Gentlemen," he began, "and Nikaso," he added quickly, "let us drink to the blessing of being Persian Jews. It is the best of two worlds, and may we never be forced to choose between them."

* * *

"You can't stop this wall, you know that," Tobiah said to Sanballat later that night after Eliashib and Manasseh had left. "It's going up this time."

Sanballat sighed. "You are probably right, although I pray to God that the stones will stay where they are."

"I'll help you in any way I can, of course," said Tobiah. "No matter what you decide to do. But we're going to lose this one, Sanballat. So I'm curious. Why not just accept the inevitable? Nehemiah's got the King's ear in this and he's bested you before it's even started. Why not let him build his silly wall? It's not as if you need the headaches of governing Yehud, much less a Yehud with a walled city at its centre. Besides, eventually Nehemiah will be re-called. We've survived much worse."

Sanballat did not answer at first. They had both loosened their belts and still lay, propped up on pillows, at the low table at which they'd eaten. Everything had been cleared except the cups from which they drank and the jug that lay within reach of both. Finally he spoke.

"Tobiah, you've got friends all through this area. Probably half the people who are going to build that wall owe either you or that father-in-law of yours money for one reason or another. Admit it. You can lean on many of them; hint that their loans will be demanded. I'm sure you hold mortgages on their lands. Artaxerxes said only that the walls *could* be built, not that they *should* be built. What if we were to harass the people? Intimidate them somehow? Mock the project and make them lose heart? What could Nehemiah do? That paper Nehemiah so boldly waves in the air cannot lift stones. He'd have to give up and go back to Susa."

The beginning of a plan hovered just at the edge of Sanballat's mind. It floated gently like a light wool cloak, soothing his wine-fogged mind.

"We'll need to keep an eye on things," he said, rousing himself.

"News will flow smoothly enough. I'm sure of it," Tobiah replied.

"True enough. But reliable news? What if we need something specific, or timely? You don't mount a campaign and trust in gossip for your intelligence."

Tobiah considered this for a moment, then yawned and said, "Send in Nikaso, your daughter. She's not known and seems sure enough of herself." He allowed himself a private grin at what he was suggesting, then added casually, "That Manasseh boy or one of his brothers can show her around and look out for her if you're worried. They all know each other well enough."

"What if Eliashib discovers her?"

"Sanballat, there is nothing sinister in your need for news, and building a city wall is hardly a private affair. Eliashib knows you oppose him in this and knows that you will not stand idly by. He'll be glad you've not tried to subvert him to your cause. Nikaso's not a spy. Jerusalem is an open city."

"A good suggestion," Sanballat answered after a minute's thought. "Between her riding clothes and plain looks she'll not be noticed."

"And no harm done if she is recognized."

"I'll tell her in the morning," Sanballat said.

Oh to be young and in love again, Tobiah thought.

Tobiah really did like to help people.

* * *

Nikaso left her horse at a tiny garden farm just outside of Jerusalem. Tobiah had made the arrangements and communicated them to her along with a long, conspirational wink. She had given nothing away, or hoped at least that was the case. She could not explain precisely why she wanted her friendship with Manasseh to be secret. They both came from good families and the only thing her father had ever remarked on was the number of suitors who had *not* pressed him for his daughter.

"You scare them off," he had once told her.

"Is it my fault that I ride a horse better than most men?"

"No, no," he had quickly retreated. "It's just that women should be somewhat delicate."

"You mean dependent."

"I mean that it's hard on a man's pride, is all."

"You did not raise me to be weak."

"I did not raise you at all," he had replied lamely. He loved his daughter passionately and knew well enough that any man made insecure by his daughter's accomplishments was not the sort of young man he would want as a son-in-law. The Sanballats were a tenacious family, and Nikaso was no exception. Two generations ago they'd still been poor. But by hard work and luck, each succeeding generation rose a little higher. His own royal appointment was proof of his family's mettle. His was a family that had worried well.

But Nikaso knew very well that family mettle did not necessarily give her the freedom to choose her male friends of her own volition. And Manasseh, she knew, was equally secretive about his feelings. Which were usually confused, and left unspoken. Unlike her own.

It was true. Nikaso loved Manasseh with an innocent frankness that was uncomplicated and ardent. She was pretty certain that Manasseh felt the same way. But the giddy thrill of young love could not completely blind either of them to the reality that marriage was still largely a thing negotiated between families.

By this time she was walking toward the city. The tallest thing on the horizon was the roof of what could only be the temple, reconstructed finally when her father was still a boy, thirty-five years earlier. It served as a useful reference point as she walked. Everyone knew about the temple and the difficulties that had attended its reconstruction. The first foundation stone for the raised terrace on which the whole thing sat had been lugged into position twenty-three years before the final bit of meagre gold leaf was hammered into place. For a building that was barely one hundred feet long by thirty feet wide and only sixty feet tall, the building of it remained an embarrassing witness to the prevailing ennui that clung to the land since the exiles had begun to migrate back to their homeland.

It was only because of Manasseh that the temple was now of interest to her. It was the visible sign of his family's importance within the community and she looked forward to inspecting it now that she felt some personal connection. She knew that her family worshipped the same God as was honoured here in Jerusalem, but also knew that they had never once come down to make sacrifice or celebrate any of the seasonal festivals.

The northern approach to Jerusalem was marked by a huge level wasteland of littered stones. Had she walked in from the west, the scene would have been the same. Many of the stones through which she picked her way were taller than she was. The smaller, more easily lifted stones had long since been carted away by energetic citizens in need of building supplies. What remained were the massive blocks, too big for the rudimentary engineering accessible in the land. Long, unkempt grass grew up like ugly whiskers from the earth's face. There was nothing natural about the stones, their squared edges reminding her that they had already played some key role in the world of humans. But for all their finished edges, they gave off the sense of having been abandoned, and now, left to their own devices, were creeping back into the earth's crust from which they'd first been dug. Their size made her think they were like the playthings of giants who had lost interest in their game and never returned to clean up their toys. Quiet, resigned decay was what they seemed to say to her.

At frequent intervals, however, were large bare patches, and only slowly did she come to see these as the places where buildings had once stood. Nothing remained except the faint depressions of where their walls had risen. They reminded her of neglected gravesites denuded of even the smallest monument that might have given some clue about the people that had once lived so close together. All that remained was the sense of mourning and loss that hovered over the open patches like the ghosts of the people who had once lived here.

After the first five hundred yards, the scene shifted again. Here were the foundations of the inner, and much older wall.

It's like an abandoned cattle pen built by drunkards at night, was her first reaction to what she saw. The inner "wall" was totally absent in many places and teetered outwards, threatening collapse in others. She could see the occasional gate, or what had once been a gate, marked by deformed timbers jutting out at odd angles wedged tightly between stones — toothpicks in a mouth full of broken teeth. Here, the anger of Nebuchadnezzar still lingered and she could only guess at the monstrous energy whose malevolent handiwork still lay strewn all around. The scene was one huge ugly dolmen to the might of the Babylonian war machine, left as a warning to other nations who might be tempted into rebellion. One hundred years later and still Jerusalem lay like a splayed-out harridan on her back, a grotesque warning to all potential rebels.

Close to one of the gates she recognized Eliashib's gaunt form standing on top of a large stone. His tunic flapped in the breeze and he was busy flailing his arms about, gesticulating apparently, to people not yet in her view. Voices carried in the air, the only real evidence that the ruins were not abandoned. She picked her way through the tumbledown gate and in doing so had entered Jerusalem. From the inside she now spotted the men Eliashib was commanding. Manasseh was among them. They were picking up stones off a huge rubble heap and moving them fifty feet away only to drop them onto another pile taking shape under their efforts. It looked no more ordered than the first pile.

So this is wall building, she marveled. The scene reminded her of chickens scurrying around the yard with no particular objective. Manasseh looked the most out of place. He wore his hair shoulder length, longer than Nikaso's, and his tall willowy frame struggled with the rocks he was picking through. He kept his face clean-shaven and his expressions changed constantly with his feelings. It was not a face that kept secrets. Nikaso thought of his long, delicate fingers and hoped they would not get injured. He had the most beautiful writing. She knew from the few small notes she kept hidden. Books were his passion. He lived in a world of words, a place where ideals and ideas were as real as the people who stood around him just now.

The decision to make herself known was made for her. Manasseh caught sight of her and in his excitement promptly dropped the stone he held, narrowly missing his foot.

"Nikaso, what are you doing here?" His voice was loud enough so that she noticed Eliashib turn in her direction.

So much for staying unrecognized, she thought. But she actually felt relieved. The idea of spying hadn't sat well with her from the beginning.

"Good morning," she said.

"I wondered when your father would send someone," Eliashib replied. He didn't seem annoyed and Nikaso was not about to be shamed where there was no cause. Shyness wasn't exactly part of her personality. She was still a governor's daughter and would carry herself in a manner befitting her station.

"It's not everyday that a city gets built. You can't blame us for being curious."

Eliashib just grunted. "Manasseh, you'd best show her around. Make sure she doesn't hurt herself. There'd be no way to explain that to Sanballat. He sees conspiracies everywhere." And then to her, "There are no secrets here." He called out again as Manasseh started toward her. "You'll be wanting food before you leave again. Manasseh knows when we break to eat. Join us." He returned to the work.

Manasseh was careful in how he took her arm until they had walked out of sight. Only then did their bodies draw slightly closer together and with every chance touch through her thin tunic delightful shivers raced intensely over her skin.

"How did you manage it?" Manasseh asked.

"Tobiah suggested it. I think he knows about us."

"Tobiah knows about everyone," Manasseh laughed. His delight at seeing her was plain. "So what do you want to see?"

"*Everything*," she said. You, she thought. I want to see you. I want to see where you work, where you sleep and eat and read and study and breathe.

"Let's start with the temple." They were only three hundred feet away from it. To get there, however, they threaded through the remains of a narrow street, past tightly packed houses in various states of disarray. In a few places stones blocked the street so that they had to climb over them. Only about half the houses looked occupied.

"There it is," Manasseh said finally. There was defiance in his voice, daring her to say something. The narrow street had ended at a piazza cleared of rubble. Ahead stood the temple, built on a ten-foot high terrace of solid stone. Broad steps on three sides led down to the square where they presently stood. But right at the bottom of the front bank of steps stood a massive slab of quarried stone supported by squat stone pillars to about waist height.

It looked almost like a banquet table except for the large bronze horns that arched up from each corner.

Manasseh pointed to it. "The altar," he explained, "where we slaughter the animals. Did you know that for the whole time we were in exile we never once could make a sacrifice?" He spoke of the exile as if he himself had only recently returned, pulling a century-old event forward into his own time.

"Why not?"

"The law of Moses forbids it. Only here, at the temple in Jerusalem, are they permitted." He continued. "And over there is the brazier where the actual sacrifice is burned." He pointed to a huge copper dish set on its own plinth.

"Where is everyone?" Nikaso asked finally. She had seen no one since they had begun walking.

"Building the walls." Manasseh laughed. "It's all that's happened since Nehemiah arrived. Come on and I'll show you." He took her hand.

They left the temple square from the far side, and entered the comparative gloom of another narrow street. Manasseh stopped in the doorway of the first abandoned house they passed and pulled her into the shelter of its stoop. She did not protest. He pressed himself tight against her with urgency. They held each other hard, the giddy sensations of an encounter that had lived too long as fantasy. Mouth met mouth, igniting a happiness in them both that consumed all other thoughts.

"We'd better keep walking," she said finally. "My father will want to know everything." Shadowed, narrow streets had never felt so kind. She linked her arm through his.

The city within the old walls was spoon-shaped. Nikaso had entered at the tip of the wide portion. But within five hundred yards the apposing walls had converged into a long narrow corridor that formed the "handle." At best, the whole city was one thousand yards in length. The narrow portion was ancient and people had come to refer to it as "David's quarters" since it was only this small section that had existed when he had first captured it.

Manasseh led her directly down to the most southern tip and they clambered up what was left of the wall to look out.

"It's magnificent," Nikaso said. Immediately past the wall the land fell sharply away into a steep valley that stretched both south and east of the city. It was a mountain view without having climbed.

"It is beautiful," Manasseh agreed, "provided you look out and not down." She followed his arm down to the valley floor.

"That break in the wall just to our right is called the Dung Gate. This is where the garbage gets thrown."

"It doesn't look very bad," Nikaso said. She had chosen all her words carefully since they had started walking. Despite the dereliction, it was clear Manasseh identified strongly with the place, showing it off with even amounts of pride and embarrassment. Nikaso had felt something as well. Perhaps it's the walls that make it feel different, she thought. She had spent her whole life in Samaria, and although it was just as ancient a city, it had no walls.[12] Her tour had the feeling of a visit to an aging aunt whose once-regal house was now a mausoleum, smelling of camphor and mothballs instead of hot bread and currants. Samaria was better rooted in the land of the living.

"How many people actually live here?" she asked.

"Seven hundred forty-eight and a half."[13]

"You're sure about the half?"

"Shallum's oldest daughter is pregnant."

"And you know this because . . . ?"

"Because our family keeps all the census lists and records the marriages, births and deaths of most everyone. We house what land deeds that have survived and even have the old caravan rosters for the past one hundred years. It's a huge collection, actually. I'll show it to you one day." He spoke with the obvious pride of a scribe and would-be scholar.

"What do you do with it all?"

"We keep it." He gave her a puzzled look. The question lay outside of what he could think. He continued. "Anyone in the whole province of Yehud could come to us and provided they knew who their father was, we could probably tell them when their family had returned from exile, in which caravan, from which Jewish ghetto — Babylon wasn't the only place we lived — and whether their family had been priests, Levites, cantors, servers — sometimes even the village their family had occupied before the great captivity."

"I'm suitably impressed, and equally awed that you have avoided my original question." She smiled and her voice was light. But not until the mention of another woman, any woman, did she realize just how much she wanted to know how he felt.

"Which was?" Manasseh's face was blank but his eyes betrayed him. He knew full well the real question that she had asked.

"Which was how you happened to know that the oldest daughter of Shallum is pregnant."

"Oh yes. That was easy. Shallum held a huge party when his daughter started to show. He's the administrator for a half district here, within the walls. The poor man has seven daughters and not one son. It'll be hard work to get them all married off. But at least the first one's found a husband and we're all hoping for a grandson."

"And are any of them hoping to find a solution to their problem in you?" Nikaso pressed. Her tone stayed light.

"I'm sure they are," he replied, his face still quite stolid. "But the question is, *am I* wanting to be part of the solution?"

"And?"

Manasseh drew her close again. They stood framed by the broken walls, with the hot wind tugging at them. He stared very hard into her face and said quietly, "And the answer is 'no.'"

But the moment could not go forward and both of them knew that nothing further could be promised or discussed. He turned and started to climb down off the wall. Steering them into safer waters, he said, "I will find some other father-in-law to make miserable. Come on, I'll introduce you to Shallum and his daughters on our way back. They're building a section of the wall on the east side."[14]

"His daughters are building?"

"We're a very progressive people, you know."

"You're all very desperate is what you are."

They walked back along the eastern wall and just as Manasseh had said, clusters of people dotted its entire length. A small corridor, free of rubble, was being cleared just inside the wall's foundation. Everywhere, people were picking up rocks only to drop them again thirty or so feet away. Nehemiah had ordered that the larger stones, especially any with squared edges, be kept separate. It was hot and sweaty work but she and Manasseh were greeted happily enough by every group they passed.

It feels like a town picnic, she thought.

"Everyone knows you," she said to Manasseh.

"Everyone knows everyone," he replied.

"Greetings, Manasseh," a voice called from just ahead. The man who called was barrel-chested and hadn't shaved in several days. A broad leather girdle encircled the waist of his dirty tunic that he wore above his knees.

"It's looking good, Berekiah,"[15] Manasseh yelled back. "But I don't see Jehohanan helping you. Is your son-in-law afraid to show up?"

Berekiah laughed. "He's a bit conflicted about things at present. Tobiah hasn't yet declared himself. But my daughter is here — just gone to get some food."

"Well, if Tobiah does object then you'll never get your section finished. Your daughter will be putting up stones on one side and her husband will be taking them down from the other." Laughter rippled at this open joke.

"Good luck!" Manasseh and Nikaso moved on.

"What was that all about?" Nikaso asked.

"Berekiah's daughter is married to Jehohanan,[16] Tobiah's son," explained Manasseh.

"Tobiah isn't going to support building this wall."

"No, and I think everyone knows he cannot."

"And so what will happen?"

Manasseh shrugged. "It's only a wall. People will find a way to accommodate each other." Nikaso did not reply.

They were passing through the narrowest part of the "handle," just before the city widened up into the northern "spoon," before they spotted Shallum and his daughters. They were working on the western part, as it turned out, and Manasseh would have missed them were it not for the walls being so close together at that point.

"You've brought another helper, I see," Shallum shouted at Manasseh as he smiled at Nikaso. Their arrival justified a break and six young girls quickly gathered to see who had come. They stood close together. The youngest — Nikaso guessed her to be about eight — was a chubby child whose curly black hair was plastered to her wet forehead. It was she who spoke:

"Have you really come to help?"

Another sister answered for Nikaso. "Manasseh has just brought a visitor." Turning to Nikaso she said, "My name is Yehoyishma but everyone calls me Yehoy. I'm the second oldest. And these are Rhoda, Miriam, Sherah, Susanna and Rachel," she said, finally pointing to the shortest one with the black curly hair.

"I'm Nikaso. My family's just visiting from the north but my father has known Eliashib for a long time."

"Would you be Sanballat's daughter then?" Shallum asked quietly.

"Yes." Nikaso stared straight into his face, daring him to comment further. He said nothing more.

"We're building the wall," Rachel spoke again. "People say that only men can build walls but my sisters say that they're wrong and that we're going to show them."

"I think your sisters are right," Nikaso said kindly, stooping to engage this talkative little child. "Manasseh has shown me a lot of the walls and your part is the neatest by far. Men think the strangest things sometimes, don't they?"

"Here we go again," groaned Manasseh loudly and the sisters laughed. "Add wall building to the list of things that women can do better than men. Is there no end to the list?"

Yehoy looked keenly at Nikaso and then, apparently having made up her mind about something, said to her: "You're welcome to help us here if you want."

"Are you sure?" Nikaso spoke to Yehoy but looked at Shallum who gave just the slightest of nods.

"She can't help today," Manasseh cut in. "Maybe another time."

"Will you bring her back?" Rachel asked.

"She doesn't need me for that. She can ride her horse right up to where you're working and climb over a low spot."

"You ride?" Yehoy asked.

"I do."

"I should like to try that some day. We don't own a horse."

"It's easier than most people say. I'd be happy to show you."

"We have to go," Manasseh said. "My father is expecting us."

"Which one is pregnant?" Nikaso asked when they were safely out of hearing.

"Oh, Deborah. She's too far along to be working on the wall. We're not cruel tyrants."

"A comfort to know," Nikaso replied. It's so easy to talk to him, she thought.

Eliashib's group had already stopped for lunch when they got back to the Sheep Gate. Lunch had been brought by Manasseh's mother. Introductions were made and Nikaso felt herself being closely inspected.

"So, have you seen enough to slake your father's thirst for news?" Eliashib asked her.

"It's a huge project," she answered.

"Long overdue. What's left to show her?" He looked at his grandson. "Don't want it said that we hid anything."

"We haven't seen the western length yet, and we only walked quickly past the temple area."

"I should very much like to see the temple, if it's possible," Nikaso spoke up.

"Yes, I don't recall your family ever coming down to the festivals," Eliashib said.

"I want to show her the scriptorium if I can," Manasseh interrupted. "The western wall can wait for another day." Eliashib grunted his permission. Manasseh and Nikaso shared a quick look. Another day together had just been achieved.

The noon break finished, she and Manasseh returned to the temple. "You can't go inside, of course," Manasseh explained. "Men only, and even then there are restrictions. But I can show you the rooms that are attached along each side. They open directly into the terrace."

"What kind of men are restricted?" Nikaso asked as they made their way past the altar with its tall arched horns and up the fifteen broad stone steps to the top of the terrace.

"Eunuchs, for one. Priests with visible deformities, and of course foreigners."

Directly ahead stood the double doors of the main entrance, flanked on each side by three pillars. They turned left and walked along the side of the building until Manasseh stopped at one of the doors that were evenly spaced along the wall.

"The scriptorium," he said, and pushed open the door. It took a while for her eyes to adjust to the dark despite the open door. Every wall was lined with small open cubbyholes and rolled scrolls lay stacked in each. Nikaso had never seen so many written words at one time in her entire life. Their own family home had at best twenty scrolls. Here, resting in quiet composure, were hundreds, perhaps more. Some were sheathed in elaborately decorated casings. Others were plain and small.

"I had no idea it would look like this," she whispered.

"We've been collecting since before I was born," Manasseh said, matching her hushed voice. "There are a few that were copied out over three hundred years ago, before Samaria was destroyed by the Assyrians.[17]

"What are they all?" She reached out and touched the ends of the ones closest to her. She touched them as if stroking the neck of a horse, caressing, ever so lightly. She felt Manasseh watching her closely.

She turned to him, waiting for his answer, and saw his face full of pride. This was his world, she thought. This small dark room that housed nothing but the washed skins of dead animals covered with the squiggly lines that had bled slowly from the ends of a thousand pens. It was a world where all of time was gathered up together.

"It's who we are," he said quietly. "We have portions of the Torah, the songs of King David, and quite a few good renderings of the more recent prophets' oracles — Amos, Hosea, Haggai and Zechariah." He pointed to a tiny collection of parchments that were housed apart from all the others.

"But the rest of these?" she pressed.

"They are the scrolls I told you about. Family ancestors, caravan rosters and land deeds. With each returning family from the exile our collection grows."

"Is your family mentioned somewhere?"

"Of course. More than mentioned. To serve at the temple is a birthright. If I cannot prove my lineage, I have no business here. It's not a matter of just wanting to serve. You have to be from the right family."

"So where *did* you come from?" she asked him suddenly. Manasseh straightened a little and then began slowly in a rich timbre quite different from how he usually spoke. Not once did his voice falter.

"I am Manasseh,[18] the third and youngest son of Joida who, because of his leprosy, could not serve in the temple. Joida, my father, was the son of Eliashib who serves as High Priest now. Eliashib is the son of Joiakim. All of those, save Joida, served as Priests here in Jerusalem after the second temple was completed.

"Before him, his father Jehozadak was taken with the remnant of Judah into exile by the hand of Nebuchadnezzar.

"Jehozadak was the son of Seriah who served before Jerusalem fell, who was the son of Azariah, the son of Hilkiah, the son of Shallum, the son of Zadok, the son of Amariah who was the son of Azariah. Before him was Johanan who was the first to serve the Lord our God in the temple built by Solomon, built on the same ground where we now stand.

"Johanan was the father of Azariah, whose father was Ahimaaz, whose father was Zadok, whose father was Ahitub, whose father was Amariah, whose father was Merioth. Merioth was the son of Zerahiah, the son of Uzzi, the son of Bukki, the son of Abishua, the son of Phineas, the son of Eleazar, the son of Aaron who was the brother of Moses."

The recitation finished and Manasseh spoke again only one more time although whether he spoke to Nikaso or to himself, she was not sure. "I am a Jew born into a priestly family of the tribe of Levi. That is who I am."

"A son of Aaron," she said quietly. "You really do know who you are." She pointed to the scrolls again. "Is our family here?"

"I have never seen them mentioned, and I have read most everything in this room. Still, it doesn't mean you don't belong."

Belong, she thought. Belong to what exactly?

The sun had started down by the time they left the temple area. "I'll walk with you back to your horse," he said. They did not touch each other the whole walk back.

* * *

Nikaso gave a full report to her father. Tobiah, who, it appeared, was staying at Beth-Horan with them indefinitely, listened too.

"I would guess that half of the houses within the old section are abandoned and damaged. Every city gate I saw was without its doors. Not every part of the wall is pulled down. The eastern section is the worst; the land falls away quite sharply into a deep valley — "

" — the Kidron," Tobiah said.

"I don't know its name but it runs almost the whole length of the east wall and all around the bottom of the city as well — "

" — the Hinnom. That's what they call it at the south end of the city," Tobiah interrupted again.

"A lot of the wall seems to have fallen down the valley side. The slope looked loose. I wouldn't risk a horse anywhere along that edge.[19] I don't know about the western side of the city. I didn't walk it, although the lower section of the city is so long and narrow the walls aren't much more than two hundred yards apart. Eliashib said I could come back again. He seemed to know you'd send someone to have a look. I'm not a very good spy, father. They spotted me the minute I was inside the city."

"It doesn't matter, Nikaso, and you've helped me a great deal. I want you to keep returning. We'll think up errands for you if we have to. But tell me, what about the people? What are they doing?"

"Just sort of clearing away a space along the inside. Getting ready, I suppose."

"Were they working hard? Did they show enthusiasm?"

Nikaso paused, wanting to be as precise as she could for her father. "They were happy," she said finally. "I heard lots of laughter."

* * *

"What do you propose to do?" Tobiah asked after Nikaso had left.

"*I* don't plan to do anything. But you, my friend, are going to march down there tomorrow and tell your friends to stop building their stupid wall."

"Just like that?"

"Just like that."

"And just what do you expect me to say that will be so convincing? 'Ignore Nehemiah. He's only your new governor whereas I'm the man who no longer has a job with any authority except in Ammon. Stop building and all come to my house for a party.'"

"Tobiah, they like you. And you know how to appeal to a crowd. Make them see how impossible the task is. Remind them that they are amateurs — that the wall will just fall over again. Remind them how long it took just to build that stone hut they call a temple. Tell them anything, just make them stop."

Tobiah looked very hard and seriously into Sanballat's face. "What's really behind this obsession of yours? I'll go. You know I will, and I'll give it my best, you know that too. But just tell me why? This isn't like you, Sanballat."

"Because they don't deserve a wall, that's why," Sanballat burst out. "They're either ignorant, slovenly peasants barely eking out a living, or they're wealthy, arrogant peacocks strutting back from the exile pretending to be the only Jews alive to have survived Nebuchadnezzar's carnage. You've seen them. Their clothes are still Persian and their names are still Babylonian. Yet they come waltzing back by the thousands as if Nehemiah were the second Joshua and they were about to re-enter the Promised Land. Their presumption makes me want to vomit."

"So you're not upset about losing control of Yehud? This is not about territory and being able to levy taxes and rule the biggest satrapy in all the Land Beyond the Euphrates?"[20]

"Of course, it's about all that too!" Sanballat raged. "What kind of fool do you take me for? But all that is just business and politics. If the Persian court wants to send out a new governor after I spend a decade looking after things without a word of thanks much less without even telling me — that's just my lot for the day. I can adjust to all that. But if you really want to know what terrifies me, I will tell you. It's not Nehemiah. He's just the biggest tick to ever crawl down my tunic. And I'd happily kill him if I thought I could get away with it. But eventually, he'll go away. It's when he does go away that I worry about. Nehemiah is many things but he's Persian, and there'll be no sedition on his watch. But what happens when he's gone? Can you imagine if some hotheaded fool rallies the people proclaiming himself a descendent of David come to free his people?"

"Like the Messiah?" Tobiah said.

"Like a lunatic. Have you observed either of Eliashib's two oldest boys? They're both bad news.[21] Violence is written all over their faces. Picture them in leadership, occupying the only fortified city between Egypt and Damascus. And do you know who will get blamed for it? It won't be Nehemiah, who is back in the king's lap being petted by his queen. It will be us who have to sort out the whole stinking mess. How many Jews have to die before we learn? How many times do we have to watch our wives get raped and our children tossed between spear tips[22] before we learn the futility of rebellion? But we never do. And it always starts with walls."

"Sanballat, calm yourself. I'll go tomorrow. You're picturing a future that will not come to pass. We shall survive no matter what happens. It's in our nature."

"Yes, Tobiah, go and do what you can. And while you're gone, I'll devise something else just in case your silver tongue fails us this once."

* * *

"Just how exactly do you propose to build this wall of ours?" Hananiah asked his brother as the two were taking a tour of inspection together. By this time there was almost a complete access corridor on the inner perimeter. The people had worked hard at clearing a working space, but so far not a single new stone had been put in place.

"I was beginning to think you weren't interested," Nehemiah said.

Hananiah had been vitally interested in the question but he had come to accept the secretive leadership of Nehemiah, who had neither the personality nor patience for leading by consensus, much less taking his subordinates into his confidence. Nehemiah had kept secrets since the beginning. Even while traveling out from Susa, couriers and visitors would often intercept their caravan, hold private conversations with Nehemiah, and either give or receive dispatches. At Damascus, without any explanation at all, Nehemiah had announced that five lumbering transport wagons were going to join them. What was in them he had never told Hananiah, only that they should be kept secure at all times.

Hananiah continued. "Just didn't want to give you the satisfaction of telling me it was a secret, was all. But I'm asking now. These stones aren't going to move themselves and we've got at best twenty masons with any kind of skill."

"Well, I do have a plan. In fact, I've been putting it together since before we left. Wasn't sure it would work, of course, until we actually got here so I couldn't say anything."

"No, admitting you might be human would be a terrible blow to your reputation." Nehemiah ignored the jibe. Instead, he pointed to a section of the wall they were walking down.

"See how the old foundations are mostly still in place?" They were walking past a portion that people called the "Broad Wall." It lay on the western side just where the city started to widen out. "I've checked carefully.

The first few feet of wall are still intact — and solid. The only place that isn't is on the Kidron side where most of the wall's gone and what's left is undercut badly on the outside slope. But everywhere else it's in good shape, and the width is pretty consistent too. It runs about fifteen feet wide." Hananiah could do mathematics as fast as most people could speak. It was an essential skill for a commissary, which had been his rank before joining Nehemiah's expedition.

"That's a lot of stone work to be building," Hannaniah replied. "After you've allowed for a plinth either side, you're still needing at least three hundred cubic feet of stone for every linear foot of wall. We don't have the materials and there are no quarries nearby."

"But that's where you're wrong," Nehemiah answered. "We've got plenty to work with."

"Give it to me all at once, please." They were still walking south, down the long narrow section of David's Quarters. The Valley Gate was on their right. Nehemiah stopped again.

"Alright. Here it is. For starters, we aren't going to build one wall. We're going to build two. Except that each wall will start about a yard in from these foundations."

"Two walls," Hananiah repeated. He did the math as he spoke. "That would make them seven feet thick in total — say each over a yard thick."

"Two walls," echoed Nehemiah. "But two *thin* walls — only a foot thick. The stones don't have to be large and the masons can jump around and do what minor cutting needs to be done."

"We don't have enough dressed stones even for that," Hananiah objected.

"True, so in addition to building *thinner* walls, we're going to build a *shorter* wall. See all those high spots where the walls weren't destroyed at all? We can dismantle say the top ten feet and reuse the stones. They're already squared, and couldn't be closer at hand. And here's the best part. Those sections of wall are still ten feet thick. That will yield —

" — one hundred linear feet of dressed stone for a one-foot thick wall."

"Exactly!" Nehemiah gleamed. "You're catching on. And between the stones that we've salvaged and kept separate from the rubble, and these sections of old wall, we've got enough. And if for some reason we don't, we can always break up the giant slabs that are still lying around from the outer wall. But I don't think we'll need them."

"Not a bad plan, I admit. But a wall that is only one foot thick — and let's say for argument's sake, thirty feet high — how will it stay up? No two stones are exactly the same shape. Every man, woman and child you've got working is a volunteer, and you want to build *two* of these? They'll fall down before we've even finished."

"Not with what's in those wagons you've been dying to know about since we got them in Damascus."

"They're filled with sacks of dirt. You think I wouldn't open one?"

"Not dirt, Hananiah. Ash. The ash that comes from a volcano. They quarry the stuff in the islands off Athens and Sparta."

"From the Greek territory? You've been trading with the Greeks?"

"And right now more valuable than if it was exotic spice from India."

"Because . . . ?"

"Because if you mix this ash with ordinary lime and add enough water until it looks like thin porridge you get —"

" — mortar!" Hananiah started to smile himself. "Nehemiah, you're one clever wine steward."

"And not just regular mortar, either. This stuff really hardens.[23] There's something special about the volcanic ash. I saw it being used at Susa for tricky kinds of building."

"You've been scheming a long time, haven't you?"

Nehemiah's face was consumed by his grin and his feet kept threatening to break into a small dance. When he got wound up about something, his whole body joined in.

"You have no idea how long I've been building these walls in my head. But it gets even better, my brother. Do you know why we're going to build two walls?"

"I'm about to."

"We fill the void in between with all the rubble that we've cleared away. We get the bulk we need for our walls *and* clean up the city in one fell swoop — "

" — and the walls will stay in place because they've been mortared," Hananiah cut in.

"And anybody can collect rubble and pack it in between the two walls. The masons can help the families that are totally inept. We'll fill as we build. You lay, say, five feet of height, let the walls dry for a day or two, fill the gap between the two walls full of rubble and you've got a firm enough platform to build the next five feet."

"Brilliant. Absolutely, makes your eyes squint, bloody brilliant! Now I see why Artaxerxes wants you back. And the gates? What engineering magic have you brewed up to solve those gaps?"

"Even easier than the walls," Nehemiah replied. "I've ordered dressed timber and the first shipment should be here within two weeks."

"From where? And who would sell it to you?"

"From Phoenecia, on the coast, to answer your first question. And from a man called Asaph[24] who just happens to oversee an old growth forest that just happens to be a royal hunting preserve."

"And he's agreed to cut down the King's park and sell it to you? He's as good as cut off his own head."

"Not at all. He's only responding to a royal writ signed by Artaxerxes himself that I dispatched to him while we were en route. Asaph is simply following orders."

"And Artaxerxes didn't mind?"

"Artaxerxes didn't even know the land was being held in the name of the empire. It was some obscure abrogation going back to the time of Cyrus when he was down this way campaigning and apparently found the area to have plentiful mountain lions. Ordered the acreage kept unspoiled in case he ever wanted to come back and hunt."

"And the timber is coming already cut?" Hananiah could hardly take in this news. It would save months of work.

"Cut in planks, six inches thick, with enough squared timbers for lintels, posts and cross pieces."

"By the beard of every holy man that ever lived," Hananiah breathed. "You've figured the whole thing out. We really are going to build these walls."

Nehemiah beamed at his brother. All the way back up the eastern side of the city they kept exchanging excited grins like twelve-year-olds who had just discovered girls. The walls they passed were already built and they could see transformation everywhere they looked.

It will still be thick enough so that the top can be easily patrolled, thought Hananiah. There's ample room to walk along the top. We'll build a stubby cornice along the outer edge for safety.

There'll be a landrush to come back and live in these homes, thought Nehemiah as he walked past the abandoned houses. Out of the ashes Jerusalem will rise again. He smiled at the joke he'd just coined. I must remember to use that phrase at some auspicious moment.

* * *

Tobiah did not go to Jerusalem to attempt his mission until about two weeks had passed. "Better to let the people develop sore backs and a few crushed fingers. They'll be more inclined to listen," he'd said to Sanballat. He set off in his best robe, and in high spirits.

He arrived back at Beth-Horan lying in the back of a wagon, quite drunk.

"Ohhhh Sanblatt, my friend," he bawled out as the wagon lurched to a stop. "Oh, oh I was so eloquent. You should have bin ther to hear me — it wassh my finest hour." Tobiah shifted his frame and tried to crawl toward the end of the wagon.

"Ahhh!" he yelped. "My ankle — the pain, the pain!"

Sanballat peered into the back of the wagon. "By the god of Marduk, what happened to you?" He tried to pull Tobiah toward him but Tobiah yelped again.

"Don't touch me, Sanblast. I am wounded."

"You're stinking drunk is what you are."

"Only a little warrior's comfort, I assure you. Medicine taken on the battlefield. But oh my lord, I came so close to winning them over. But there's no stopping him now, Sanblah. He's outfoxed you every which way — "

Tobiah started to laugh — or whimper. "That's pretty good," he gurgled to himself. "Outfoxed. That's what happened to me alright."

Sanballat willed himself to speak very slowly and calmly all the while resisting the urge to leap into the wagon and choke the news out of his friend.

"Tell me who hurt you, Tobiah. Who did this to you?"

"Oh Sanblaat, I was so close; gathered a group around me — got them to stop their work and I could tell they were listening. I crooned. I cajoled. I was commanding. Told them the task was futile, that the walls would not stay up — that they had no clue what they were doing. I reminded them that we'd always lived together without walls — that the time would be better spent repairing their own houses. It was going so well. And then — ”

" — yes?”

"And then for emphasis I jumped up onto this small mound of stones — for effect, you see. And I said 'see what do think you're building? Why, if even a fox jumped up here he would flatten it.'" 25

"Yes?" Sanballat repeated.

"And that's when I fell. The stones moved and I fell right over and down the back of the rubble heap. Fell right out of sight. It broke the spell. They started to laugh. A fox! See? We got outfoxed. You and me both.”

Tobiah stopped talking, reliving the scene in his mind. "It was rather funny, I suppose. One minute I'm a powerful orator holding forth and the next minute I'm up ass over kettle, flat on my back. It took ages for them to find the cart and they didn't want to move me until it arrived. I just had to lie there looking up at all those faces and try not to cry.”

He put his hand down close to his ankle and rocked back and forth again. "It hurts so badly. I shall never walk again. I'm sure of it.”

Sanballat did not press him for any more details. He motioned the servants to deal with this large, drunk, and now injured three hundred odd pound problem that lay helpless in the cart.

* * *

Nikaso kept returning to the city. She would have gone even if her father did not seem obsessed for news. She did not understand his dark animus that brewed stronger with each bit of information she provided. Only once had she asked him about it, but he had told her harshly that she could not hope to understand.

"They're not bad people," she had said.

"It's not about being bad," he replied. "It's a matter of being easily led astray.”

"But Jerusalem was an ugly eyesore before. They're cleaning it up, making something of it. Where is the harm of that?"

"And after it's all cleaned up and the gates are back on their hinges and soldiers are pacing the top of the wall — what then?"

"But they need a wall for protection. Everyone says so."

That was when Sanballat raged. Anger jumped out of his face like oil spit up from a hot griddle. It shook his body and narrowed his eyes into slits of flint. She had never seen him so angry. "Protection from what?" he shouted. "Protection from the Persian troops who keep us safe? Protection from the Egyptians who have not once ever invaded us? Or from the Greeks whose nearest army is a thousand miles away and who don't even know we exist? Just what is it that is so threatening?"

"I don't know, but leaving it so broken feels wrong." It was the best she could say. To Nikaso's mind, building the wall seemed so natural. It was like cleaning up a stable or clearing away the dishes after a large meal. Jerusalem was messy, and barren. Cleaning it up was just something you did if you could. And this Nehemiah person had been able to get people to work together as a team. It didn't need to be justified or objected to. You just did it, and felt better as a consequence.

Sanballat answered his own question. "I'll tell you what they want protection from," he ranted. "It's me! Every stone piled up is another slur on my reputation. They might just as well be throwing them at me. Yet have I waged war on them? Am I a monster come from the depths of Sheol to devour them? Do you see our home full of Jewish slave girls, whom I snatched away from their mothers?"

"No, of course not," Nikaso said. "And they must know you have been fair with them. You even helped when you did not have to. The walls are not meant to be an insult. I don't think it's about you at all. I think it's more about them. Building those walls is doing something to them. You can see it. Straightening the walls seems to straighten the people. Walls will make them a people."

"That is where you're most wrong," her father had shouted. "Walls do not make *a* people — they make *two* peoples! Do you have any idea what kind of gift the Persians have given us? For three million square miles there is peace — real honest-to-goodness lasting peace to live out our tiny lives undisturbed. For eighty years now — since Cyrus first allowed it — this land has made room for anyone who wanted to come home. Everyone adjusted to the newcomers. There was lots of land to be worked. But no! By some black philtre Nehemiah poured into the cup of King Artaxerxes our one chance to be united has been cut in two, sliced by that damn wall."

"But how, father? Why will a wall do that to us? I don't understand." Nikaso's voice was that of a small, frightened child facing blind anger that might at any moment turn in her direction.

"Because it will divide us Jews again, Nikaso. I know you think those people down there welcome you. But don't think for a minute that they're welcoming you as one of them. And when those gates are slammed shut in your face for the first time, when those same trodden down, dispirited people you feel so sorry for sweating over the rubble heap — when they're standing on top of the thirty foot wall jeering down at the rest of us, how will you feel then? How will you feel when they tell you that you're not one of the *real* chosen people?"

"We worship Yahweh. We're Jewish too."

"Not once those walls go up. We'll just be the people living on the outside. We'll be the offspring of the 'bad figs'[26] left rotting in the land because we weren't worth taking to Babylon."

Nikaso could not reply. Bigotry, exclusion, a divided society just because of where your ancestors had lived; these things just did not exist in the straightforward world she thought she lived in. And, if those things were not heavy enough for her, Sanballat hurled one more acerbic barb before he stomped out of the room.

"It won't stop with us either, daughter. One of these days those Jews living in their safe little bastion will start to think that the Persians aren't good enough for them either. And that's when the real killing will start."

* * *

"Sanballat, you can't be serious." Tobiah, leaning heavily on a stick the size of a small fence post, could not believe what he had just heard.

"I am most serious. They will all be here within a week. Geshem will ride with at least fifty men. I've sent for another thirty from Samaria, and Phineas has promised no fewer than forty. He'll probably arrive first since he's closest. Ashdod is only two days' ride and they'll be traveling light. And I expect some of your local constables to show up as well. By the time everyone arrives, we should have over two hundred men."

"You're mad!" For once Tobiah did not mince his words. "Nehemiah is your equal. Attack him and you've as good as attacked Persia. How long do you think it will be before Megabyzus learns of this and marshals federal troops? He's got easily a thousand troops he can call out, and they aren't provisional volunteers like we are. It won't be Nehemiah's head they come for, either. It'll be yours…. And mine too." All of Tobiah's usual bonhomie had drained from his face. He was plainly scared.

Sanballat gave him a weaselly smile. "Megabyzus already knows. I wrote him."

"And said what exactly?"

"Gave him a full report on Nehemiah's progress, of course. Told him that the wall was being built in an orderly manner and would probably be finished within a month."

"That's all?"

"Not quite. I also said that rumours had reached my ears that certain more zealous Jews, mostly newly returned from Susa, were openly discussing independence; that Nehemiah enjoyed huge popularity and was doing nothing to quell such public enthusiasm. In short, I suggested that the embers of sovereignty thought to be safely extinguished showed signs of re-igniting. He'll catch my drift plainly enough. He's barely taken his armour off from dealing with the Egyptian uprising."

"What did he reply?"

"I didn't ask for one, and none has come. Told him I could handle things since it was still a purely local matter and the walls weren't even complete. I even admitted that I had no hard proof that Nehemiah was planning to accept the crown of his people — just that I had an instinct for trouble and meant to be proactive. Wanted him to know of my plans in advance of any one else telling him."

"But you're raising an army, two or three hundred men. Why?"

"It's time those people got reminded of who their neighbours are, Tobiah. If we can't talk them nicely into giving up this project, perhaps we can remind them of who still controls everything beyond their walls. Right now, from all the news that Nikaso and you bring me, the people are only thinking about how their precious walls will keep people out. It's time to remind them that those same walls can just as easily keep people in."

"You're planning a siege?"

"I prefer to think of it as a theatrical demonstration of who is really in charge. Let them see the glint of a hundred spear tips dancing round about their city. Remind them that we stand between them and their fields and vineyards. They'll figure out soon enough what's in their best interests."

"Don't do it, Sanballat. I beg of you. Too much can go wrong."

"What can happen? We show our strength. They discover a strong yellow streak of enlightened self-interest, drop their stones and fade back into the countryside. Nehemiah goes back to Susa where he belongs and we all go back to the way things were."

"Would you actually attack them?"

Sanballat put his lips hard together for a minute and stared at his friend. "Tobiah, I'm angry, not stupid. And Phineas isn't either. He's a governor just like me and knows where the limits are. But, my friend," he pushed his face quite close to Tobiah's bulk, "for this show to work, no one must know it's a show."

"And Geshem? Aren't you forgetting he's Arab? And you know how he loves to fight; he's always been a bit of a brawler. And he's not bound the way you and Phineas are. His territory's not part of Persia." [27]

"All true. And those desert nomads he leads are quite wild. But he won't put his own treaty terms at risk. No, he'll be content with just baring his teeth and reminding the whole bunch of us that Arabia still has the biggest jaws."

"So you think he'll control himself?"

"If a few reckless hotheads catch the edge of a sword — well, it's not the first time we've had to kill the odd local troublemaker."

"Sanballat, you're playing a dangerous game of brinksmanship."

"I'm not playing."

* * *

There were no secrets in the land. Sanballat didn't seem to care how wild the rumours grew about what he intended to do once his coalition army had gathered. An arrogant swagger now marked his walk and, in public at least, his face wore a contemptuous scowl. He seemed to grow naturally into the role of chief antagonist in the impending drama. Nikaso had not seen this side of him and shrank from it. Only his most personal slave knew just how badly his bowels were betraying him.

The city too was changing. The energy created by Nehemiah's arrival and the thrill of his grand plan had been intense. But true to his own prediction, it was not sufficient to carry them through to the end and now showed signs of running out. People had done little else but move rock for weeks and fatigue was encircling the city just as surely as Sanballat's army soon would. Nikaso noticed it. There was no laughter and in some spots along the wall, fewer people were helping.

* * *

"What's to be done?" Hananiah asked his brother on one of their now twice daily tours. "We're getting tired. All of us."

"What's the latest news of Sanballat?"

"That his army grows bigger each day. Their tents are easy enough to count and last evening three men got roughed up a bit on their way back home. If that keeps up we'll lose workers. The people helping us will be afraid to come in each day from their villages. We need them to finish."

"That's easy enough to fix. Pass the word. Every worker from outside will be billeted inside the city until the walls are up. Their families should come too. We'll provide the food for everyone."

"You could be feeding a few hundred people — free food for a month is a generous gift under any conditions. And you've already waived your governor's tax. Who will pay?"[28]

Nehemiah threw his brother a wry little smile and Hananiah caught what he was thinking. "Well there goes our family inheritance," Hananiah groaned in mock despair. "But what about Sanballat? Right now he's winning the propaganda war. People are nervous. Fatigue and fright — it's a bad combination."

"I'm working on a plan."

"You could always send a message to Artaxerxes. He could order out the nearest federal garrison."

"On what grounds? Sanballat's not attacked us."

"Yet."

"Come on, Hananiah. He hasn't, and he won't. It'd be his own death warrant if he did. The real trouble is that he doesn't *have* to attack us in order to win. All he has to do is intimidate us enough. The minute we've dropped our trowels, he's won."

"What we need is an army of our own," Hananiah mused.

A tiny sparkle of light started to play around the edges of Nehemiah's eyes. "What we need to do," he replied, "is to find a way to make Sanballat's army work for us."

"You're not going to tell me what that short little brain of yours is scheming, are you?"

But Nehemiah had already turned his back and was trotting off in the direction of his headquarters. "I've got some letters to write," he called over his shoulder. "For now, get those Immortal Guards of yours up on their horses and have them patrol the outside perimeter — lots of show. Be conspicuous."

* * *

Nikaso watched as men kept arriving at Beth-Horan. Brutality and hard living pocked their faces. At night she could hear their raucous carousing. There was not a single true soldier among them. These were just tough drifters, drawn to an easy fight. She pictured these uncouth brigands coming upon Shallum's daughters. She thought about Manasseh's lean form trying to dart to safety between their horses, or worse, standing his ground with only a rock in his hand. Her father talked only of tearing down the wall. He never spoke about the people who would fall along with it.

He's wrong, she thought. There isn't one person that I've met who hates him. The walls are not the threat he takes them for.

That, at least, was what she thought with her head. Her heart only knew one thing. She could not lose Manasseh. And so head and heart between them forged a plan that was both terrifying and exhilarating all at the same time. She lay awake that night listening to what now to her ears sounded like truculent tigers hot on the scent of pillage. By morning she was convinced. She would act on her plan.

Head and heart nodded to each other in silent satisfaction. The heart especially.

* * *

Nehemiah decided to write his letter to Artaxerxes himself. It was not just that he did not trust the scribe, seconded from the temple staff. He hoped that his own handwriting would add just the right amount of personal intimacy and match the tone of his dispatch. Artaxerxes had his sentimental side and Nehemiah was not above exploiting it. He began:

> *Longimanus:*[29]
> *Forgive the impertinence of your childhood name but it was not just a random jest of God that He made your right hand extend longer. It is from that hand that I have already received more beneficence than I deserve. Cyrus, your grandfather, might have been called "Yahweh's Anointed"[30] for having first released our people but you surely are God's right hand of goodness. For it is by you, and you alone, that the walls of our city will rise again.*

Nehemiah paused. It's a little thickly laid on, he thought. And Artaxerxes will see that, and also know that I know that I'm reaching. But he will also be flattered. No, it's a good introduction. I'll leave it. He continued to write.

> *The work is three quarters complete, although it does not look it and the people are understandably weary. They could not know that preparations are always more onerous than the actual building. At present, though, those who oppose me in this work are marshalling armed and mounted irregulars and mean to attack*

*us, or at least would like us to think that they will. Sanballat, your
governor, is at the centre of the intrigue and does everything he can
to threaten me. He is so desperate that he even bribed two local
nabis who came to me with a supposed "word from Yahweh." Had
I listened, the matter would have led to committing a sacrilege
within the temple.*[31]

*I had feared that his hold over the people and the enormity of the
task might at last carry the day and we would lose heart and energy
to finish. These people are so broken themselves, poor not only in
spirit but also in purse. Many had sold their own children into service just to raise their tribute, their fields being already pledged.*[32]

Nehemiah paused again. Careful, he thought. I don't want him to feel
guilty. He'll just get angry if he thinks I'm trying to blame his taxes for the
plight of these people. He started again.

*But like your own heart, God softened the hearts of those rich
Jews who had so shamelessly exploited their own kinsmen. I was
able to convince them to forgive all debt owed to them by a Jew.
In this I led the way. Even if you had doubts I would return
to you, be at rest in that matter, for I have sold almost all my
family's estates and bought back all the Jews who had been sold
into Gentile servitude.*[33] *But you taught me well and in this I
have only followed your own counsel. For leadership to be trusted,
it must always cost the leader something personal. And I have no
regrets.*

*Still, the open barbs and mockery Sanballat hurled on us ate
at our morale. It is his latest move, however, that will betray him
and serve our purposes just as surely as if he were on our side. For
if you are the right hand of God, then Sanballat is his left, though
he remains blind to it.*

*You will hear (or perhaps you already have heard) that I am
plotting to rebel against you, that I seek to resurrect the broken
throne of David and sit upon it in defiance of your lawful right
to rule over us — a wobbly throne, to be sure! This is the rumour
that Sanballat spreads to justify his intimidation and the gathering of an army.*[34] *Who knows for sure what he truly believes? He is
many vile things, and I make no secret of my contempt, but he is no
traitor to Persia. And in that lies my salvation and the providence*

of God. For he cannot — he will not — attack a fellow governor without the hard proof of my rebellion.

His army will do for me the very thing I seek. It will bring us together — unite us against a common foe, and elevate the drudgery of lifting stones into a holy mission. There is nothing quite like the threat of war to energize a people, especially when no one will actually die. So, Longimanus, my small request of you is simply that on hearing wild reports of my insurrection and equally tall tales about Sanballat's intended savagery, you simply do nothing. Sanballat has done more to stiffen the resolve of us Jews than anything I might have done. To play at being soldiers lies in the breast of every farmer, merchant, priest or poet. My workers will take up what swords can be found. Hananiah will distribute military chevrons. They will sew your colours on their tunics, all the while hailing each other as comrades-in-arms. On their simple leaders I will bestow military rank, and their mouths shall be full of the glorious taste of victory, food that will feed us until the last gate is hung. Blessed be both the right and the left hand of God. Our mission is already complete.

Your obedient cupbearer,

Nehemiah.

* * *

They met on the south side of the temple terrace. On that side, the various chambers that abutted the main temple building offered a number of secluded niches where they would not be seen. Nikaso had entered the city from where Shallum's family worked and then excused herself after a few hours. Not everything that she told Manasseh was news to him. But the intensity with which she spoke was its own message — both urgent and ardent. His heart listened to it without defence.

He told her of the preparations being made. Nehemiah had put the city on high alert and now had a trumpeter constantly at his side for signaling.[35] The entire length of wall could not be defended at the same time. But then, Sanballat's rabble also could not attack except in one spot. At all the high points along the wall, Nehemiah had stationed sentries, teenaged youth, if the truth were told, but all with keen eyes and fast feet. The plan was that whoever saw Sanballat's advance would run to Nehemiah's command post. The trumpeter would race back to where the attack was anticipated and sound the alarm. Everyone would then mass at the threatened point. Nehemiah had insisted that the entire city practise the maneuver several times. "Military preparedness," was what he called it.

The first few times the trumpet had sounded the results had been comical, with breathless and out of shape civilians dashing through the narrow streets in search of a sound that proved surprisingly hard to locate. On one such exercise, a portly man who had been the first to arrive panted about proudly until it was pointed out to him that the scabbard strapped to his waist was missing its sword. In his haste, it had fallen out and he was a day finding it again.

But Manasseh confirmed that the mood was better. Putting the whole city on a wartime footing had birthed an energy and camaraderie that surpassed even the initial days of wall building. Patriotism ran riot. Puffed up egos prated loudly that they would die before they let Sanballat desecrate one sacred stone of their city. Building teams were split into a rotation so that there were always some men standing guard. Everyone who had swords wore them. It didn't matter that few really knew how to use them. Nehemiah praised everyone he saw for the battle-hardened soldiers they saw themselves to be. Work on the wall had actually quickened despite the reduced people available for the building.

Nikaso loved listening to Manasseh describe a scene — any scene. He had that artist's gift of being able to stand outside of a thing yet still feel its moods and colour. It was serious business, her father's army. But from inside the wall, there was something endearing about the people's resolve.

"Why have you come?" he asked finally.

"My father thinks that this wall will destroy us somehow. That once it's built the people inside will disown the Jews outside. Only those who can prove they came back from the exile will be considered real Jews. The rest of us — me, my family, Tobiah — we'll be considered no better than Gentiles."

"You have not answered my question."

She gazed straight into his face. "Marry me. Take me as your wife. Show my father he has nothing to be afraid of."

"I should marry you just to prove a point?" For once she could not read his face.

"Marry me because I love you."

He put a finger to her lips before she could say anything else. Then, slowly and with great deliberation, he pressed his mouth tight against hers. It was a long, probing exchange. She felt herself being held by his body against the wall where they stood. She felt all of him against her, his chest pushing in her breasts and those long arms of his encircling her shoulders, reaching round back of her, drawing her in. It was a kiss that ran from her feet to her head. It was a kiss that bound them more tightly than any hurried words a priest might say over them later. She received his answer and gave him back the assurances he needed in return.

Finally he drew back. His eyes sparkled. They were the kindest glitters of light she had ever seen. Years later, that moment would come back and comfort her when nothing else could. Their marriage might prove a point. It might not. But he would marry her because he loved her too. He cupped her gently by the chin and said with an impish grin, "Usually it's the men who do the asking, Nikaso." Then, grabbing her hand, he tugged at her. "We're going to talk to my grandfather. This isn't going to be easy."

"I'm taking Nikaso for my wife," was how Manasseh started the conversation. Eliashib's face remained as stony as the wall against which he stood.

"I'm not your father, and you are of age. I cannot stop you, and permission is not mine to give or withhold. But your news is not a complete surprise to me."

"Oh." Manasseh, who had been ready for fierce resistance, was not sure now how to proceed.

Eliashib continued. "I'm old, Manasseh, but I'm not entirely blind to your affairs. Besides, Tobiah alerted me to this possibility some time ago. We have already discussed its implications to the larger picture."

"Tobiah?" Nikaso gasped. "What did he tell you?" And who else has he told? My father, probably."

"It is not your business to know," Eliashib replied curtly, "even as it is not mine to ask why the two of you are intent on marrying." He waved his hands dismissively at their immediate protests. "Oh, I know. You're marrying out of love, or you believe foolishly that no one in the entire world has ever felt the way you do. Or, perhaps you rush to marriage because Nikaso is already pregnant. Frankly, I do not much care. But tell me, Nikaso, has it penetrated your star-struck gaze that your father has raised a small army and parades it in front of us this past week, meaning to attack us?

"I'm just curious, you see. Curious to see if you've given even one minute's thought to what you will do after you've found a priest willing to officiate — what then? Will you ride out and join your father? And you, Manasseh; did you then plan to stay here and defend yourself against your new bride?"

Hot anger instantly seized Nikaso's face. "My father fears this wall; he is obsessed that it will divide what few Jews remain in the world. My marriage will show him he has no need to fear. Do not insult me by treating me like a child who does not comprehend the larger affairs that threaten us all."

Eliashib ignored her anger and when he spoke, it was in the quiet measured tone of reason. "Let me ask you both something. Has it ever occurred to you that Sanballat might be right?"

No one spoke. Clearly it had not occurred to them. Eliashib continued. "I see it has not. Well, my children — no, no — don't protest, for that is exactly what you are — you both are. I for one believe that Sanballat sees clearly into the future. This wall is only a beginning. Oh, it will make us a people again; it will be the morning star that guides the exiles back from the east. And on the face of it, there is no reason the city should not be restored. But Sanballat is not alone in seeing a dark future. Nehemiah's housecleaning will not stop with the debris in our streets. He will not rest until the people are as clean and upright as are our walls."

"Clean and upright according to whom? According to Nehemiah?" Manasseh asked.

"You have asked the essential question, Manasseh. And the answer is still in front of us all. But make no mistake, the walls are only the beginning of a much bigger reconstruction."

"And you?" Nikaso asked. "Where do you stand?"

"If Nehemiah and his zealots carry the day, do you have any idea how hard your marriage will be?" It was as if Eliashib had not heard her question.

"And if no one resists?" she answered. "Sanballats are not cowards. I name Yahweh as my God. So does Manasseh. That makes us both Jews."

Eliashib smiled for the first time. "And I agree with you. The future that I dream about but which I will not live to see is a land that is big enough for us all. I dream of the day when the nabi's words will be true — that the temple shall be a place of prayer for all people; that the lost tribes that were scattered will be gathered together."[36]

"You could name me as your successor! As the next High Priest I could bring this future to pass."

"You are not tough enough," Eliashib replied bluntly, and then with more kindness, "it is why Nikaso loves you and not your older brother Johnathon whom I will anoint. You have a good heart, Manasseh — pure. The politics of office would destroy it. There is no dishonour in being who you are."

"Will you help us tell my father?" asked Nikaso.

"You both have courage. And I will publicly support you. People should know where this High Priest stands, old though he is. And it will be a warning to Nehemiah to tread softly. And as for your father," he said directly to Nikaso, "do you want to be married before, or after I would speak to him?"

Nikaso looked at Manasseh and saw that the decision was hers, and hers alone. "Before."

"Then go and find Meremoth.[37] He's the priest on duty. It's unusual, to say the least. But we are, after all, under threat of attack — by the bride's father, no less. Come back when you've signed the certificates and Meremoth has entered it in the temple record."

"I'll write it in myself," said Manasseh. "Meremoth's hand trembles when he's nervous."

"And I'm certain he'll be that. Tell him I approve of what you ask."

The rest of the day took on dream-like qualities, but by evening everything had been accomplished. Still, neither Manasseh nor Nikaso felt truly different from the way they had felt that morning. Not until Sanballat had been confronted would either of them feel truly married.

"I could ride out tonight and tell him," Manasseh suggested.

"No. He would take huge offence and think that I was afraid. I'll *not* have that. And willing though he might be, it is hardly Eliashib's job to tell him. He's *my* father. I should go myself."

"I won't let you. There are men wandering all over the countryside. You'll be detained, and worse. Send him a note. The courier can bring back his reply if there is to be one."

"It's the best that can be done. Can you find someone willing to ride this time of night?"

"You write the letter. I'll find a rider." He left her at a small escritoire, clutching a sharpened stylus. When he returned she silently handed him a small packet of papyri already sealed.

"You found someone?"

"I did, and will take it to him now. Afterward I've got some preparations at the temple that I must attend to. I'll be on duty myself soon. Sorry; but I'll hurry through them." They shared a kiss, but they both felt its awkwardness. It was all either of them could do not to look around to see if anyone was watching.

* * *

Should we have waited? he wondered. This feels so strange; good but unfamiliar. And tonight I sleep with her. A week ago I did not even dare hope, yet now that it is possible, I'm nervous.

* * *

Does he regret it, she wondered? He holds himself so rigid. And what will tonight be like? The temple rituals were so quick I hardly dare believe that sharing a bed is now expected of us. We've been secretive for so long. Will he be disappointed?

* * *

About a half mile from Beth-Horan, Manasseh stopped to light a large lantern tied to his saddle. He did not want to be the target of some overanxious sentry thinking he was a spy. Only once was he challenged to which he curtly replied, "Urgent dispatches for Sanballat. I've ridden from Ashdod." He knew exactly the house where Sanballat was and handed Nikaso's letter to its doorkeeper saying, "Sanballat is to get this at once. Wake him up if you have to. Tell him that Manasseh, grandson of Eliashib, waits by his door for a reply."

Sanballat was still up and recognized the handwriting. Not until then did he realize that he'd not actually seen Nikaso all day. He stomped irritably while a stronger light was found and he began to read:

Father,

Manasseh is now my husband.[38] *We married in haste this after-noon, for the city fears that the next time your army appears it will be successful in entering the city. What you look upon as faceless, arrogant Jews intent on snubbing you, I know as good-hearted, innocent people, each one with a name. They have hopes and fears about the future, just like us. I could not persuade you with words from your conviction that this wall will destroy us. Perhaps my actions will. Today one of Jerusalem's leading families has accepted me into their household. Jew has married Jew, and Eliashib will make known his support.*

This wall has only the power that we give to it, and today Manasseh and I have shown how it can be so easily breached. It takes only the courage to follow our heart's love.

Perhaps now you will relent and not attack the city. These people will not prevail against your army, and wives and children work alongside the men. Many will die if you press us. I beg of you, father, believe in a future that can hold together all of us who name Yahweh as God. Believe that the love Manasseh and I have for each other can prevail. I know you cannot object to his family. Please do not object to him whom my heart has chosen.

Nikaso

Sanballat slumped back. I drove her to it, he thought. She truly believed I meant to attack the city. Tobiah warned me of trouble but I never saw this. What have I done?

A servant coughed quietly in the doorway. Sanballat looked up.

"What?"

"I was to tell you that the man who delivered the dispatch is waiting should you wish to see him. His name is Manasseh, grandson of Eliashib. He made clear he wanted you to know his name."

Sanballat's whole throat came together like a sprung trap. He fought for breath and found just enough air to say, "Have him wait." His whole body entered one long agonizing convulsion. He was aware that his lungs would not expand and that his breathing stopped somewhere just below his throat. I've got to get control, he thought. He began with his breathing, counting slowly each breath, willing his body to accept a little more air with each succeeding effort. The fit passed slowly. Only when he was quite certain his body would not betray him, did he get to his feet and start toward where Manasseh was waiting.

"I could kill you, you know," he began. "It would serve Eliashib right. I give you hospitality all these years, open my home to you, and this is how you repay me. You secretly abuse my daughter and then marry her in haste without the courage to confront me first."

"That's a lie," Manasseh flashed hotly. " We have not yet been intimate." He blushed at his admission but of everything that Sanballat had said, it was that slur that cut deepest. Sanballat regretted his accusation. There are some things a father did not need to know and Nikaso was hardly one to engage in anything she did not want to.

"Did Nikaso send you?"

"She does not know I am here. She thinks I am out making preparations for my temple duty that could not wait."

"Why did she not come herself?"

"She wanted to, but I would not let her. Your newly arrived visitors can be troublesome if met on the road at night. She might have come to some harm."

"You have a point," Sanballat grunted. "So then, why are *you* here?"

"We need your blessing."

"Do you, now. I'd say it's a little late for that. Besides, Eliashib approves. I'm just a lowly hanger-on from the ten lost tribes of the north. Whereas you — you could well be the next High Priest."

"This is not about whose family is more noble — or more Jewish, for that matter."

"Isn't it? I think that is precisely what this is about. You think I should be grateful that the High Priest's family has stooped to welcome a Samarian Jew into their collective bed?"

"I think the High Priest's family should be grateful that a Persian governor would link his family with theirs."

Sanballat's tone softened slightly. "You're a clever one with words, Manasseh. You always have been. And now you and Nikaso think you will make everything right; that Eliashib and I will each stand on tippy-toe to shake hands over the wall and be led into a happy future by our newlywed children?"

Manasseh allowed a small grin. "That is about how Nikaso hoped it might go — or at the very least, that you would not kill us all."

It was Sanballat's turn to smile a little. "She's persistent when she gets an idea into her head, isn't she?"

"Yes. Quite."

"But you should have asked first."

"That's what I said, too."

It took Sanballat a second to take in the meaning of Manasseh's remark. His face was now the face of a frustrated father dealing with a strong-minded daughter. "She's not the usual submissive type, Manasseh. I should warn you."

"She loves her father more than she loves me," he replied.

"Do you have any notion of how hard your lives are going to be?" Sanballat asked. "Not everyone will approve of this union."

"Eliashib thinks there could be trouble ahead."

"Well, he and I agree for once, then."

"Your blessing," Manasseh pressed.

"Alright, you have it. There, it is done. Now get back to your wife. You have no business being this far away from her on your wedding night."

He stood in the doorway of the house and watched his son-in-law mount up and recede into the blackness.

It was time to send the army home.

ENDNOTES

1. Sanballat seems to have done a remarkable job both in managing his province and passing on these skills to his children. His direct descendants remained in charge of Samaria for the next century (*Oxford History of the Biblical World*, p. 313).

2. That Sanballat had a daughter is attested to in scriptures, but she is not named. Josephus names her in his story of Nehemiah's activities and this is the name I have used.

3. Precise information about Persia's political administration is hampered by Greek and Babylonian texts rendering the precise Persian word "satrap" (protector of the realm) to the more general word "governor." The Persian king Darius (522–486) consolidated the Persian administration into twenty satrapies, ruled by royal princes. Megabyzus was one such appointed viceroy, although history indicates he wielded substantial power. Within each satrapy, however, smaller provinces were also established and both Sanballat and Nehemiah were court-appointed "satraps" for their respective jurisdictions. Both satrapies and provinces were of assorted sizes and had been frequently established along ethnic demographics, or the results of military campaigns. Control over provinces was maintained by the royal court as a safeguard against overly ambitious viceroys who might seek independence. The reference in Esther 8:9 to one hundred and twenty-seven provinces stretching from India to Ethiopia probably refers to the number of provinces within the twenty satrapies.

4. The Immortals were a federal army corps consisting of ten thousand mounted troops under the personal direction of the King.

5. Traditional scholarship holds that the Assyrians deported large numbers of Jews in a forced resettlement scheme designed to make subsequent rebellion impossible. It should be noted, however, that Assyrian documents record that only 27,290 people were taken as captives, hardly enough to permanently scatter the ten northern tribes of Israel. It is possible that a sizable population remained in the land, and could identify themselves as true Israelites (*International Standard Bible Encyclopedia*; see article on Samaritans).

6. Most scholars estimate that about 4,600 adult males were deported. Neither before nor since had God's covenant people ever been reduced to such a tiny remnant.

7. Tobiah's offspring remained a powerful family for almost three hundred years. The family's palace still survives in Jordan and resembles something of a small palace surrounded by a dug lake, built for ornamental effect. The presence of Jewish religious symbols on the interior cornice is strong evidence that the clan were practising Jews.

8. Malachi 1:10ff. Traditional dating for Malachi's ministry is about 470 BC. It is perhaps black irony that his oracles are the last book in the Old Testament. What followed was four hundred years of prophetic silence until John the Baptist began his ministry proclaiming the coming of Jesus.

9. Nehemiah 12:11. This is the only reference to Eliashib's son and this passage only includes him in reciting the High Priestly lineage. If he was ever High Priest, we know nothing of his activities. The biblical narrative and Josephus' history suggest that the office of High Priest passed directly from Eliashib to one of his grandsons. A few historians even refer to Johanan (Johnathon), Joshua and Manasseh as the sons of Eliashib, not the grandsons.

10. Mount Gerizim ("the mount of blessings") together with its twin mountain Ebal ("the mount of curses") is located about fifty miles north of Jerusalem and ten miles to the southeast of Samaria. Jacob's well (John 4:6) where Jesus encountered the Samaritan woman (John 4:20) is located in the valley between them. The ancient town of Shechem is at the base of Mount Gerizim. Mount Gerizim became the centre for Samarian worship, and a temple was built at its base in the fourth century BC.

In Deuteronomy 27:1–9 Moses instructs the Israelites to cross over the Jordan and build an altar of natural stone on Mount Ebal. The words of the law were to be chiseled into rock dolmens placed prominently on the mountainside. This location was understood to be the central place of worship. The two mountains are again mentioned in Joshua 8:30–35 and Deuteronomy 27:11–13. These scriptures describe a national liturgy in which the people positioned themselves on both mountains, creating a natural amphitheatre. Those on Mount Gerizim would shout the "blessing formulas" while those on Mount Ebal would respond with appropriate "cursing formulas."

Adherents of the Samarian (later, Samaritan) sect worshiped Yahweh, followed Torah, and claimed Moses as their prophet. They also asserted that in the original versions of Torah, Moses had chosen Mount Gerizim as the central place of worship, and not Mount Ebal as our English language texts read. Samarian tradition holds that it was Ezra who deliberately changed the words of Torah to undermine the Samarians' claim to be legitimate Yahweh worshippers and part of the Jewish community. Whereas in Jewish traditions Ezra is revered as a prophet second only to Moses, in Samarian history he is an infidel, guilty of having changed the words of Torah. The meaning of Samaritan is "keeper of the faith" and the Samaritans' Jewish roots are traced back to the northern tribes of Ephraim and Manasseh.

While certainty is impossible, there is some weight to the Samarians' claim. It seems unusual that the Mount of Curses would be where Moses ordained central worship, rather than the Mount of Blessings. Textual evidence is divided. A report issued by the United Bible Society concluded that ". . . the original text of Deuteronomy 27:4 cited Mount Gerizim but we are tentative in our conclusions" (D. Barthelemy ed. *Preliminary Report on the Old Testament Text Project*. New York, United Bible Society, 1979).

11. Ezra 4:7 cites a certain Tabeel who was among the civil rulers who frustrated the rebuilding project five years earlier. Both Tabeel (Aramaic) and Tobiah (Hebrew) mean *God is good*. Some scholars have identified both names as referring to the same person.

12. Under Persian rule, provincial cities did not have walls. Fortifications built by earlier rulers had been dismantled. Samaria was no exception. This was both to make insurrection difficult to take root and to be a sign of the overall security of the empire. During the Persian period, military presence was by way of small fortified garrisons strategically located along the major roads. Housed with federal regiments, their main task was to maintain safe travel. That Jerusalem had been granted permission to rebuild its fortifications was unique.

13. Population estimates for the time period are based on both incomplete data and methodology that is open to criticism. *The Oxford History of the Biblical World* (page 289) says that Jerusalem's population could have been as low as 475 to 500. The population for all of Yehud is placed at about 10,000. The combined biblical census lists (Ezra chapter 2 and Nehemiah chapter 7) suggest a population of about 50,000 for the province, but it is difficult to know exactly what time period these lists cover (see John Bright, *A History of Israel*, page 378).

14. Nehemiah 3:12.

15. The person they encountered was actually named Meshullam, the son of Berekiah: Nehemiah 3:4,30; Nehemiah 6:18. Since a more prominent character with the same name appears in a later story, I have substituted the father's name here to avoid reader confusion.

16. Nehemiah 6:18.

17. The demise of Israel as a sovereign state happened in two stages. Shortly after King Solomon died (930 BC) the twelve united tribes split into two nations. The ten northern tribes were ruled from Samaria and the tribes of Judah and Benjamin formed their own state, ruled from Jerusalem. In 722 BC, the Assyrian Empire invaded and destroyed the northern kingdom, deporting a large part of the population to various other parts of their empire. The southern kingdom survived until 587 BC when Nebuchadnezzar, the Babylonian king, destroyed Jerusalem and took Israel's last king into captivity.

18. Nehemiah 12:10 cites the list of Priests from Manasseh's brother to Jeshua.

The other names cited are in I Chronicles 6:3–15. See also I Chronicles 9:10,11.

19. Nehemiah 2:13ff: In fact, when Nehemiah made his first inspection of the walls (at night) he was forced to dismount and descend to the valley floor from which he made his inspection of this portion of the wall.

20. Some scholars conclude that prior to Nehemiah's arrival, Sanballat had formal charge over the province of Yehud. Accordingly, his opposition to Nehemiah could be interpreted as jealousy over the loss of territory. While this is a convenient slur on Sanballat's character, archeological evidence confirms continuous independent governors in Yehud from 538 BC to 408 BC. The simplistic explanation that Sanballat's actions were motivated by his desire for political and economic power has to be considered carefully. A case can be made that Sanballat, for some periods of time, had informal care of the province, at least insofar as remitting taxes, the maintenance of roads and maintaining civil order. But Yehud was not and never had been part of Sanballat's formal jurisdiction. Bluntly put, in opposing Nehemiah, he risked his very life for dubious economic gain, if any. What is astonishing is that Sanballat did not suffer reprisals from the Persian court for such a clear violation of Imperial regulations. Not only was he not recalled (or worse), but his sons were appointed as his successor.

21. Sanballat's concern about the quality of Jewish leadership, and their bias towards violence, is not simply literary fabrication. According to Josephus, a first-century Jewish historian, Jonathon brutally murdered his brother Joshua in an argument over who would serve as High Priest. Worse, the murder took place inside the temple. That any religious shrine would be desecrated in this manner was enormously offensive to the Persians who imposed a punitive tax on the Jews for seven years. It is dark irony that foreigners would have more respect for the sanctity of Yahweh's temple than did the Jewish High Priest. (*Jewish Antiquities*, Bk II, Ch. 7).

22. A typical Assyrian form of brutality.

23. While the construction methods Nehemiah used are not known, lime-based concrete had been used at least as far back as the Egyptian pyramids in 2500 BC. The basic recipe is lime, sand and water. Volcanic ash was used from at least as far back as the Roman Empire. It was this technology that enabled the building of the Roman Coliseum. While they did not understand why using ash was an improvement, it was actually the silicone that reacts with the calcium hydroxide in the lime to increase the hardening properties of the concrete.

24. Nehemiah 2:8. Asaph is called the "keeper of the king's forest," although his location is not known. Nehemiah would probably have requisitioned lumber from as nearby as possible.

25. Nehemiah 4:3. The exact words of Tobiah are recorded as ". . . if even a fox climbed up on it, he would break down their wall of stones."

26. Jeremiah 24:1–10: In this perturbing vision received by Jeremiah, Yahweh calls those Jews who remained in the land "bad figs" whom He would abandon in favour of those who were exiled into Babylon. While other scriptures promise a more encompassing definition of God's peoples (Isaiah 44: 3–5, and especially Isaiah 56:1–8), this passage in Jeremiah is both stark and clear in its intent.

27. The Arabian desert was never brought under formal Persian control. A treaty required some annual tribute, but Geshem enjoyed considerably more latitude than Sanballat or the (Phonecian) Governor from Ashdod. Geshem was steadily pushing north and west of his historic lands into the territory formerly occupied by the Edomites, long-time enemies of Israel. He therefore had an immediate and personal stake in the success of Sanballat's mission. If Geshem had ridden from his home base at Dedan, then he would have crossed two hundred miles of desert in order to assist Sanballat. The rebuilding of Jerusalem's walls was seen to have far-reaching consequences.

28. Nehemiah 5:17–19. Persian administration authorized provincial satraps the right to levy taxes for the operation of their households and administrative staff. As a result, governors were, as a rule, quite wealthy. Waiving the "governor's tax" may be thought of as having the same effect as a local municipality abolishing property taxes, leaving only federal obligations. For the poor and frequently indebted population, this "tax holiday" was an act of generosity without precedent.

29. Prior to his ascending to the throne, this was the personal name of Artaxerxes. Some scholars think it was a nickname from the fact that his right arm was noticeably longer than his left.

30. Isaiah 45:1–8. Cyrus is the only foreign king to have been so singled out.

31. Nehemiah 6:10ff.

32. Nehemiah 5:1–20. Through a series of bold and self-sacrificing initiatives, Nehemiah brilliantly gained the confidence and support of the wealthy Jews who were critical to his success. This chapter remains a stellar account of "leadership by example" that would find a place in any current management textbook.

33. Nehemiah 5:1–13.

34. Nehemiah 6:5ff.

35. Nehemiah 4:16ff.

36. Isaiah 27:12, Isaiah 56:1–8.

37. Ezra 8:33: Meremoth, the son of Uriah, the son of Hakkoz (I Chronicles 24:10). I have included this man because his own lineage could not be proved for a time and he was barred from priestly duties (and revenues). Nehemiah 7:61–66 and Ezra 2:61 describe a small group of returning priests (that included the descendants of Hakkoz) who could not prove their ancestral purity. Ezra and Nehemiah mention at least three men who were barred from service. Meremoth's two companions, it would seem, were never re-instated, owing to missing ancestral records.

38. Nehemiah 13:28.

REFINER'S ASHES

Ezra In Prayer.
Gustave Doré (1832–1883)

"But who may abide the day of His coming? And who shall stand when He appeareth? For He is like a refiner's fire. And he shall purify the sons of Levi, that they may offer unto the Lord an offering in righteousness."
— Spoken by the nabi Malachi at the time of this story.

When Ezra finally left Jerusalem, people either blessed their sons or cursed their dogs with his name. But whether he was revered as a holy man or despised as a religious incendiary, no one's life was ever the same after his visit. That included Katannah,[1] a woman who braided the hair of wealthy women living in their newly restored Jerusalem homes.

Katannah's family were farmers, or at least tried to be when the drought and locusts let up enough for there to be a crop to harvest. Her village lay about eight miles to the east of Jerusalem, settled by Ammonites whose roots were already dug deep into the land when the Israelites were still slaves in Egypt. Katannah had never been further than ten miles away from the hovel she called home and she was utterly poor.

But despite these hardships, Katannah regarded herself, when she thought about it at all, as living a life that had been hugely blessed by the gods, and as a consequence she was both happy and grateful. Her particular blessings were two in number. The first was that she was still free and had not been sold into indentured labour by her parents so as to raise money for the annual taxes. Many of her childhood friends had suffered that fate and were now scattered throughout the surrounding provinces, likely never to see their families ever again. The second blessing was that she had married a man called Caleb[2] whom she passionately loved and who returned her love in equal measure. There was a third blessing the gods had granted her. Katannah was beautiful. But since no one in the village owned a mirror she could not comprehend the extent of this gift and so could not dwell on it.

Poverty was so prevalent and widespread among the villages that, as with her natural beauty, Katannah grew up largely unaware of what wealth actually was. Not until Jerusalem had been brought back to life by the zealous breath of a man called Nehemiah, not until rich Jews came in waves from a land called Persia on news that their ancient city of David once again had both walls and temple, not until she saw the bulging caravans of richly carved furniture, panniers gorged with huge bolts of embroidered silken draperies and the shimmering linen tunics made from Indian cotton that graced the sleek bodies of the women she served, not until one of her clients gave her a small coin made of silver that first taught her about this thing called money, and not until the transformation of Jerusalem from an abandoned refuse pit to the new cosmopolitan centre of Yehud — not until all of this happened did it dawn on Katannah that she was desperately poor.

But as part of that education, Katannah saw her reflection in a polished tin mirror owned by a client, and she came to understand just how beautiful she actually was. Katannah possessed a natural beauty that all the lotions of Persia could not create. It was an outer form that made old men pause in mid sentence and forget how to start again, and made young men go slack-jawed when they saw her in Jerusalem's streets. Her face radiated a glow that seemed to come from some inner light, and her black eyes twinkled with kindness. She usually wore her own hair in a modest long plait tied in place with a scrap of cloth. But sometimes she would let it cascade down in sensuous oiled coils that hid her shoulders. There was not one part of her body that had not been perfectly sculpted, and her rough tunic, worn only to the knees, could not hide either her firm round breasts or slender thighs that flitted ever so briefly into sight when she walked.

But her real beauty, the kind that stayed with her long after her skin had wrinkled and her breasts were stretched from the suck of infants, rested in a spirit that remained content even after she realized just how poor she was. The gods had been kind to her. And as a consequence, the fragrance of gratitude covered her like the finest spun gossamer.

She had met Caleb by accident. Walking through the narrow streets one day, she heard the sound of someone singing. There were no instruments, just a pure melodic voice that filled the still air between the crowded houses. Intrigued, she followed the voice until she was standing in the large open square that surrounded the temple. There, standing all alone on the elevated terrace on which the temple itself was built, stood the singer. What few other people were in the square seemed to take no notice. The singer's face tilted up exposing a squarish, clean-shaven chin. His eyes were closed and he seemed oblivious to who might, or might not, care to be listening. His arms hung loosely at his sides as he swayed slowly in response to the cadence of his own voice. Katannah drew closer until only the ten broad stone steps connecting the temple terrace to the square separated them. Katannah had no preparation, much less defence, for what she heard. She did not recognize the language. But words and music together were like some grand and wild bird in flight swooping down low over her head, describing what it felt to be free from the earthen obligations that ensnared her feet. It was an invitation into something so pure and yet so passionate all at the same time that, had she been able, she would have left everything that was her life just to see the world as the singer's voice told her it existed. She stood utterly still. Each new note that entered her ears plucked at some feeling Katannah did not know lay inside her until that very moment. Hope, longing and fulfillment suddenly sprang to life, fully formed inside her, and danced with the music until there was no more space inside of her to hold his song. Her chest was tight and her breath came in short, shallow gasps. In one brief song, courtship and conquest were completed.

Caleb stopped and looked down into Katannah's upturned face. She said nothing but only continued to stare back at him. He noticed her chest heaving and her gaze was so intense that he wondered if she actually was looking at him. He waited.

"What were you singing?" she asked bluntly. She asked her question in Aramaic. It was by far the most widely used language throughout Persia. It was also the only one she knew. He answered her in the same.

"Hebrew," Caleb said. "It is a song in praise of Yahweh." He gestured back at the temple doors behind him. "It thanks him for having made our world and everything in it: sun, stars, moon, the day, the night, the wind and even the rainstorms and lightning."

"Why were you singing it?"

"Because singing is what I do, and this — " he pointed to the temple again patiently, " — is his temple. Why were you listening?"

She flushed and Caleb instantly regretted his bantering question. Wherever it was his music had taken her, even he could see that she was not entirely returned to where she stood.

"Am I not allowed?" she asked, quite seriously.

"Of course, and I'm flattered that someone would pause and honour my practising."

"Practising?"

"Yes. There is a small festival of sorts in two days' time and I have a solo part. But I like to practise out here in the bright sunlight when I can. It's freer and fits the music better. My name is Caleb, by the way. I'm a cantor."

"I'm Katannah," she said, willing herself to breathe normally again.

"Pleased to meet you."

"What does a cantor do?" Katannah had no embarrassment about admitting her own ignorance about anything. It allowed her to ask the most direct of questions in a way that disarmed people.

"Why, we sing. We sing prayers and praise anthems, recite parts of the Torah too. There are only six of us who get paid. But there is a larger choir that comes together for special occasions. The rest are volunteers, just people who like to sing. It's part of how we worship. We're not all about killing helpless goats and turtle doves on the altar, you know." Even to Caleb's ear, his answer didn't sound very intelligent. What his mind was saying was, "I'm a singer. But do you have any idea how beautiful you are and please, please don't go away until I find out who you are."

Katannah spoke again. "I'm not Jewish."

"I guessed as much. But don't you sing — at your own temple?"

"We haven't got a temple." She pictured the three small clay figures that stood on a shelf in her parents' hut. They were rude representations of the only gods she knew. She had no words to connect her meagre experience with this huge temple she now stood in front of.

"Oh." Caleb had reached an impasse, but had no intention of ending the conversation. "So what do you do?" he asked bluntly.

"I arrange women's hair; cut it sometimes if they want me to, and braid it."

"You must be very good at it."

"How can you tell?"

"Because your own hair is beautiful."

Katannah flushed for the second time and now Caleb regretted his question not a bit. He smiled. "Do you ever do men's hair?" He shook his own roughly cut mass that had not seen a comb for some time.

She smiled back. "I don't do it for free."

"Oh." It was Caleb's turn to flush, for he had virtually no money himself and he suddenly realized that he had no idea how much having his hair done might cost. Arranging women's hair was as foreign to him as cantoring was to Katannah. But his natural wit saved him and he said, "I could sing for you in exchange."

Their eyes, locking directly ever so briefly, betrayed both of them. They would see each other again.

"Where should I come to look for you?" she asked.

"I'll meet you here, tomorrow, about the same time."

People would have said that they were the happiest two people in Jerusalem, except that both were so poor and inconsequential that in truth no one took any notice of them. Caleb's parents had come from Babylon about twenty years earlier. He'd been five years old at the time and the memories of the long trip overland were simply the vivid fragments a young child retains without context. His mother had died somewhere on the way and he remembered his father, also a cantor, standing over a mound of earth crying out a haunting dirge while clutching Caleb's tiny hand. They'd started for Jerusalem in response to rumours of a flourishing singing guild said to be expanding there. But as in most tales of the Promised Land, vision far exceeded reality and Caleb's father had finally returned to Babylon to ply his trade in one of the half dozen established synagogues that flourished in the eastern part of the Persian Empire. Caleb had chosen to stay. Eventually he was taken on by the temple staff and given a tiny room and food enough to live in exchange for his songs. He was in essence an orphan, adopted by the temple and those who ran it.

Marrying Caleb had been a simple matter and followed soon after they first met. He had no family that might object. Her own parents were delighted at the prospects that they imagined Jerusalem might afford Katannah, and a husband who was "on the temple staff" had, to their simple minds, the ring of a royally appointed position. Katannah moved into Caleb's tiny room. And sometimes, when the moon would give them light, they would sit, cross-legged on his bed, facing each other and Caleb would fill her heart with ancient love songs in a tongue she did not understand while touching her hair and caressing her breasts ever so lightly. What their respective gods had seen fit to give them, they gave in turn to each other without reserve — his voice and her beauty —and it was all they needed for happiness.

* * *

Of all Katannah's clients, her favourite was an old woman called Fetneh. Not just because she was Ammonite, like Katannah; Fetneh embraced life with an exuberance that was contagious, and treated Katannah more as a sister despite their difference in age. Fetneh was not just old; she was old and fat, had a conspicuously missing front tooth, and dull grey hair that she refused to let Katannah colour.

"The only thing worse than an old hag is an old hag who doesn't know she is one," Fetneh would chortle whenever Katannah would broach the subject. "No, I've had my time twisting men's hearts out of shape and still live off the memories."

She had once been beautiful, or so she said, and Katannah believed her. Fetneh had an intricate tattoo on her front: a large image of Ishtar, the ancient fertility goddess who went by various names throughout the Fertile Crescent. Ishtar's head started just in the vee between Fetneh's cleavage and descended in great detail until her trailing gown receded finally somewhere in the vicinity of Fetneh's thighs. She even volunteered that in the early days, when she sat astride her husband, he would gaze up and imagine it was the goddess herself who attended to his every desire.

At least that was how Fetneh said it had been. Now, the rolls of fat that spilled everywhere made it impossible to see the tattoo clearly at all and the one time Katannah had occasion to see it while helping Fetneh change, the tattoo looked like some misshapen ink blot that could not be washed away.

Yet for all her ugliness, Fetneh kept the earthy musk of fertility that ran deep in the Ammonite soul and lived in a profound, happy conviction that all of life was a sensual affair. She made people happy just to be alive one more day. Her name meant "seduction" and she would shock the produce merchants in the market by scandalously swinging her ponderous breasts — with the heft of melons — asking if the merchants' produce was as ripe as hers. Then she would cackle with delight at their embarrassment. It was all good fun as far as she was concerned — "and anybody who said sex wasn't important was either a hypocrite or just very unlucky in whom they'd married."

Fetneh's husband, Jehiel, could not have been more opposite and Katannah could only guess at what had brought them together. He was one-third her weight, already had a slight stoop, and a head that looked permanently down lest he have to meet someone's eyes. Katannah had seen kitchen mice with more personality. Jehiel was Jewish and had arrived while still a baby, born somewhere on the overland route between Babylon and Jerusalem. His father had been a stonemason by trade and had devoted his entire life to the building of the temple. There was not much to show for his life. The temple rested in the middle of a massive raised terrace of quarried stone, one hundred feet wide, two hundred feet long and not quite ten feet high. Jehiel's father had died before even this rudimentary foundation was finished.

"He just keeled over dead one day, chisel and hammer clutched in his hands. Heart, I suppose, or heat, or just plain discouragement," Fetneh had explained to Katannah one day. "And Jehiel was never the same after that, seemed to shrink a little each day. But if you had seen the old Jehiel, the one I married, before his father died, you would understand. And it's the old Jehiel I love, and pray to the goddess whose image I'll take to my grave that some day he'll be given back to me." Over time, Katannah saw that Fetneh's zest for life was partly because she was living for two: herself and the husk of a man whose soul seemed to have vanished with the death of his father. It was like a perpetual invitation to rejoin life, and Fetneh loved her poor Jehiel so much that she would never stop trying to revive him. "Besides," she said to Katannah with a sad little laugh, "how can I give up on him? I'm not called *seduction* for nothing."

But if Fetneh and Jehiel were a mismatched pair, their one son, Shecaniah,[3] could well have been a foundling for all the resemblance he bore to either of his parents. Katannah met him by accident through her husband.

"Can you help a friend with his hair?" Caleb had asked her abruptly one day. She had brought him a lunch and they were standing on the north side of the temple terrace where there was at least a little shade.

"Of course," she answered, thinking it was another singer to whom Caleb owed a favour. "I'm free later."

"No, now. He's working just around the corner."

"But my shears are at home."

"It won't matter, he's got a knife."

"What?"

But Caleb was already steering her toward the east side of the terrace. A series of small chambers was being built along the back wall of the temple building itself. When finished, they would match the rooms that already flanked each of the long sides of the temple and be used for storehouses, living quarters and the like. Each chamber had a door that opened directly onto the massive stone terrace. About twenty men grunted in the hot sun, shifting dressed stones that Katannah could see would eventually become the chamber walls.

"Shecaniah," Caleb called out, "I've brought her; this is my wife, Katannah."

A square mass of a man, leveraging a stubborn stone with brute force, looked up, gave the iron bar he held one last gigantic push, and moved the stone the final few required inches. Only then did he move slowly toward her. Tiny rock crystals covered his entire body and where they had mixed with his sweat, stuck to his skin like glittering but grotesque scabs.

His arms are as big as my legs, thought Katannah, and she was not too far wrong.

"Thank you, Caleb," the man said softly, avoiding Katannah's face. "This tuft at the back of my neck is driving me crazy and I can't get my knife back to cut it off."

"You don't cut hair with a knife," Katannah said.

"So it would seem." Shecaniah spoke to the space just below her eyes. "Or at least not all of it." Only a very long time later would she understand his gaze to be shyness instead of rudeness. His hair looked about as ruined as Jerusalem had been before the reconstruction. It was short so that most of it stuck straight up, except in patches which stood longer like wheat sheaves that had escaped the harvest.

"I keep it short because of the work," Shecaniah explained, seeing her stare. "Stone chips are hell on a man's scalp and if you're mixing mortar at the same time it's worse. Caleb says you do hair. There's something scratching my neck every time I move; can't concentrate and I can't leave this crew." He jerked backwards with his thumb, although whether he meant the crew or his neck, Katannah couldn't be sure. "Otherwise I'd get it fixed tonight."

Shecaniah's whole upper body was so full of muscles it was easy to see how the back of his neck was unreachable by the tree trunks that were his arms.

"Let me see," Katannah said. He shuffled around, moving his feet several times to complete the turn. "You'll have to sit down," she said. "You're too tall."

He sat down on the closest stone. Just as he said, a matte of hair hung down at the nape of his neck, encrusted with what looked like tar, now mixed with stone chips. He offered her his knife without speaking and in one clean stroke she cut the clump from his head.

"Ah," he said shaking his head sideways, testing the sensation. "Much better." He held out his hand for his knife, which was how she saw that two of his fingers ended in mangled stumps.

How does he even hold a knife? she thought. She'd noticed him watching her take in the details of his hand but seemed quite unconcerned with her stare.

"A sacrifice to the gods of stone," he laughed, waving his hand toward her. "Thankfully, they didn't ask for the whole hand. I worship Yahweh now. He is more reasonable in his demands." His scrabby face grinned at his own subtle joke, inviting her to join in, and this time he met her eyes with frank openness. "Thank you, Katannah."

"I could come again later, with my shears and — " she stopped just short of completing her thought, which was to say "and make you look presentable." Instead, she finished with "and your whole head would be cooler." But she had not quite been quick enough.

"Don't like my own styling, eh?"

"Well, original as it is, I'm not too worried you'll steal my customers."

He chuckled again, the chuckle of a shy boy pleased to find someone who understood his sense of humour.

"Caleb knows where I live. Come over some evening." He returned to the crew.

Katannah and Caleb retreated from where Shecaniah and his crew were working. "You have some interesting friends," she said.

"You don't know who that is?"

"Am I supposed to?"

"He's Jerusalem's biggest builder; probably rebuilt or renovated a third of the houses. This is only one of the crews he has working for him in the city."

"He's big, I'll grant you that."

"And smart. Don't let that horse of a body fool you. Or his shyness. He's not like that when it comes to his workers. He went around and bought up as many of the abandoned houses as he could shortly after Nehemiah arrived. He's done all right for himself. Owns a few market stalls too. When he speaks, however softly, people listen."

"What's he doing for the temple? It looks expensive."

"He's building another run of chambers at the back. And I've heard that he's doing the whole thing for free. That comment he made about worshipping Yahweh wasn't just a joke. He loves the temple. His grandfather was part of the crew that built the plinth we're standing on."

"What's his mother's name?" Katannah asked suddenly.

"Fetneh, and his father is Jehiel. You cut her hair."

"But Fetneh isn't Jewish. She's Ammonite, like me."

"Well, Shecaniah is as Jewish as they come. Can't wait for Ezra to arrive."

"Is he married?" asked Katannah.

"No."

* * *

"He'll be here in less than a month. Your father's sent me a long dispatch." Manasseh burst into the room where his wife, Nikaso, was having her hair washed. Her head hung off the end of a low couch and Katannah was slowly kneading soap into her scalp, forming a rich lather. Of all Katannah's clients, Nikaso's hair was the easiest to manage since she insisted on wearing it short and off her shoulders. Nikaso sat up abruptly and Katannah rushed for a towel to catch the soapy drips. It still shocked her to see how casually her clients treated their furniture.

"Tell me everything. Is my father well?" Nikaso's father was Sanballat, governor of Samaria, the next province north of Yehud. The union of Nikaso, daughter of the Samarian governor who had done everything short of all-out war to stop Nehemiah from rebuilding Jerusalem's walls, to Manasseh, grandson of the High Priest who was first to help Nehemiah build that very same wall, had been a controversial matter. But since both families were powerful, any criticism that lingered was now little more than whispered gossip. Manasseh, a full-ranking priest, assisted his grandfather in the temple administration.

"He writes of nothing except Ezra. Apparently the caravan is huge — at least two thousand people and there are more groups traveling behind."

"Did they meet each other?"

"You mean your father and Ezra? Yes, it would seem so. Sanballat offered an armed escort through his territory, which Ezra declined. Ezra said that Yahweh's protection was sufficient, or some such thing.[4] He's carrying a gift from King Artaxerxes that sounds big enough to run the temple for a decade, even with the increased staff. And the plate and serving vessels that Nebuchadnezzar plundered from us are being returned. Think of it, Nikaso. We'll actually touch the very same bowls that King David himself touched."

"But two thousand people — where will they stay? And what will they all do?"

"Some will have land claims or clan members already here. It will take months to establish their lineage and catalogue whatever documents they've brought with them. And for certain the temple staff will swell. A lot of them came from families that have served in the temple since the beginning, since Solomon built the first one. Each one will have to prove it, of course."

"But these people were all born in Babylon, or Susa or who knows what other Persian city. It's been a hundred and fifty years since the Babylonians carted their forebears into exile. And it wasn't as if they were forced to live all bunched together. There are Jews sprinkled all over the Persian Empire. How can people possibly have kept track of who their ancestors were?"

"Nikaso, have you forgotten all those scrolls that fill our library? No sooner does a cartload of exiles roll through our gates but their leader presents himself to me, clutching scraps of papyri or leather parchment that confirms them to be legitimate Jews. It's both poignant and pathetic, in a way. I mean, why else would they have pulled up stakes in the east and trekked two thousand miles to start life all over again if they *weren't* Jewish? But I see how important these lists of names are to them — it's an obsession. They arrive still wearing their Persian cowls and speaking Aramaic far better than their supposedly native Hebrew tongue; but keeping track of the family histories is everything. As the name of a man clings to him, so men cling to names. It's a miracle that there are any pure Jews left anywhere, yet they survived. They'll come with their lists, sure enough. It's their entrance ticket back into the Promised Land."

"So will Ezra be your new High Priest? That seems hardly fair to Eliashib, your grandfather. He's the one who's worked so hard just to keep the temple open all these years. Is he going to be pushed aside by all these newcomers?"

"I don't know what privilege Ezra will claim. And yes, my grandfather does his best to hide his anxiety. But he's ready to retire anyway. It's my brothers who are fearful. They've been waiting for ages to become the next High Priest. If Ezra takes over, that will ruin their chances. Still, family histories cut both ways. The job's been in our family since Moses and we can prove it. But it's not clear that Ezra means to make Jerusalem his home. He might only be visiting."

"Still, I feel sorry for Eliashib. Everyone always fawns over returning exiles like they're long lost family heirlooms. And your grandfather was so supportive of us when we were married."

Nikaso's face darkened. "Is your job safe?" she asked suddenly. By this time she had stood up and wrapped the towel around her head like a turban. Katannah had retreated to the edge of the room, back pressed tightly against a wall. She had not been dismissed, so she could not leave, but for the moment she did not exist.

"No it's not," Manasseh replied. "No, no, it doesn't matter," he said seeing her concern. "You knew I was never in the running for High Priest and I'm no good at supervising even our small staff, when it falls to me. Ezra is sure to reorganize how the temple will operate and no doubt he'll have someone who is good at that sort of thing. I'm happy enough to give up all that. It's only the library I really care about."

Nikaso looked at her husband's excited face that was utterly incapable of hiding anything he might be feeling. With each detail of his impending job loss his eyes had grown brighter.

"Ezra's bringing books with him! Admit it!" Nikaso exclaimed.

"Wagon loads! O Nikaso, they're way more valuable than the money everyone is fixed on. The rumour is that all this time in Susa, Ezra's been building a library; not just collecting, either. He's reconstructed sections of Torah thought to have been lost forever. Said to have gathered every last scrap of parchment thought to contain even one word of Moses. And not just Torah either. He's compiled two histories — one is called *Annals of the Kings*, and the other is called *Chronicles of Israel*."

"And you can't wait to see them, can you." Nikaso laughed. "Manasseh, you're about ready to dance with anticipation. But I'm glad you're happy."

"Nikaso, it's as if the heart of our people is coming home. Think of being able to read the entire Torah, knowing that there are no missing sections. For the first time in two hundred years, we'll hear the complete words of Moses!"

"If my father was not also in love with old scrolls, I would think you quite mad," she said lightly. And then, leaning forward to kiss his forehead, she added, "As it is, I just find you adorably eccentric. Now leave me so that Katannah can finish my hair. She'll probably have to start over again because of you."

Nikaso closed her eyes as Katannah resumed massaging her scalp, normally a soothing ritual. But for some reason what came to her was the gaunt and tired face of Eliashib.

Faithfulness never prevails against fads, she thought.

* * *

"Ezra's somewhere just north of Samaria," Hananiah said, making his daily report to his brother, Nehemiah, governor of Yehud.

"He's actually going to make it," Nehemiah said. "All these months I had hardly dared hope — and coming with more temple loot than anyone could possibly imagine."

"Should I ride to meet him with troops?" Hananiah asked.

"No. Sanballat will see that he stays safe enough. He can't afford any more public embarrassment after his 'wall' fiasco."

"You quite enjoyed outmaneuvering him on that one, didn't you."

"Loved every minute of it," Nehemiah smirked. "And getting Ezra here will cement the victory."

"Oh?" Hananiah had long learned not to press his brother for details. There was no question that Nehemiah was a brilliant leader and strategist. But it was also well known that he took no one into his confidence, and if he were not such a selfless promoter of the Jewish public weal, people might have regarded him as the tyrannical autocrat that was actually his style. Hananiah thought of a question that might be safe to ask.

"Is he coming to replace you? I've heard he carries an official writ bearing the seal of King Artaxerxes."

"No, he's not replacing me, but yes, he's got the backing of the Persian throne. And his writ of office is unique; unique and quite brilliant, I might add."

"You had a hand in it, no doubt."

"Wrote the draft personally. And I don't believe that Artaxerxes changed a single word of it; I sent it to him almost a year ago. Brother, I've prayed so hard for this. And Yahweh has heard my prayer."

"So who exactly is he, and why did you send for him? Surely you can tell me, now that your brilliant plan is almost at our gates."

Nehemiah smirked again. He'd guarded his reputation for secrecy — part of what made him an effective leader, he said — but he also desperately wanted to tell someone about his plan that he'd kept to himself for over a year. He would tell his brother, he decided, and then bask just a little in his admiration.

"Ezra is only the greatest scribe and priest since Moses.[5] And his family lineage is uncontested; he traces his family right back to Aaron.[6] I discovered him in Babylon, oh, twenty years ago during one of Artaxerxes' visits to that city. He was running a small but elite school for Jewish scribes. He's got to be at least seventy years old by this time, but he's spent his entire life collecting and editing Hebrew writings. King Artaxerxes granted him access to all the Royal archives — "

" — at your suggestion, no doubt."

Nehemiah just smiled, and continued. "There isn't a man alive who knows more about Torah than Ezra does."

"But what's your interest in having him here at Jerusalem? Our temple already has a High Priest; don't forget that Eliashib was your first volunteer to rebuild the walls. He's not obstructed you in any way. Why send for another priest?"

"Not a priest, brother. Ezra's writ goes way beyond the temple. His official title is *State Secretary for the Implementation and Oversight of Jewish Regulations by Order of the Persian Throne.*" Nehemiah let the cumbersome title roll off his tongue majestically with as much pomp as he could muster. He stopped, waiting for his brother to grasp the implications of what he had just uttered.

Hananiah began slowly, hardly believing where his mind was taking him. "Which means that all the laws of Moses . . ."

". . . now carry the weight of Persian legal code," ended Nehemiah. "Insofar as any regulation is not contrary to Persian interests or security, the faith of our fathers is now part of our civil ordinances. His writ even lets him appoint magistrates in the villages."

"How did you pull this off?" Hananiah was astounded.

"I wasn't Artaxerxes' personal cupbearer all those years for nothing. And in the early days, we Jews were somewhat helpful in keeping him secure on his throne. The king likes me. Besides, it's a shrewd bit of public politics to demonstrate Persian beneficence and tolerance to those who suffered at the hands of the Babylonians. It engenders loyalty. And with Jerusalem so close to Egypt, loyalty is a good thing to foster."

"Will he report to you then?" Hananiah asked.

"Not at all. Look, my brother, I'm not entirely without eyes. It's true I can get things done, mobilize people to work together by appealing to their enlightened self-interest. But following Torah again — for that you need to capture a man's heart and I don't touch people that way. I'm too — "

" — prickly?" finished Hananiah.

"I was thinking secular."

"And Ezra's got the personality to change our hearts, has he? He's going to arrive and pour a little religious zeal on the altar and ignite a bonfire of Jewish purity?"

"Don't mock, Hananiah," Nehemiah said seriously. "This is the man who will make us a nation once more. Moses brought us out of Egypt. Ezra brings us back from Babylon. A city — well, that's an easy enough thing to rebuild; but to build a people — for that you need a priest. There's something about this man that I'd give half my life-span to possess. It's true that he carries the stick of Persian authority. But he won't need it. You watch. He makes a man want to live better than he is. It's leadership of a kind I can't hope to emulate. How do you think he recruited so many people to come with him?"

"And the wagonloads of temple gold? How did you manage that?" asked Hananiah. "And incidentally, how much is actually coming?"

"I didn't manage it," said his brother quietly. "And as for how much, not even I can believe what I've heard. There's said to be twenty tons of silver alone. This is none other than Yahweh himself moving the heart of our king. There is no other explanation for his largesse. I think it's his genuine acknowledgement that we Jews worship a living and powerful God, one whose favour should be curried if at all possible."[7]

* * *

Jerusalem launched into a frenzy of preparations for Ezra and his entourage. It felt like the frantic actions of a newlywed bride entertaining her in-laws for the first time. Houses and apartments were being restored in record time. Several far-sighted farmers erected a holding pen not far from the gates for a small herd of prime sacrificial livestock that would be required and for whose purchase there would be ample funds. Meremoth, the priest who had married Nikaso and Manasseh, also served as exchequer for the temple treasury and was doubling the size of his strongholds.

Caleb grew more ecstatic with each day. He'd heard that no fewer than fifty cantors were in Ezra's party and that none other than Jezrahiah[8] had charge of them.

"And who exactly is Jezrahiah?" Katannah asked him one day.

"Hugely famous — if you're a singer, that is. He's composed wonderful anthems for mass choirs and instruments. His melodies are arresting. We only have a few of his works, but he's written hundreds of compositions."

"You'll find advancement?" she asked.

"It won't matter," he replied.

"But you might?" she pressed.

"I think of it more as a chance to push my gift to be the best it can possibly be."

She admired her husband's pure and transparent love for his music, but all the same she harboured a wifely hope for his future prospects.

Eliashib, to his credit, held a meeting for everyone who worked at the temple and confirmed what everyone already knew about Ezra's coming. But his public remarks went further: Yes, Ezra was coming. But Ezra was a holy and righteous man, whose family tree could be traced all the way back to Aaron, brother of Moses and the first priest of Israel. And with Ezra would come changes to the temple organization. Rites and rituals would change. And such changes as would be suggested by Ezra were not to be obstructed.

Where does that man find such dignity and grace? Nikaso wondered when she heard what Eliashib had said.

"Why is Eliashib so quick to defer to Ezra?" she asked her husband. "It's as if he thinks Ezra could be some kind of second Moses, or even the Messiah."

"Not Moses, and certainly not the Messiah, I don't think," he answered.

"Then what?"

"Eliashib is hopeful. And old and tired though he is, he hopes that Ezra might be the fulfilment of a prophecy."

"By whom?"

"By the nabi Malachi, thought to be still alive but who hasn't been seen in public for almost two score years. It was the last oracle he proclaimed before he withdrew."

"And it says?" Nikaso pressed impatiently. She knew who Malachi was. Her father had several small scrolls in his collection containing some of Malachi's words. They were for the most part scathing diatribes at the infidelity of God's people.

"It says that in the Day of Yahweh, He will send back the prophet Elijah[9] and he will turn the hearts of the fathers to their children, and the hearts of the children to their fathers."

"All Jews living together in peace as a unified people," Nikaso said.

"Something like that," Manasseh agreed. "Or at least, a time when what a man feels in his heart is given more weight than whether he can prove where he came from."

"And Ezra could be the man to bring this to pass? Give us a sense of unity?"

"It's the thing Eliashib hopes to see before he dies. Yes, Nikaso, and that, I believe, is why he's so quick to get out of the way."

* * *

Ezra arrived and all of Jerusalem instantly fell in love with him. An air of courtly courtesy surrounded him. His very entrance through the Horse Gate was modest. It was the wagons piled high with wealth, lurching towards the temple, whose clattering wheels were drowned by the bleats of a hundred goats, that caused the sensation. Ezra had brought only a hundred men with him for this first appearance. They presented themselves quietly to Nehemiah, who stood in the Temple square, and then got on with the work of surrendering the silver, gold and sacred articles to Meremoth, the temple Exchequer. Solemnly each item was ticked off against the inventory list and as everything on each page was accounted for, Meremoth would carefully place his seal of receipt on the hefty papyri. Eventually, these would find their way back to King Artaxerxes. It might have all belonged to Yahweh, but it was still a prudent thing to verify that Yahweh's property had been delivered without shrinkage.

Only then, their long journey officially ended, did Ezra and his group present their sacrifices. The burnt offerings were substantial, just three animals shy of two hundred, and included twelve prime bulls, raised especially for this purpose. It was sacrifice on a scale that the Temple had not received before, and everywhere procedures creaked under the stress of such an oblation. Blood ran thick into the altar's gutters, which soon overflowed and had to be scooped up and carted away in barrels. Dozens of braziers belched smoke as portions from each animal were burned as a savory scent to Yahweh. Eliashib had plunged the knife into the first of the twelve wild-eyed bull calfs presented and then withdrew to stand at the top of the steps. Behind him the six pillars that graced the temple entrance made an imposing backdrop. He stood impassively, not moving when clumps of thick smoke swirled around him. He could just as easily have been guarding the temple doors against invaders as preparing to surrender it to his replacement.

Eliashib watched Ezra separate himself from the crowd and slowly climb the stone steps. Compared to Eliashib, he looked almost patrician. His robes were unadorned but unmistakably expensive. The two men stood for a moment, each examining the other, two old men who knew all too well just how short the span of a man's life really was. Whatever their differences were going to be, they shared a common certainty that Sheol would soon claim them both and the burden of Jerusalem would fall on the backs of others.

But until that moment comes, Eliashib thought, this temple is in my care. And I have done the best I can with what I was given. My life, too, has been spent in the service of Yahweh. Surely there is still some small place for me.

"Ezra, son of Aaron," Eliashib said quietly, acknowledging Ezra's priestly credentials.

"In Susa they call me 'Ezra the scribe,'[10] and I am too old to take up another vocation." He tilted his head ever so slowly toward Eliashib and then straightened up, looking keenly at Eliashib to make sure that the gesture had been understood.

"We *are* in need of instruction," Eliashib replied solemnly.

"Almost all my students have come with me," Ezra said. "They are fine teachers in their own right. We have been studying the Law of Moses together for some time."

"News of your scholarship precedes you," Eliashib said. "It is said that you have assembled all of Torah — that the words of Moses have been recovered by your efforts."

Ezra smiled softly. "I believe that to be so."

"Yahweh be praised," Eliashib said.

"Yahweh be praised," Ezra repeated. "We have several full copies for your temple scriptorium, in addition to other books we have compiled."

"They will be welcome, as are you."

"My thanks, but I will reside elsewhere. It would only confuse matters. Nehemiah has found me chambers in the south of the city. But there are many who came with me hoping to find service at the temple, perhaps join the rotation. Their credentials are all quite in order. And I particularly commend one person to you — Meshullam, son of Bani[11] — by far my brightest and most diligent adjuvant."

"Tell him to seek me out. He can help me absorb those whom you've brought. We are open to change. But what help can I be to you?"

"Send me students." That same soft smile crept over Ezra's face. "It was our hope to start classes for the instruction of Torah. I've ample enough scribes for the job. And I hope to organize the public readings during the feasts."

"Not in my whole lifetime have the words of Moses been proclaimed. I am ashamed of the scrolls we have, valued though they are by us." Eliashib's voice caught a bit. "And Ezra...." Eliashib paused.

"Yes?"

"Thank you."

Ezra retreated back down the steps, leaving Eliashib alone once more to preside over the sacrifices.

Ezra will not occupy the temple, nor crowd me out, Eliashib thought. I'll take on his young scribe, Meshullam, and give him a senior position. It will send a strong signal to everyone that Ezra and I have no quarrel. Thanks be to Yahweh, for mine eyes have seen the salvation of his people.

* * *

Down below from where Eliashib stood, two young priests bent over the body of a goat that had been transferred from the altar to the charcoal brazier that they tended. One priest lived in Jerusalem. The other had arrived with Ezra. It was fast-paced work, hot and messy. Together they stretched the goat, getting ready for that first, long pull down the soft underbelly of the animal.

"Agh!" grunted the Jerusalem priest, dropping his knife and holding up his hand quickly. "I've just nicked my finger."

"I'll find someone to replace you," said the priest from Persia.

"No matter; it's not deep and will close quickly enough," the Jerusalem priest said.

"I'm glad you're alright, but still, you'll have to be relieved."

"And why would that be?" the Jerusalem priest asked. "Look, it's almost stopped bleeding already." .

"Because the Law of Moses forbids it; not until you're fully healed are you permitted to serve again. But surely you knew that."[12]

The Jerusalem priest stared blankly but already the Persian priest had left to search out a replacement.

What else had Moses forbidden?

* * *

Change blew through the city; everywhere people opened their windows to embrace it. It was as if there had been a void, unrecognized until now, that Ezra and his people filled naturally, like missing pieces in a puzzle that made the whole picture so much grander and majestic. Ezra's coming did not so much put people down as elevate them to where he stood. The leaven of Ezra penetrated everywhere.

But to Katannah's practical mind, the Laws of Moses — *Torah* was what people called it — were a decidedly odd collection of enjoinders. It seemed to her that the foreigners, for that is how she thought of the Persian transplants, had arrived with a chest full of elaborate costumes and all of Jerusalem played dress-up as if preparing for an elaborate masquerade. The changes seemed almost random. Pork, along with rabbit, badger and camel meat, vanished from the market stalls. They could still eat meat, of course, and they could still drink milk, but suddenly they could no longer do both at the same meal.[13] Tattoos were suddenly frowned on and although they had not been hugely fashionable, those Jews who had them kept them covered up where possible.[14] Caleb started to grow out his forelocks,[15] and one day without warning asked her if she thought any of his clothes might have wool and cotton mixed together. She didn't think so, but he came home one day with the buttons all cut from his wool jerkin. Someone at the temple had apparently told him that cotton thread had been used to attach them. It didn't matter whether people understood the "why" of a thing. *"The Law of Moses requires it"* was all the incantation necessary for some new custom to have authority.

Passion, jocularity, mixed with vast amounts of ignorance, produced the most heated of debates. The hip roast from animals, for example, was now taboo out of deference to the memory of the thigh of a man called Jacob who had lived even before Moses. Several versions of the "Jacob story" circulated.[16] But what people now debated was whether it was permitted to buy hip roasts as long as you stripped the meat off for stew. Everyone knew that all butchered animals had to be slaughtered according to new rituals.[17] But if a butcher wasn't Jewish, yet still adhered to the new procedures, did it count? If a garment could not be made of both wool and linen, then was it still permitted to wear a woolen item if it came in contact with a cotton item? Could, for example, your tunic be cotton and your belt wool?

A whole new cuisine sprang up and people called it "kosher." Recipes and rules were traded with the intensity of gossip. The rituals of table and the rituals of temple now shared the same religious aroma.

Katannah could not be certain if what she observed was like some momentary madness that frequently swept over a people. She had seen certain kinds of hairstyles first embraced and then abandoned with equal intensity, and wondered if these Laws of Moses were simply the latest import from Persia like the small hoods and cowls that had been embraced a few years earlier. This latest bout of change all carried a religious gloss that confused her. The river of religion, once a neat if meagre stream, seemed to have overflowed its banks and had spread a fine layer of silt over every detail of a person's life.

Among the exiles came new clients for Katannah, and by far the most interesting of these was Arémeté, wife of Meshullam who had indeed been hired by Eliashib and was now Caleb's new boss at the temple. Arémeté was interesting, not just because she had lived in Susa and Babylon — cities with populations of several hundred thousand people — but because she was pure Persian and made no effort to hide her lineage. If she found Jerusalem and its citizens parochial or peasant-like she never showed it, but entered into what entertainments the city offered with genuine interest. Nikaso became her special friend, as did their husbands who worked together at the temple.

Jerusalem was not the first colony of Jews that Meshullam had worked with, Arémeté told Katannah. "He is a brilliant organizer. And his own scholarship will match that of his mentor Ezra one day. I am certain. And I follow him," she sighed in mock despair. "It is worse than being married to a military man. These missionaries of Yahweh go anywhere there are Jews needing instruction." Her pride in Meshullam's work was obvious.

One thing was certain: the couple was not poor and Katannah got the impression that it was Arémeté's money that kept them in their regal habits. He's married a princess, Katannah thought, and it might have been true. Arémeté was a little too short, and a bit too chubby, to be considered beautiful, but there was an element of durability to her.

It was from Arémeté that Katannah learned new hairstyles, Persian in design and popular among the younger women of Jerusalem. Arémeté wore her hair bobbed short, clear of her shoulders, but it didn't hang loose in the way Nikaso wore hers, but rather as a forest of tiny braids. To get the desired effect, Katannah learned that the hair had to be grown much longer first, in order to make braids.

She also had free rein to investigate the endless pots of crèmes and powders that Arémeté possessed, some containing mysterious plant extracts made in India. One of these was a depilatory that when carefully applied would remove unsightly hair. Katannah did not actually believe such a thing was possible until she actually saw it work.

"Do your priests make that?" she asked Arémeté.

"Hardly," Arémeté laughed, "and a good thing too. They would charge twice as much and probably forget to put in the essential compounds. It's readily available from any good apothecary."

Katannah tried to imagine a city where seemingly magic potions could be had simply for the asking in the local market. If Arémeté kept such power so carelessly in her boudoir, what other powers had these sophisticated foreigners brought with them?

In the small antechamber that was Arémeté's dressing room and where Katannah washed her hair, stood two small delicate statues, clearly images of deities. They were mostly ivory, or perhaps white marble, that had been painstakingly carved. Some of the features were in relucent gold that shimmered in the sunlight. That they shared the same elaborate base clearly indicated that the two figures were part of the same scene. At one end, suspended on a bent gold shaft, hung a creature with oversized wings, talons pointing forward as if about to seize its prey. The face of the creature, however, was human and on its head was a crown. Wing tips, claws and crown were all gilt-edged. Beneath it, and in front of the winged creature, was a two-wheeled chariot pulled by charging horses with golden manes that undulated in some imaginary wind. Their every muscle strained in the act of pulling the chariot forward. So life-like was their pose that Katannah half believed she would see them move if she watched them long enough. In the chariot stood a person, one hand held high grasping a sword. On the back of the figure hung a quiver of arrows, each tiny tuft complete with perfect golden feathers.

The chariot, though just in front of the bird, was not the bird's quarry; rather, both were joined in the pursuit of some common foe. It was a scene that shouted of a story, but it was not Katannah's place to ask about them. Her interest in them, however, was plain enough.

"They are the gods of my people," Arémeté explained one day, "or rather, images of them."

"What are their names?" Katannah asked.

"The bird is *Ahura Mazda*, the god who rules above all other gods. By him the whole earth was made. He is the god of all that is good. He is also the god of light."

"And the one in the chariot?"

"*Mithra*, who is my particular patron. He is the god of covenant and contract who watches over the promises we make and who guides us in all truth. He protects those who keep their word and punishes those who do not. Speaking the truth and keeping our oaths: they are virtues among us Persians. All children are taught this from an early age.[18] Where I come from, it is a terrible thing to lie."

"They are chasing something," Katannah ventured shyly.

"They are hunting down *Drauga*, which in Aramaic would mean *The Lie*. He is the god who seeks to destroy truth and cause men to break their covenants one with another."

"Do they live at Susa, in your city?" Katannah asked.

"They live everywhere."

"But they have houses, a temple such as Yahweh has here in Jerusalem?"

"Yes, there are several; at Susa, at Babylon, and of course at Persepolis, though I have seen only the first two."

"And do they demand sacrifices the way Yahweh does?"

"Yes, but not in the same way. We sacrifice anywhere the ground is unpolluted, and the portions we burn are smaller, always mixed with a little sweet grass. Our prayers must always be the same; we pray for the good of all Persians and do not ask any special favours for ourselves."

"But you have priests who help you?"

"We have our holy men, like Ezra and like Meshullam will be one day. We call them magi. They study the heavens for wisdom."

"Like Ezra studies his books."

"Just so. And he is held in high esteem by the magi at Susa."

"So do you worship Yahweh too?"

"Yahweh is not mine to worship," Arémeté said firmly. "It is my husband who is in his service, for which I am proud."

Katannah paused, trying to find the right words for what she wanted to ask. The conversation had strayed into personal territory, yet Arémeté was not dismissive or demeaning. And for all their differences of caste, they were at that moment both foreign wives whose husbands served the Jewish God Yahweh. This thing that lay on her mind felt so pressing and at the same time so confusing. It had to do with Caleb, that much she knew, Caleb and the changes that were happening at the temple.

A few nights earlier Caleb had removed his shirt to reveal a small white rectangle of cloth that hung over both his chest and back. From each of the four corners hung a tassel braided of blue and white cords.

"What is that?" she had asked curiously.

"It's called a *tallit*,"[19] he had answered stiffly.

"What is it for? Where did you get it?"

"One of the new cantors gave it to me. It is to remind us of all the commands Yahweh has given us lest we prostitute ourselves and yield to the lusts of our hearts and the lusts of our eyes." The words had rolled flatly out of Caleb's mouth.[20]

Those are not Caleb's words, she'd thought. He has been given them along with this tallit he both defends and is ashamed of. Why else would he wear it beneath his clothing?

"In accordance with the Laws of Moses," she had finally whispered gently. He did not reply. She'd continued. "It's handsome on you, Caleb, and I will take great care when I wash it. You're learning much from your new friends and I'm happy for you. Finally you are among men who value your gift of song."

Caleb removed the cloth and folded it carefully on top of his tunic.

We will speak more of this tonight when we lie together, she'd thought. He will tell me what these lusts are that he is so frightened of transgressing. And I will help in this. But that night when she'd reached for him, he'd turned away.

It was impossible to tell Arémeté any of what had happened. On the face of it, Caleb was wearing a new garment given to him at the temple. What was the harm of that? What was there even to ask about? "My husband sings at the temple," she said finally.

"Caleb is his name," Arémeté answered.

"You know him?"

"Meshullam has mentioned him. His voice is powerful for a singer still so young." Arémeté looked keenly at Katannah and then continued, "Your husband has a special gift. He will go far in his calling. My husband has already taken note of his abilities. You can be proud."

"As you are proud," Katannah said softly.

"Yes. I know there are many men who earn their bread in the service of gods yet for them it is just a job. It doesn't matter the god, either; Yahweh, Mithra, Ahura Mazda, Ishtar, Marduk — it is the same in every guild. There are those who serve because it is easy pay. But to them, the gods remain as silent and lumpen as the stones from which their images are carved."

"I have met some like that. Not all of Caleb's friends sing the way he does."

"But there are some, men like our husbands for whom their gods are alive, men who will give their whole lives over to the service of something that is bigger than they are, bigger than any of us."

"That is how Caleb looks when he is singing," Katannah said.

"It is how Meshullam looks when he reads Torah," Arémeté replied. "Perhaps they recognize the same thing in each other."

"Sometimes," said Katannah, "when I hear Caleb sing it is like light so pure and so white that I feel it could consume me if I got too close to it. I do not understand the words, and wonder sometimes if that is a good thing, the thing that protects me. Yet at the same time I want to understand, even if in the next moment I was destroyed. It would be worth it, to know this thing that Caleb serves, that so invades his heart."

"It's lonely being their wife, isn't it?" Arémeté murmured, more to herself than to Katannah.

"It's not that I'm jealous," Katannah whispered, "only afraid. Afraid and shut out of something stern and terrifying, yet more majestic than anything I thought could exist. But there isn't room for me."

* * *

It was Ezra's voice that gave public definition to the wave of tribal pride that rose higher with each passing week. It was a wave that had no shore on which to break, storing up energy that was visible only in its power to sweep things away. One such tiny bit of detritus burst into the apartment of Nikaso and Manasseh long after it was polite to call on neighbours. Meremoth, the priest in charge of the treasury, who just two months ago had so conspicuously been part of Ezra's welcome, now stood in front of Nikaso and her husband, oblivious to the signs that they had been roused from bed.

"Manasseh, I need your help. I've been removed."

"Come in," Nikaso said lamely, pretending to ignore the breach in manners. She turned to light some lamps.

"What do you mean, removed?" Manasseh asked. "From what? There is nothing amiss at the treasury, is there?"

"I've been removed from the temple; thrown out — literally. They told me this afternoon. And I'm not the only one. Hobiah and Barzillai have lost their jobs as well."[21]

"Ridiculous," Manasseh exploded. "It's your right to be a priest. On what grounds could they do this? Is there something wrong at the storehouse — a theft?"

"No, nothing."

"So?"

"So it seems I can't prove that I'm from the family of Hakkoz — and word's come down from the governor that you've got to have proof."

"Proof of what?"

"Proof that I'm from a priestly family!"

"That's absurd. You've been serving for years. You married us. You built the wall next to my grandfather![22] Of course you are a priest."

"Absurd or not, it's what's happened. No proof, no job. No exceptions. Manasseh, you've got to help me."

"I'll talk to someone. Is Meshullam behind this? Do they want to get rid of the old guard and make room for their own?"

"No, Meshullam isn't involved. I'm not sure who started the investigation or raised a fuss. Not everyone was investigated."

"But everyone knows you're from Hakkoz's family."

"Knows it, yes. But knowing something and proving something are not the same. Manasseh, you've got to help me." Meremoth was frantic and his voice showed it. And Manasseh, while he did not actually believe that Meremoth's story was true, could see that his own incredulity was only making things worse.

"I'll help you of course. What would you like me to do?" This whole thing is crazy, he thought. Meremoth had misunderstood something that someone had said to him. Eliashib would sort this out.

"Search your scrolls. Search the temple archives for me. Find some old list that says I am who I say I am. You know those scrolls better than any man in Jerusalem. Manasseh, those scrolls are the only hope I've got."

Manasseh and Nikaso did what they could to calm their friend who left finally, still whimpering like a bewildered puppy that had been harshly punished without explanation. Under different circumstances, it would have been funny. It left them feeling as black as the night into which Meremoth had retreated. His words were an ill harbinger.

"What are you going to do?" Nikaso asked.

"I'm going to help our friend, and then I'm going to have a talk with whoever is behind this madness."

It took Manasseh three days of searching, but he found what Meremoth needed, and when he handed over the tiny, tightly bound and quite brittle scroll, Meremoth began to cry.

"You've saved my life."

Manasseh brushed it off. "Tell whoever is behind this perversion that if that scroll is damaged in any way, I shall call down curses on them and all their children — the Laws of Moses notwithstanding. That scrap of leather you are holding is five hundred years old. King David's scribe wrote it,[23] and it contains the twenty-four priestly families confirmed by King David himself. Hakkoz, your ancestor, is halfway down the list. Let them argue with that."

But Meremoth wasn't listening. He held the scroll, cupped in both hands as a child might hold a newborn chick fallen from its nest. "I will take great care," he said, without looking up. "I will bring it back once I have shown it to someone in authority from the governor's staff." Suddenly he looked up. "But what of my friends, Hobiah and Barzillai?"

Manasseh shook his head. "Nothing. It didn't help that Barzillai took the name of his wife's family. Makes it look like he was trying to inherit some land through her side. Priests can't do that.[24] Whatever the reason, I hope it was worth it because it's cost him his job. Still, I'm sorry for them both."

Meremoth only nodded. "I'll be back soon."

I saved one at any rate, Manasseh thought watching his friend scurry away, his hands still cupped together over the scroll.

* * *

Nehemiah and his brother Hananiah were walking the western section of the wall between the Old Gate and the Tower of Ovens. They stopped halfway along a straight section called the Broad Wall and looked east over the city. Jerusalem resembled a large, misshapen delta spilling out of a narrow river; in the south, the walls were scarcely one hundred yards apart. But about halfway up its length, the city debouched into an irregular roundish pond. Here, in the north quadrant, the city widened to about six hundred yards. Ever since the two brothers had arrived — almost four years ago now — they had toured at least some section of the walls each day. They had worked hard rebuilding Jerusalem, and had overcome long odds. What had once been a silent scape of grey, disheveled stone was now tessellated ordered squares of rooftops. Separating them were the narrow streets and laneways, shadowy arteries carrying the lifeblood of the city. No two rooftops were the same. Already about half had gardens planted and some of the more energetic homeowners had hauled up small palm trees. Hananiah could only wonder at the ongoing effort needed to keep them watered. Fabric awnings, not yet faded by the sun, dotted the scene like so many tiny bright flowers recklessly growing in defiance of the hot sun. Occasionally, occupants had painted the cornice moldings of their houses, making for an elaborate selvage that defined their particular patchwork of roof within the bigger tapestry. Across from where Hananiah and Nehemiah had stopped, on the far side of the city, stood the temple. Its pitched roof jutted up above the neighbouring buildings. The hammered gold frieze of its commanding portico glittered like the crown on the head of a proud young athlete. From below, the street noises, muffled slightly by the buildings, drifted up in a pleasant buzz that sang of health.

Our city is alive, Hananiah thought. Life has taken root again. It's home. He stood silently, letting what filled his eyes, fill his heart as well.

"I've been talking to Ezra," Nehemiah said, breaking into his thoughts.

"Oh?" Hananiah for once would not let his brother disturb the tranquility of the moment.

"It's time to solidify our gains; begin the next stage. Ezra agrees. And he also agrees that the city is ready."

Hananiah sighed. Ever since Ezra had arrived, Nehemiah had remained conspicuously absent from public affairs. His brother had wondered how long it would be until Nehemiah broke under the stress of being at rest.

"What did you have in mind?" Hananiah asked, resenting for once his usual role of awed audience, struck dumb in mute amazement while Nehemiah revealed his latest parlour trick. It was both Nehemiah's greatest strength and weakness, this need to improve whatever lay in his path.

"It's time for our city to celebrate — really celebrate. We're going to dedicate these walls."

His brother turned and stared suspiciously into Nehemiah's face. "That's it? Just a celebration? That's your next stage?"

The corners of Nehemiah's mouth turned up ever so slightly. "Well, not a celebration exactly; it will be more like a festival."

"How long is it going to last?"

"About a month."

"Why do something small if you can do it big, eh?" Hananiah smiled wryly, knowing his curiosity had once again hooked him into another one of Nehemiah's grand schemes.

Nehemiah laughed and clapped him on his shoulder. "And you thought I was going to do something rash like go to war with someone."

"Why are you telling me?" Hananiah asked suddenly. "What do you want from me?"

"Well," Nehemiah began pan-faced, "the way Ezra and I see it, in order to dedicate the walls properly, we want to organize a monstrous procession — actually two processions — say, a few thousand people in each."

"A few thousand people? On the walls?"

"A few thousand each," Nehemiah replied hurriedly. "Plus whoever wants to just tag along in our trains. I'll lead one, of course, and Ezra will lead the other. He and I have already walked the route. We'll both start out at the southern tip, where the city is narrowest, by the Dung Gate. I'll take my group up this western side while Ezra will lead his group up the eastern side until we meet again just north of the temple. Jezrahiah — that famous composer Ezra brought with him — will train two mass choirs, one for each of the groups. And Ezra figures that there are at least four hundred musicians available — say two hundred for each group. We can stop at each of the gates and sing an anthem, or blow the trumpets and bash the cymbals; lots of music and gaiety — that sort of thing."

"You could hold contests to see which group can sing the loudest," Hananiah suggested. But Nehemiah, for whom music was an utterly foreign concept, appeared to take him seriously.

"A great idea. I'll suggest it to Ezra. We can get something written and sing it antiphonally." Nehemiah's tongue tripped a bit over that last word, proof that it had only recently entered his vocabulary.

"There's an ancient ballad about Joshua that might be appropriate," Hananiah continued. "You must know it — about how he marched around and around the walls of Jericho until the walls fell down."

Nehemiah stopped. "That's hardly funny. You don't think that's possible, do you?"

"You *were* in a hurry to build them, and it was all volunteer labour."

"You're joking."

"What happens when everyone reaches the Sheep Gate, the one closest to the temple?" Hananiah chose to ignore Nehemiah's look of momentary panic. Let him worry a bit over those walls, Hananiah thought. Do him good.

Excitement seized Nehemiah again as if by his very words the procession he imagined would magically appear. "Well, our thought was that the choirs — and the musicians — would stay massed on the wall while everyone else would descend from the walls and fill the temple square. Ezra would read the Torah appointed for the day[25] and then preside over the sacrifices."

"A credible celebration," Hananiah said —

" — that would end in a kind of citywide evening meal,"interrupted his brother.

"Free food and good wine for all, no doubt; dancing in the streets. But the whole thing is only a day; you mentioned a month-long event."

"The dedication is only the opening ceremonies. Next comes a Festival called the Feast of Booths.[26] Ezra wants to celebrate it strictly in accordance with how Moses first prescribed it, just like in the old days. It's not been held in over a century. And combined with that will be a public recitation of the entire Law. It's not been read this way since Josiah was King.[27] Not one person in Jerusalem will have heard it before. They won't want to leave."

"This Feast of Booths," Hananiah confessed, "it's supposed to be a kind of harvest thanksgiving isn't it?"

"Yes, but also a reminder of how our forefathers lived in temporary shelters while wandering in the wilderness. Still, Ezra tells me it will be quite a party. But right after the Feast, Ezra wants to sponsor two weeks of city-wide teaching; a huge public Torah school. It's a logical follow-up to having heard the Law read. People will have endless questions, and Ezra wants to capitalize on the public momentum."

"Enough," Hananiah cut in. "I can wait for the rest. I get the general idea. He turned to go, but not before Nehemiah caught his arm and peered anxiously into his face.

"None of it will fall down, will it?"

"Just keep an eye out for families that helped build the wall but who don't want to join your procession. It will be their sections you'll be wanting to have a look at." He chuckled to himself all the way back to his quarters.

* * *

Caleb burst into their tiny apartment, laid his package carefully down on the table, then grabbed Katannah by the waist and danced her round three times. "I have a solo part! They've chosen me to sing a solo!" He kissed her, a loud smacking noise, then drew his face away and twirled her round again. "The whole city will hear. They chose me. Can you believe it?"

Katannah hugged him hard, still dancing with him. "Caleb, I'm so proud, what great news! But when, and what will you sing?"

"The walls are being dedicated. We've less than a month to get ready. Jezrahiah is arranging new music. There will be two huge choirs — oh, and Katannah, they've picked me to sing. My part will be at the very end. I'm to be the last cantor in the programme. Look —" he turned to the parcel he had dropped on the table. "They've given me a special surplice to wear."

Katannah touched the brilliant white linen smock, edged in dark blue on the sleeves and neck. "It's magnificent!"

"You need to shorten it for me."

"Of course. Try it on."

He needed no second invitation. In an instant he shucked his own rough tunic and put the robe on over his head. He stood in front of her, arms slightly raised, eyes shooting out sparks of happiness that brightened the whole room.

"You are a prince," she said.

"I am a cantor; a cantor who has been given a solo anthem in the biggest assembly that will ever happen in this city. Oh, Katannah. All this time I thought that Yahweh was displeased with me because I didn't know the Laws of Moses well enough or that my voice was not good enough for him."

"It's surely a sign of his favour. And I am both happy and proud."

* * *

All of Jerusalem embraced the task of getting ready with unbridled enthusiasm. From the very start, it would be a celebration in which everyone could participate. Word went out for musicians of any proficiency to come forward. People rummaged through their households for musical instruments long since laid aside. Cymbals, harps, lyres, zithers, trumpets, drums, tambourines, bells and double piped flutes were restrung, dusted off or polished, then brought bashfully by their owners to the temple. All were welcome and none were turned away.

A general summons went out to every village within a day's walk of the city for the entire corps of priests, Levites, singers and servers to assemble a few days in advance both to undergo their lustral obligations and to receive detailed instructions about their allotted task. Nehemiah had fallen prey to his own self-inflicted obsession that some portion of the wall might in fact give way under the expected weight of people who meant to throng it. Hananiah being of no help in the matter, it was Shecaniah who took one of his crews and carefully inspected the walls.

His father Jehiel helped him. He had taken a genuine interest in all the new Jewish customs that Ezra had brought with him, was growing his forelocks out and had ceased to eat pork. And he was walking a little straighter. They were all encouraging signs and Fetneh was pleased.

"They're stout enough," Shecaniah reported to Nehemiah, "but the parapets are too low to be safe; a person could be shoved off by accident — the press of the crowd. We'll build a wooden barrier, especially at the south end where the ground falls away. Take it down afterwards, of course. And there's one or two of the stairs leading up to the walls that could stand a little re-enforcement. People will stand anywhere they can to get a good view."

"And the walls?" Nehemiah asked.

"Won't come down in our lifetimes," Shecaniah grunted. "You built good, governor; not sure why you had concern."

I'm going to throttle my brother, Nehemiah thought. He knows I can't *not* stop myself once I start to worry about something. He abuses me shamelessly.

Shecaniah had not left.

"Yes?" said Nehemiah encouragingly.

"My grandfather built the temple plinth, you know."

"Yes. I believe I knew that about your family."

"People don't remember them — those that worked before you. They didn't finish but that doesn't mean they didn't work — or serve Yahweh same as you do."

Nehemiah grasped instantly what was troubling the man. "We'll honour and bless everyone's work, Shecaniah. Past and present. They are all worthy of the same recognition. I know what we can do. Can you find the names of the men who worked with your grandfather?"

"Should be easy enough. Manasseh will have it somewhere in that library of his."

"We'll write them all out, a special list of honour and read it from the temple steps. The priests will sprinkle the holy waters on the terrace just the same as they will on the walls. They were builders just like us. You can read it."

Shecaniah seemed to have something suddenly catch in his eye that needed urgent attention. "My father's the one who should read. He was there. I just heard about those times."

"As you wish. You bring me the list and I'll see that Jehiel is included."

Shecaniah turned to leave. "You've done a good thing for us all, Nehemiah. Made us Jews again, even if you had to shove a few people out of your way to do it. Don't go believing any different."

"Thank you."

* * *

Katannah shortened Caleb's tunic and pressed it ever so carefully. Then, with a little money of her own, she searched the markets until she found new sandals for him. Sturdy enough so he won't worry about his footing, but just as elegant as his robe, she thought. Her heart overflowed with gratitude, like a river in spring flood that infused everything she did with happiness. Whatever dark numen that had once lain between them seemed to have vanished.

"Where should I stand?" she asked Caleb one night. "I want to hear you clearly."

"And I want to see you, or at least know where to look for you. Take up a place in the Temple square. That's where it will all end. You won't see much of the procession along the walls and will probably have to wait most of the day, but if you try to follow us along the wall you won't find room at the temple when you want it. I'll see you from the wall, where I'll be singing."

"I'll go with Fetneh. She won't get jostled and she's easy to spot in a crowd."

The festival was loud, exuberant, majestic and solemn all at the same time. Later, people would talk about the day of dedication as the day when Jerusalem's heart started to beat again. True to Nehemiah's forecast, people kept climbing up on the walls, pressing together until the city was rimmed by a colourful garland of people who called her home. The streets bulged as people craned upwards following the choral processions. Those who were too old, or too young to endure the day, mounted rooftops to participate as well as they could.

Great care had gone into the planning of the day's events. At each gate, a senior priest intoned a benison, specially written for that gate. His words were Hebrew, of course, part prayer, part proclamation, part praise. Then, the families who had built the walls closest to the gate chanted the same benediction in Aramaic, their voices carrying down to the people who stood in the streets below.

> *Peace be upon the Valley Gate.*
> *Peace be on all who pass through it.*
> *For it is Yahweh himself who has built it.*
> *It is Yahweh himself who watches over our city.*
> *For Yahweh has chosen Zion as His home.*
> *He desires it for His dwelling.*[28]

A special litany had been written for each stop the procession made along the walls. Once, when the eastern choir stopped at the Great Projecting Tower, both groups fell silent at some prearranged signal. A cluster of flutes started a melody — dirge-like, played in minor key, the notes floating in the air like injured birds. Then a single soprano voice began to sing:

> *By the Rivers of Babylon, we sat down*
> *and wept when we remembered Zion.*
> *There on the poplars we hung our harps;*

Our captors demanded songs of joy saying
'Sing us one of the songs of Zion'
But how could we sing Yahweh's praise in a foreign land?
So we wept, while our tormentors taunted us.
If I forget you O Jerusalem,
May my right hand forget its skill.
May my tongue stick tight in my mouth if I should forget you,
O Jerusalem, my highest joy.
May Yahweh never forget the assaults on His city,
May Yahweh never forget our enemies.
On the day Jerusalem fell, they rejoiced and cried
'Tear it down. Tear it down to its foundations!'[29]

The recent immigrants were easy to spot. They knew the words. Grown men wept openly as they relived the pain of an exiled people. Those who had long been in the land reached out to embrace the recent homecomers and cried along with them. It didn't matter when a person had returned, or even if their forebears had never actually left. From that moment on, the exile into Babylon became a shared experience. The last plaintive note ended and the entire city stood for a time in silent tribute to a pain that not until that moment had been acknowledged.

But the pain of exile was not the end of the story. Today was homecoming. Jordan had been crossed a second time; a people who for six generations had wandered the desert of Babylon now fell into the arms of their waiting city like two brothers who had not seen each other since childhood. On cue, the western orchestra started in, this time with drums and cymbals and trilling trumpets. People started to clap to the beat and the more energetic in the crowd danced a little. The western choir began this song, and line by line it was repeated by the eastern voices:

But when Yahweh brought back the captives
    But when Yahweh brought back the captives
We were like men who had dreamed a dream
    We were like men who had dreamed a dream

Our mouths filled up with laughter
Our mouths filled up with laughter
Our tongues with songs of joy.
Our tongues with songs of joy.
Then the nations round about us
Then the nations round about us
Bowed their heads in awe,
Bowed their heads in awe,
"Their God has done great things for them"
"Their God has done great things for them"
It's true, Yahweh's done great things for us
It's true, Yahweh's done great things for us
And we are filled with joy.
And we are filled with joy.[30]

Katannah and Fetneh had camped out in the Temple square since before the procession had even mounted the walls. The square filled up early with others who also wanted to get a good view of the final celebrations. All through the day snippets of songs and music had reached them like heralds in advance of the royal party. It was early afternoon when the choirs finally arrived. Everything at the temple had been polished to a mirror-like finish so that when the western sun finally touched them it was as if each bronze brazier, each oblation bowl, even the altar itself, joined in the great dance.

Ezra and Nehemiah, each at the head of their respective throngs, bowed low to each other. Then in slow deliberate movements, Nehemiah knelt in front of Ezra. Meshullam, never far from Ezra's side, proffered a vial of sacramental oil, and, taking the flask, Ezra held it high over the head of Nehemiah. The clear thick liquid poured down over his hair and beard, soaking into his robes, and finally onto the stones on which he knelt. It was a simple ritual but all who watched felt the moment. Just as the city itself had been blessed, so also would its citizens receive the sacrament of holy unction.

Standing again, the two men joined hands and raised them high over their heads. Moses and Aaron — the temple and the state — once again united in theocratic governance. The crowd roared out its approval, so that even the cobblestones on which Katannah and Fetneh stood pulsated in sympathy.[31] It took over half an hour just for Ezra, Nehemiah, and the cluster of priests to descend the wall, push through the crowd and make their way up the broad stone perron to stand again looking out over the temple square that was now jammed with people. Not until Ezra finally bowed his head as if in prayer did the crowd quiet its exuberance, momentarily checked.

This is the moment, thought Katannah. This is my husband's solo part. She looked up toward the wall, and sure enough, there he was. The harps began the melody, low and dulcet so that people strained forward to catch the notes. Then, the melody having been established, Caleb's voice confidently joined.

> *How I rejoiced when they said to me,*
> *Let us go to the House of Yahweh.*
> *And now our feet are standing in your gateway*
> *O Jerusalem.*
> *Jerusalem restored.*
> *Our city is one.*
> *Here the tribes have gathered, come up;*
> *The tribes of Yahweh; Yahweh's people.*

Caleb finished the first stanza. The harps asserted themselves again as if repeating the words in a different language. Caleb stood with eyes closed but head tilted slightly, catching the full afternoon sun on his face.

> *We have come to praise Yahweh's name*
> *As He has ordered us.*
> *Here true justice can be found,*
> *Here is David's royal throne and sceptre.*
> *We praise Yahweh for His statutes are among us.*
> *We praise Yahweh according to His law.*[32]

Caleb's voice was a thousand fiery arrows that people eagerly took to their hearts, piercing the squalid limits of their self-absorbed worlds. It was the voice of Yahweh, come to quicken the hearts of His people, to both break and bind them in the same song. It was the voice of their God setting eternity in their hearts, mixing the glory of Jerusalem with tinctures of His own glory. It was the pillar of fire from the days of Moses, come again into their midst, inviting them to embrace a holy holocaust.

Katannah felt as if a thread had attached itself to her heart: Caleb's voice, a thousand tiny timbrous fibres that stretched across some huge divide. He had crossed through the refiner's fire and now stood on the other side inviting others to exchange their hearts of stone for living hearts.

Caleb began the third and final verse. It was a closing benediction.

Pray for peace in Jerusalem.
Prosperity to your houses,
Peace inside your city walls
Prosperity to your palaces.
Since you are all my brothers and friends
We exchange the kiss of peace.
Since Yahweh is here among us
I pray for our happiness.

The song ended and Caleb stepped quickly back into the choir.

Thank you, thought Katannah, although to whom she directed this, she had no idea.

Nehemiah stepped forward. "Citizens of Jerusalem," he began, "men of Jerusalem — " The crowd shouted back at him in agreement so that he finally raised his hands for silence.

"Today we have dedicated our walls. We have blessed the work of the hands of those who built them — your hands."

The crowd broke out again. He could get not much more than two or three phrases out before the crowd would respond. There was no stopping them.

"It will be a day of slow speeches," Fetneh shouted into Katannah's ear. "I hope it doesn't put poor Jehiel off. He's nervous enough already."

Nehemiah raised his hands again. The people reluctantly quieted. "But we began our task on the shoulders of those who came before us. Some of you with grey hair will remember the early days — the days of King Cyrus, long may his memory be among us — when we were first granted our freedom. It wasn't just broken walls and derelict houses that awaited them. The very Temple of Yahweh had been laid waste.

"But Yahweh gave them stout hearts and strong backs. This is a day that honours them as well." It was about as much continuous speech as the crowd could endure without interrupting with their own feelings. Tomorrow would be a day of raw throats but no one really cared just then.

Shecaniah, who had managed to find his mother in the crowd, put his face close to Fetneh and growled, "This is it. Jehiel is about to be called up." He pointed to where his father stood on the first step, nervously fidgeting with his papers.

"He'll do well," Fetneh shouted back. Shecaniah did not withdraw his bulk. Instead, he wrapped one arm around Fetneh's shoulders and squeezed her close; two solid but otherwise small and insignificant people, pressed in by thousands. The moment they anticipated would be mostly forgotten by the end of the day. The plinth that Shecaniah's grandfather spent his life building was, truth be told, unremarkable. But for one old fat Ammonite woman who loved her husband without reserve, and for one burly Jewish stonemason, this was a holy moment.

Nehemiah was speaking again, and motioning for Jehiel to join him at the top of the steps. "I have asked Jehiel, father of Shecaniah, a descendant of Elam, to read the names of those who prepared the way for us — brave pioneers whose work we bless." He raised his hands, calling for silence, and nodded to Jehiel.

Jehiel's thin voice stilled the crowd more effectively than any of Nehemiah's hand gestures. People hushed and leaned forward to catch his words. "These are the names of the families who first returned from Babylon, who were the first to come home, who, in the first year of Cyrus, King of Persia, in fulfillment of the prophecy spoken by the nabi Jeremiah, came up out of captivity and built our God's temple."[33]

He took a deep breath and started in. "The family of Parosh, of Arah, of — "

At the mention of Arah a small cheer went up from the edge of the square. Jehiel looked up from his papyri, startled as if perhaps he'd pronounced it wrong.

" — of Shephatiah — " and again a cheer, louder this time, and from a different location.

" — of Pahath-Moab." More shouts, this time from a group of people standing on top of the wall. It dawned on Jehiel that the shouts were coming from the families whose forebears he was reading. And, with each name he read, the cheers grew more assertive, as if to outdo the shouts that had preceded them. He started in again.

" — the family of Bebai." A single voice responded and everyone laughed. But the pattern had been set and the crowd listened carefully to each name Jehiel read out, waiting to show the strength of their clan. Jehiel relaxed, smiled shyly out over his audience, and rose to the occasion.

" — of Zaccai . . . of Adonikam . . . of Netophah . . . of Azmareth."

The descendants of each family were seldom standing together, and voices would respond from all over the courtyard and along the walls and rooftops.

" . . . of Micmash . . . of Elam."

Shecaniah and Fetneh bellowed their satisfaction, joined by others who claimed Elam as a forebear. They turned to each other, stomping their feet and pummeling each other's large arms. Fetneh turned and drew Katannah into the moment. And so it went until Jehiel finished reading the list, ninety-four names in all. He bowed bashfully toward the crowd and received his own cheer of thanks before descending from the steps to join his wife and son.

Fetneh's gesture of congratulations pulled her husband full off his feet as she enfolded him against her fleshy chest. "You were magnificent," she chortled. "The crowd loved you."

Jehiel beamed. He looks taller, Katannah thought, watching Fetneh fuss over her husband's accomplishment. She offered her hand and said, "Congratulations, O son of Elam." He only grinned back at her, still too full of the moment for words.

Ezra moved forward to take over the proceedings. Meshullam, never far from the side of his mentor, stood just to Ezra's left, holding a large scroll, already open at some predetermined place. "Sons and daughters of Jerusalem," he began, "Children of the Exile." He paused and gave a slight nod to Meshullam, who lifted the scroll slowly up, presenting it to the people.

Ezra continued. "The words of Moses appointed for this day: A reading to guide us in purity lest through our ignorance we defile ourselves." The crowd remained silent. It was Ezra's first public address. "We read Torah each day because Yahweh has commanded it, for in the reading of it, we gain wisdom; wisdom and a blessing. Some of you, I know, think that Torah is like some magic incantation, housed in the temple storehouse lest it be plundered by our enemies. But today I proclaim to you the truth of Torah. The truth of Torah is that Yahweh would have all his children know His laws, for when we know Torah, we know Yahweh.

"Hear what Moses himself said about learning Torah." He closed his eyes and recited from memory: "These are the commands, decrees and laws the Lord your God directed me to teach you to observe in the land that you are crossing over Jordan to possess, so that you, your children and their children after them may fear the Lord your God as long as you live by keeping all his decrees and commands that I give you, and so that you may enjoy long life. Hear O Israel: the Lord our God, the Lord is one. Love the Lord your God with all your heart and with all your soul and with all your strength. These commandments that I give you today are to be upon your hearts. Impress them on your children. Talk about them when you sit at home and when you walk along the road, when you lie down and when you get up. Tie them as symbols on your hands and bind them on your foreheads. Write them on the door-frames of your houses and on your gates."[34]

Ezra glanced again at Meshullam who now lowered the scroll and positioned it so that Ezra could read from it. Ezra began:

"The lesson for this day:

'No one who has been emasculated by crushing or cutting may enter the assembly of Yahweh. No one of illegitimate birth, nor any of his descendants may enter the assembly of Yahweh.'"[35]

An uneasy stir rippled across the people as a cat's paw of wind might suddenly sweep over an otherwise still pond. Ezra, if he sensed anything, gave no notice of it and continued. His tone was measured and he paused after every sentence as if to allow it to be received.

"No Ammonite and no Moabite or any of his descendants may enter the assembly of Yahweh. For they did not meet you with bread and water when you came out of Egypt but hired Balaam, son of Beor, to curse you. Do not seek peace or good relations with them as long as you live. But do not abhor the sons of Edom,[36] for he is your brother. And do not abhor the Egyptian, because you lived as an alien in his country. The third generation of children born to them may enter the assembly of Yahweh."

Perhaps it was because Katannah had been listening to everything so intently that the words penetrated her so easily. Her body heard and understood the words far better than her mind. She sagged a little as her knees weakened. Her vision narrowed so that she saw only the robe of the person directly in front. If she breathed at all, she was unaware. She felt her insides constrict violently, making themselves small, and she fought hard against the urge to void her water where she stood. Her balance betrayed her as did her legs that refused to move so that she swayed and would have fallen completely had Fetneh not grabbed her.

Only once before in her life had her body taken charge so completely over her mind. It had been very early morning and she had been walking to Jerusalem from her village. A mountain cat had suddenly come out of the field beside the road and stopped directly in front of her. Its eyes were the calculating eyes of a hunter assessing its prey and the safety of making the kill just at that particular moment. The lion vanished with the same speed with which it had appeared, retreating toward the hills against the advance of the sunlight. But Katannah's body had braced for disaster then, just as it was doing now.

She sagged into Fetneh, who took her weight easily.

"It's time to go," Fetneh whispered close to her ear. "I'll take you home."

Whether Fetneh pushed through the crowd or whether the people moved aside as if to speed their departure, Katannah did not register. She felt only the lion's hard unblinking eyes now multiplied a hundred times, gazing at her with every step Fetneh took. Her muscles locked themselves tight as if by hardening they might withstand the claws of the large cat that stalked her. Only when she and Fetneh reached the shelter of the first narrow laneway did strength seep back into her frame, and gradually she began to walk on her own. Still Fetneh did not let go of her.

She steered them to Katannah's small apartment and only relaxed her grasp when Katannah was sitting on the edge of their low bed. Ever so gently,

Fetneh removed her tunic and rubbed her body dry of sweat. Katannah felt the rough warmth of a new shirt pulled down over her head and did not resist as Fetneh guided her down until she lay on her side, curled up tightly into herself. Fetneh stayed on the side of the bed, stroking her hair in a long steady caress.

Neither spoke. Katannah closed her eyes. All sense of time fled.

Eventually Fetneh said, "I must leave you. Jehiel will worry. Caleb will be home soon, I am sure." Katannah made no reply.

She opened her eyes again when it was Caleb's hands that were touching her and it was his voice that repeated her name over and over.

"Oh Katannah, my precious Katannah." It was the voice of a frightened child tying to give comfort to someone equally distressed. Only then did Katannah begin to cry. She leaned up and burrowed her face in Caleb's lap, sobbing into the fine white linen tunic that she had so carefully adjusted on him as he had left their apartment an eternity ago that morning.

He stroked her head as only a husband can, bending low and kissing the side of her head. "I'm sorry. I didn't know," he kept repeating. "I didn't know the words were there. I'm sorry." A cadence crept into his voice until the words became a lullaby he sang gently down over her. "I didn't know, I didn't know. I am so, so sorry." She lay crying, her arms now tightly around his waist, pressing her face into his warmth.

She spoke at last but did not lift her head. "What will happen now?"

"I don't know." They did not speak again, nor did he move until Katannah fell asleep.

* * *

Caleb and Katannah never spoke of her exclusion from public worship. In the two months that followed he was rarely off duty, involved in some public event almost every day. But at night they clung to each other with a feral fierceness they had not known before, as if the gulf that now divided them could be squeezed back out of their lives by the press of their bodies. It could not, of course, but together in the dark Caleb would enter her with frantic urgency as if by his very penetration he might erase their differences. Katannah opened herself freely, believing — at least while she still lay in the dark — in the ancient power of marriage that truly made two people one flesh. By the end of the first month, Katannah suspected she was pregnant, but said nothing.

The content of what Ezra had read did not force all that many changes. There was total agreement that Egyptians would be immediately welcomed into all public assemblies. Of course the last Egyptian known to have lived in Jerusalem had been old Ebed-Melech, the Ethiopian eunuch who had hauled poor Jeremiah out of the slime pit into which he'd been tossed to die. That had been one hundred and fifty years earlier and it was certain that Ebed-Melech didn't have any children.

The same unequivocal welcome would be extended to any Edomites who might be sufficiently stupid as to wander up out of their own province into Jerusalem. As for the few hundred Ammonites and Moabites who called Jerusalem home, well, the rain fell on everyone, and being excluded from public assemblies wasn't meant to be taken as a personal slight. The Laws of Moses had to be respected.

Fetneh was quite sanguine about the whole affair. "Every religion has its own rules," she said to Katannah one day, "and the Jews are no different. Where would we be if we couldn't tolerate each other's peculiarities? Live and let live. Besides, Jehiel is happy. Happy and proud. Becoming a Jew again is what's done it."

Katannah wasn't so sure. Three good customers all discovered that they no longer needed Katannah's services, and made this discovery all in the same week. They were all Jewish. It was an unfortunate confluence of bad luck. In contrast, Arémeté asked for more of Katannah's time, and even Nikaso, whose continuous disdain for her hair was shockingly public, suddenly said that Katannah should come more often.

"You are the only hope I have at elegance," she had laughed. "Manasseh says that I spend more time grooming my horse than I do myself and I can't have my horse looking better than I am."

It was all so matter of fact, this subtle redrawing of social loyalties. But Katannah could not help but feel the herd being culled, foreigners ever so slightly being edged to the perimeter. She wondered if Arémeté and Nikaso's actions weren't a gesture of closing ranks in the face of an ill wind. She said nothing to Caleb, not even daring to ask if anything had changed for him at the temple on account of his Ammonite wife.

But the exclusion of a few hundred people from public assemblies wasn't the main thing that occupied people's minds. For the first time in living memory, the shroud of mystery surrounding Torah had been stripped off and stood in all its robust and repristinate splendour, inviting examination by all. The people of the book had been brought face to face with the book of the people and the encounter was charged with intrigue. What exactly does the whole Torah say? What other instructions does it hold? What else are we doing wrong? Ezra could not have asked for a more motivated group of students and was not slow in taking advantage of the situation.

It was on the first day in the month called Tishri that Ezra's school officially opened and all of Jerusalem showed up to be enrolled. Shechaniah's men had built a wooden scaffold over the Water Gate, and the usual market stalls that stood cheek to jowl just inside the gate had been cleared away by order of Nehemiah. The result was an elevated platform from which Ezra could speak down into a large open-air classroom to accommodate his students. If anyone noticed that the place from which Ezra taught was at the opposite end of the city from where the temple stood, no one said anything. The temple square would have been a much more suitable location, and Ezra could have read from the top of the steps instead of the rude makeshift pulpit. But like the snubs Katannah felt, but could not confront, Eliashib and the other priests could not protest about a slight they could not prove. Nonetheless, Torah clearly had no need of the temple.

In the predawn light of that first day of Tishri, Shecaniah padded around the base of the scaffolding, a carpenter's bib wrapped around his broad waist, testing the trusses for any movement.

Not the prettiest thing I ever built, he thought, but it'll do the job. He wished that Nehemiah had given him more time for the task, to build something that was, at least to Shecaniah's builder's eye, more fitting for the occasion.

"You're here early too, I see." It was Nehemiah's voice. Shecaniah just grunted, still checking the structure.

Are you coming to the reading?" Nehemiah spoke again.

"Nothing could keep me away. You know, Governor, all my life I've felt like I was waiting for something and not even sure what it was. Just always felt like there was something important missing. And today, well, today feels like I'm on the brink of discovering something big. I can't explain it."

"Ezra is a powerful man."

"Powerful men come and go." Shecaniah was not ready to commit to the explanation. He would wait for the day to unfold.

Even before the grey, predawn light had fully departed from that first day of the month of Tishri, Ezra and Nehemiah, surrounded by a score of Ezra's scribes, gazed down into a tightly packed square of sober, upturned faces.

Nehemiah spoke. "It gives me joy that the citizens of Zion are eager to hear the words of Moses. There is no better way to mark this, the first day of a new year. I declare as Governor that for the entire month this space shall be reserved as a public place of assembly until the Torah is proclaimed. Word of the respect you have already shown Ezra," — he paused, looked the crowd over slowly and then continued — "and will continue to show, will please

King Artaxerxes when he learns how favourably his royal envoy has been received, and with what care you have attended to his words."

Nehemiah left. His message had been delivered. The watchful eye of the Persian court would follow the proceedings. Ezra was a great and holy man. True enough. He also held a Persian writ of office.

It was Ezra's turn. He stepped forward and began without any preamble. "Hear O Israel, the LORD our God is one."

In unison everyone stood. "Amen, Amen," they responded.

Ezra closed his eyes and stretched out his hands. "Blessed art thou, O God — blessed be your glorious name and may it be exalted above all blessing and praise. For you alone are the LORD. It is you who made the heavens — "[37] Noises from below reached his ears and he opened his eyes to see what was happening. Everywhere people were starting to kneel down, bending low so that their faces touched the rough paving stones.[38] There had been no instruction to do this.

They are already taking in the words, he thought. He could not yet trust himself to start speaking again, gripped by the silent humility he was witness to. This is not my doing, he thought. A holy dread stole into his chest. Yahweh has been before me. Truly, God was in this place and I knew it not — this is none other than the work of His hand. What dust am I that I should be His instrument of salvation?

His eyes blurred completely, and, seasoned orator that he was, he still could not find speech. Slowly he knelt himself and removed first one sandal and then the other. Just as slowly he stood again, head bowed, tears now streaming down his face, a thin leather sandal clenched in each hand.

Quietly he tested his voice. "We will start at the beginning," he said. "The words of Moses — the words of Yahweh — are many. But there is no need for haste." Meshullam was now by his side and Ezra reached out and grasped his arm. They looked at each other. He knows, thought Ezra. He turned, probing the faces of the other young men who clustered on the stage

— Mattithism, Shema, Uriah and the others[39] he'd so carefully nurtured at his school in Susa — all protégées who had faithfully followed him to this moment. They understand. It was for this moment that Yahweh raised them up and gave them to his care.

A deep happiness swept through Ezra. I have passed the torch, he thought. My hands did not falter all those years. Torah is safely in the hearts of the next generation of teachers. He grinned suddenly, the grin of a grand old master smiling at his students on graduation day, welcoming them into the scholarly guild as equals. And to a man they smiled back at him. This was their day too and they would bring honour to the man who had rescued Torah from extinction.

"We shall start at the beginning," Ezra said again, "for the history of our people does not start with Abraham, ancient though he is. For even before Yahweh called Abram and brought him out of the land of Ur of the Chaldeans[40] — even before this, Yahweh was speaking."

One of the young scribes had by this time positioned himself slightly in front of Ezra, a scroll open, and Ezra looked down and began to read.[41]

"In the beginning God created the heavens and the earth. And the earth was without form and void, and darkness was upon the face of the deep. But the spirit of Yahweh was hovering over the water. And God said, 'Let there be light, and there was light.'"

The shrill voice of a child suddenly cut across Ezra's sonorous voice. "Who did Yahweh say that to? There wasn't anyone else around."

The entire square started to laugh. It was time for school to start.

"He has a point," Meshullam said to Ezra, while waiting for the people to settle again. "And the makings of a good scribe."

"He'll be in your classes, not mine," Ezra replied, and good luck to you if he's asking that kind of question at his age."

He turned back towards the crowd. "To ask questions is good. It shows respect. And these men — " he pointed to the scribes standing around him " — can give you answers. So here is how we will proceed. These men will come down and stand in the square — divide yourself into groups around them so that you can talk among yourselves and have your questions answered."

Meshullam was first off the platform and got no further than Shecaniah's bulk before stopping. They greeted each other formally.

"I have much to learn," Shecaniah said.

"Your love for the ways of Torah is already well known, Shecaniah," Meshullam replied. He cut off the man's attempt to protest with a wave of his hand. "Oh yes, Nehemiah has been quite specific in his praise of you. And a zealous heart towards Yahweh's law fulfills the first and greatest commandment."

"But are there not over six hundred statutes, not counting the customs and general prohibitions?" Shecaniah replied.

Meshullam laughed. "Six hundred and thirteen, to be precise, and none of them as important to Yahweh as keeping the first." He grinned. "But they do give us scribes a lot to argue about."

The teachers dispersed through the crowd and Ezra resumed reading. "The heavens and earth were spoken into being and Adam, formed from the dust of the ground, was made in the very image of Yahweh." Ezra's pace was leisurely and he stopped frequently so that people might ask questions of the nearest scribe. The pattern would continue all month. Like daylight on a cloudy morning, Torah stole softly into people's hearts.

Early in the month, Ezra had read the instructions concerning the Feast of Booths.[42] Except for the ancient words of Moses and a few suggestions from Ezra, there were no traditions to encumber people's earnest enthusiasm to properly enter into this Feast. As a consequence, there was a certain adolescent excitement that came from approaching a thing for the very first time. In less than two days the entire city looked to have become one giant leafy cabbage. Cart after cart staggered in through the gates filled with the cuttings of olive trees, myrtle bushes, palms and cypresses. In a flash people would seize them, scampering back like busy squirrels to add them to their huts they would occupy for the next seven days. The fresh smell of forest mingled with the smoky incense of roasted meat cooked slow and succulent in open braziers. Nehemiah, having personally donated some two hundred goats and sheep to the festival, strolled the streets, beaming at the contentment that lay like a cozy wool blanket pulled up tight under the greasy chin of Jerusalem. Not since the days of Joshua, successor to Moses, had the Feast of Booths been celebrated with such gusto.[43]

But whether by accident or deliberate cunning, Ezra destroyed the postprandial somnolence with just one short reading. Three days after the feast had ended, Ezra quietly climbed the scaffolding as usual.

"The reading of the day are the words of Moses to our forefathers, instructing them on their relations with nations who dwelt in Canaan before Yahweh gave it to his people. These are the regulations: 'You are to make no treaty with them. Do not intermarry with them. Do not give your daughters to their sons or take their daughters for your sons. For they will turn your sons away from following me to serve other gods. Yahweh's anger will burn against you and will quickly destroy you. For Yahweh has chosen you — only you — to be his people, his treasured possession.'"

Ezra stopped reading, looked down into the stunned, upturned faces and said, "That is sufficient Torah to consider for one day."

It didn't matter whether people had attended the reading or not. All of Jerusalem learned of it before evening. By next morning a dozen engagements were publicly repudiated much to the humiliation of certain prominent, but nonetheless, foreign families. And if the point had not been clear before, now everyone knew it: The Torah had teeth.

* * *

Tension so filled Katannah and Caleb's tiny apartment that there was room for nothing else. It did not leave room even for words to talk about this new reminder that somehow their marriage was an offence to Yahweh. Caleb rarely met her eye, looking more like a fugitive in hiding from some monstrous crime he had committed. And confining as their one room was, Katannah found that going out was even worse. Caleb might feel criminal. She felt like a leper.

Lying beside each other at night was the hardest. What had once been their place of intimate exchange became a place of daily purgatory. The low bench on which they slept was not wide and each involuntary meeting of flesh on flesh sent them both retreating to the edges of their horizontal prison.

They lay on their backs, staring up into the blackness, feigning sleep, each locked in their torment: two desperately frightened, confused and insignificant people. Only once did Katannah try to touch him, reaching out in the dark to find Caleb's arm and stroking it ever so gently from his shoulder to his elbow. Her body was turned toward him so that she lay on her side, face within inches of his cheek. In that one slow caress she had said everything she could ever say, and risked all that would ever matter. Despite her flimsy sleeping shirt, she lay utterly naked and vulnerable, offering everything she had.

"Caleb," she whispered. It was more supplication than summons. She waited, feeling his body tense. It would have taken only the slightest turning of his head, less than half a turn before he would have found her willing mouth, and from there her willing body. One small turning of his head and the chasm of a hundred miles that stretched across their bed would have vanished in the sweaty passion that would engulf them both, sweeping them to safety.

But he did not turn. Instead he said only, "I am tired."

Never had Katannah cried herself to sleep in such silence.

* * *

She lost more customers, and this time they did not even bother to make an excuse. And among those who did retain her, foreign wives mostly, like herself, she noticed that they all wore the wary veil of apprehension. Nikaso, usually bursting with energy, now sat silently, yielding to Katannah's hands without protest. Some cruel and random plague settled on all of them. Katannah ever so delicately tried to engage Nikaso.

"Your family — in Samaria — are well?" she ventured.

"They are fine enough," came Nikaso's flat reply.

"Your husband is not sick?" Katannah asked again.

Nikaso roused herself. "My husband, Manasseh, is fine; my father, Sanballat, is fine; the servants are all fine; even my favourite horse is fine. And I, I am fine as well." She sighed, submitting to Katannah's soothing fingers as they massaged her scalp through a rich lather of soap. "The problem is that although I am fine, it would seem I am not Jewish. And because of that, nothing is fine." She sank back into the couch and then murmured "But then, you understand. You are not fine either."

"But you worship Yahweh." Katannah's voice was barely above a whisper. "I am Ammonite. It's to be expected that I should be shunned. But you, you even look the same as them. And your husband is grandson to the High Priest. Surely that is enough."

"It is not enough to look like them or to worship the same God. And that I should have sullied one of their priests seems only to increase my sins. No, the only people who are 'fine' in this city are those that did not come from here. Only if you came from Persia — with your precious lineage intact — only then are you fine."

"I'm sorry. My husband too is made to feel ashamed because of me, though we do not speak of it. We did not know this would happen."

"My father had a premonition that something like this would come to pass, that our marriage would not be accepted. But to his credit he does not remind me of that. His letters offer only great love and a home for Manasseh and me, and even an armed escort to ride with us if it should come to that."

"Mistress Nikaso," Katannah started in tentatively, "you know I have never brought gossip about others into your home, neither have I ever taken any out."

"What is your news that you can no longer keep inside you?" replied Nikaso, rousing herself from her own thought.

"Not news, but rather a question, about another couple who..." Katannah paused, searching for the right phrase. "... Who are like us," she finished finally.

"Who are they?"

"The husband is Meshullam. He is shown respect by everyone and is always seen in the company of the holy man who came from Persia."

"Yes, Meshullam. I know him and his wife as well. My husband has many dealings with him at the temple, and admires him. It is thought that he will take Ezra's place when the time comes. They come often to our home. We are friends."

On hearing that last sentence, Katannah quickly retreated. "It is not my place to ask about your friends. I am sorry."

"Ask what you want," Nikaso said who now appeared to be quite interested in the question that Katannah would eventually find words for.

Katannah pressed on. "His wife, Arémeté — she is not Jewish, yet her husband is not made to feel embarrassed — or rather," she corrected herself hastily, "what I know for certain is that his wife is the same as she has always been. It is as if what the holy man read in the square does not touch them."

Nikaso let out a long, noisy breath, part laugh, part lament. "Ah yes, Meshullam and his exotic Persian wife who, it seems, live out their lives under a special dispensation. A loophole in Torah has been provided them. Who would have imagined such a thing?"

Katannah waited. Nikaso continued. "You are perceptive, and quite correct. Arémeté and Meshullam — and there are others too — claim special exemption. You see, Katannah, a very long time ago, over one hundred years, when Jerusalem was destroyed by King Nebuchadnezzar, the very best of our people were taken to Babylon."

"The ancestors of those that have returned," said Katannah.

"There have been six generations of our people born in captivity. And to these people was granted permission to take wives and husbands who were not Jews."

"Who gave them such rules? This Torah they are bound by, it speaks clearly against such things."

"A nabi called Jeremiah, who it would seem did not actually go to Babylon himself but who wrote a letter to those who had, not only gave them permission to marry others not from our tribe, but actually encouraged them to do so. At least that is how they interpret his words."[44] Nikaso's voice had taken on a brittle bite, making it clear what she thought about such a convenient letter.

"And those who did not go to Babylon? Did this man — the prophet who stayed behind — did he speak of them? *Of you?*"

"Yes," Nikaso answered softly. "The letter of the holy nabi Jeremiah speaks of those who remained behind in the land. His words were quite clear and leave no doubt to their meaning. Those who did not go into Babylon are like the figs on a tree that are too rotten to harvest, so bad that we are of no use."[45] She paused, then added, "His exact phrase is that Yahweh would make us objects of horror and a reproach among the nations, at least that is to be the fate of those that survive at all.[46] For Yahweh it seems has hidden his face from those of us who remained in the land."[47]

"I am sorry for your troubles," Katannah whispered. " I did not know that you too have been afflicted by all the words that have flown into our city."

"The locusts strip the fields of rich and poor alike," Nikaso tried to laugh, failing miserably. "Not even a Governor's daughter is beyond their reach."

"And are you certain that this Jeremiah said such things? Perhaps someone steals his name for his own dark purpose."

"Yes, Katannah, I am quite certain. I am certain because the words of Jeremiah were preserved in Persia[48] and Ezra has brought them back with him. Meshullam gave a copy to my husband for the temple scriptorium." And then, in a voice Katannah could hardly hear, Nikaso added, "And no one ever forgets being told that they are no better than rotting fruit."

"There is no hope for us, is there. Either of us."

"No," answered Nikaso. "It is just a matter of time before we are dealt with — we and the men who married us."

* * *

Torah school remained open and as the month of Tishri progressed, Shecaniah intentionally stood close to wherever Meshullam was stationed. A mutual respect marked their frequent and often spirited debates. Meshullam's knowledge was equally offset by the intensity with which Shecaniah applied himself to the ways of Torah.

"There is no end to your appetite," said Meshullam. "Once you've latched on to any part of Torah, you consume every bit, however small."

"What is the point of listening if you are not willing to change how you live?" Shecaniah had retorted. The subject had been whether Sabbath regulations permitted any merchant to remain open on that day. Meshullam had suggested that the merchants who were not bound by Torah should be free to choose. Shecaniah had favoured the forced closure of the entire market.

"But you cannot succeed in making people keep the outward appearance of Torah if they do not first wish to keep it in their hearts," Meshullam had argued.

"Perhaps," Shecaniah countered, "but why should we make it easy for people to stray from the ordinances of Yahweh? How else will they see the wisdom of our ways except in the doing of them? And for once, our city leaders have both the power and the inclination to make our entire city pure."

"So you would seek a civil ordinance to close the markets?"

"Of course, and to be frank, Meshullam, I do not understand why Ezra has not yet done so. He has the power of Persia behind him. Why does he hold back?"

"And if Ezra imposed the words of Moses on our city, how long do you think it would last? You can't legislate a pure heart, Shecaniah."

"You can't tolerate disobedience. Do you think I've listened all this month and learned nothing from the history of our people? How long can we test the patience of Yahweh before he will once again bring disaster down on our heads — and rightly deserved. Do you think these walls cannot be destroyed yet again and our people carried off into yet another captivity?"

"Shecaniah," Meshullam answered with quiet intensity, "may I ask if others in the city share your beliefs?"

"Yes, you may ask freely, and the answer is that there are many." He smiled slyly at his friend before adding, "This business of understanding Torah is far too important to trust entirely to you scribes, you know. The men of the city — we meet often to discuss what needs to be done."

"And?"

"And what we want is a chance to show where we stand, prove that we've heard Torah and will change our ways as a result. We want some kind of declaration."

"And you think people would agree to live by its regulations?"

"We are eager for it."

Thanks be to Yahweh, Meshullam thought, for he has heard our prayers.

* * *

The signing of the Jerusalem Covenant,[49] as it came to be called, was an event gorged with pomp and ceremony. Nehemiah seized on the idea with the zeal of an out of work actor suddenly given a leading role again. Truth be told, he had found Tishri a hard month to endure, the focus being entirely on Ezra. But getting consensus on the actual details of the covenant had been surprisingly hard. To Nehemiah's delight and Meshullam's unease, some prominent citizens argued for regulations that would be binding on all citizens of Jerusalem without exception. In the end, though, the covenant remained a voluntary ordinance, binding only on those who signed it. Eighty-five of Jerusalem's most powerful families[50] strutted proudly up the temple steps to a large table where Nehemiah sat in front of an elaborately decorated parchment. With great care, the signet ring of each family was pressed into the waiting hot wax until, by the end of the day, there was more wax than words on the creamy white skin used in the making of the scroll.

But as Nehemiah had shrewdly calculated, this voluntary arrangement enforced the regulations far more powerfully than if they had been imposed. Elitism has always engendered emulation and no family wanted to risk the social stigma of not following the lead of those they envied.

The covenant itself was simple enough. No one who signed it would engage in Sabbath trade, and the financial needs of the Temple would be provided for with gifts of both coin and provisions. And of course, any *future* marriage to a foreigner was no longer permitted.[51]

But the proclamation of the covenant marked a change in the mood of the city, as if finally the weather had committed to a new season. Like clear ice that finally skims a pond on the first cold night of winter, the covenant coated everything with a glistening veneer. Meshullam was uneasy, unsure within himself. From all outward signs, Yahweh had turned his face once more upon the city of David. People's appetite for learning Torah exceeded the scribes' capacity to teach. Rituals were embraced with energy. Temple tithes were collected without coercion. Meshullam tried to be both grateful and content. But he could not shake a mounting sense of unease. It was as if the brilliance of purity that now encased the city sparkled from some harshness, like the glitter of glass shards that would cut you deep even as they twinkled brightly.

Not until Arémeté confronted him did he fully appreciate the personal manifestation of the corporate piety that was his daily curriculum.

"This covenant, recently proclaimed," she began one evening as they ate, "you were a signatory to it, I believe?"

Meshullam, long accustomed to her direct speech, answered in kind. "Yes. A remarkable document, coming from the people themselves. Ezra was encouraged by it, as were we all."

"Tell me, what does it say concerning the market stalls?" Arémeté pressed.

"Only that they will remain closed on the Sabbath."

"That is all? There was nothing else?"

"No. Why?"

"I was refused service today," Arémeté replied. It was the tone of a highbred woman who had suffered an insult beyond what she would accept.

"I am sorry. But you are certain it was a refusal? Might it not have been just a misunderstanding?"

"Both the merchant and I spoke Aramaic," she said, "until the end, that is. His final insult was hurled at my back in Hebrew. Even I know their word for a dog. Meshullam, what is happening in this city? I have a right to know."

"What exactly did he say to you?" Meshullam turned his paling face fully toward her. This is a serious matter, was what his faced showed to her. What touches you, touches me. She sat, staring back at him until she was satisfied his concern was genuine. Then, a little more kindly, she continued.

"I had stopped over a piece of jewelry — a gold chain fashioned on a pattern I had seen once at home. I asked its price only to be told it was not for sale. It clearly was."

Meshullam waited. Arémeté had no trouble expressing herself. She had paused only long enough to rein in her recollected anger. "I asked why, and was told that, as a devout Jew, he sold only to other Jews and that followers of Marduk should look to the stalls in Babylon for the things they needed."

"Marduk?"

"Yes, Meshullam. He took me for a Babylonian; probably thinks that Nebuchadnezzar still sits on the throne though he's been dead a hundred years, and their paltry god, Marduk, was melted into Persian coinage some eighty years past. These people know nothing of what lies beyond their borders. This is a narrow world you have brought me to, Meshullam, occupied by narrow and brutish minds." It was a reflection of Arémeté's breeding that she was angry rather than intimidated as a result of the encounter. Arémeté knew exactly both who she was, and who she was not, in the ever-changing constellation of nations. And while she respected her husband's equally well-defined identity, she would not countenance even the slightest suggestion that her Persian blood was socially inferior to anyone's.

"The man probably thinks that Yehud is an independent sovereignty and that Nehemiah is its king," she snorted, giving vent to her husband.

"Your news is disquieting; to insult you is to insult me," he sighed, adding, "and it shows that we have failed to teach the full meaning of Torah. Men seek to bend it to their own prejudices."

"I'm not entirely ignorant of your work, husband," she replied. "It does not become you to try and hide from me the fact that this Jerusalem Covenant you have signed forbids foreign marriages such as ours."

"It forbids only future marriages," Meshullam spoke sharply. "If it said otherwise, I would not have supported it, much less signed it."

236

"It's a fine line you tread, Meshullam. The Jews who lived in Persia are not the same as the Jews who now live in Jerusalem, though they are the same people."

Their conversation only paused. Both knew there was more that needed saying. But not until the safety of their bed when they lay together did they pick it up again.

"I *am* uneasy," he said to her, finding her hand in the dark. "More than uneasy. Jerusalem is unlike anywhere else I have taught. We have started something here that is no longer in our control. Purity of heart is what Yahweh asks of his people, not this fixation with rules."

"For six generations Jew has married Persian, and you Jews have only increased in both numbers and devotion. You borrowed our clothes, our language, our foods, our libraries, even our names, and you still stayed faithful to Yahweh."

"It's true," he answered. "But here, there is no distinction between the spirit of a thing and the outer form."

"It will not stay only with future marriages, Meshullam. Let's not pretend otherwise and betray the honesty between us. Would that I could convert to this god of yours. Once, in Susa, I might have, but then it was not required. Now, it is required but not possible. Even if I did, I would remain a problem."

"You and your family have done much for me — and Ezra."

Arémeté laughed gently. "A good thing we have more to live on than the pay Ezra finds for you." Then more seriously she added, "It is our nature to tolerate all gods. Many speak for the same virtues as ours."

She turned toward him so that their blunt words were softened by the touch of their bodies. This was not the first threat that their marriage had faced. "This Torah you have studied all your life; it is a covenant that Yahweh upholds. Mithra too champions the sacredness of contracts. You cannot deny this, clever man that you are." The anger of the day had been talked out of her and she relaxed more into him, finding her usual spot just under his arm.

"What will become of us?" he whispered.

She stretched up her face to kiss his chin. "Enough troubles for one day, Meshullam. Surely between Yahweh and Mithra we will not be asked to break the promises we have made to each other. Their reputations depend on it."

Still nestled against him she fell asleep quickly. Meshullam, however, did not.

* * *

Arémeté was right. The quest for purity spread like a bitter balm, each of the offending families targeted like pox marks on an otherwise pretty face. Shecaniah, flush with his role in creating the Jerusalem Covenant, was emboldened enough to seek what he knew to be the only, and final, solution. He bypassed Meshullam, something telling him that his thoughts would not be received with enthusiasm. Instead he sought an audience with his friend, Nehemiah. The Governor wasn't afraid of making tough decisions.

"We need to go further," he began bluntly. "The changes you've made so far are all well and good, Governor, but there is more that needs doing and you're the only one with courage to do it. Ever since you stood up to Sanballat and his rabble, everyone knows you're not afraid of fighting for what is right."

"Your flattery is welcome," laughed Nehemiah, which was actually quite true. "What is your concern?"

"It's the foreigners who live among us. They don't belong here anymore now that we know what it means to be Jewish."

Nehemiah's face gave no hint of his emotions. *Yes!* was what he wanted to shout. You and I agree. There is no need to present your reasons. Let's do something. He resisted the urge to jump up out of his seat and seize some part of Shecaniah's bulk in a clumsy lumbering dance of glee. Instead, he only said, "It is a delicate matter you raise. They do not disturb the peace, and neither incite disobedience nor avoid paying their tax. At present there is no law they have transgressed."

"You are right," replied Shecaniah evenly. "No law at present." The two men eyed each other like two merchants who knew that a deal was about to be consummated. Finally Shecaniah added, "But of course you have the power to change that."

Careful, thought Nehemiah, I cannot lead beyond where the people will follow. "On what grounds would you suggest I introduce new ordinances, assuming of course that I would entertain the idea?"

"They are an offence to Yahweh — the God you serve, the God of this city, the God of this land. Torah declares it. There is no other reason needed."

"Shecaniah," Nehemiah said, "when you refer to the foreigners who live among us, do you mean just the families who live within our walls that are not Jewish?"

"I do not. They are no threat. And it's no fault of theirs that they weren't born Jewish. So long as they stick to themselves, *and their own kind*, their trade is welcome."

"To whom do you refer then?" was the cold question. Say the words, Nehemiah pleaded inside himself. Name the sin that stains us; you have only to be clear this one time and I shall do the rest. Everything can happen as you want but you must speak the words I long to hear.

"I refer to those foreigners whom certain of us have taken for wives. They have no place among us any longer."

"So you would send them away — by an act of civil decree? You would enforce divorce?"

"A farmer does not raise a pure herd from mixed breeding stock," said Shecaniah, "any more than I build a stout house from a mixed load of stone, or," he pushed his head out and down so that it was level with Nehemiah's and just a little closer than it should have been for normal conversation, "you build a nation with half-breeds. Everything that's meant to grow needs pruning. It is the way of all life. This isn't personal."

"You are right in one thing," Nehemiah countered, choosing not to commit himself just yet. "The families I have observed, those with foreign wives — their children seem stubbornly resistant to Torah. The wives do not convert, and the children learn no Hebrew.[52] It was not like that in Persia." He stopped suddenly. Shecaniah was himself the child of just such a marriage.

But to his relief, Shecaniah just laughed. "Yes, it is no secret who my mother is. But Yahweh has protected me and perhaps more. Who knows but for this moment I was saved, for who better to speak against the pollution of foreigners than someone who will suffer along with the rest?"

"You are Jewish to the core," replied Nehemiah. "Yahweh has given you great devotion. But not all the offspring of these unholy alliances have been so fortunate. "

"We see the same problem, then."

"The problem, yes," said Nehemiah, "but not the solution. In truth, Shecaniah, what you ask for exceeds my authority. This is a religious matter flowing from Jewish law, not Persian."

"The seed of Abraham must not be polluted," came Shecaniah's obdurate reply. "The Jew in you recoils at the thought. Deny it if you dare."

"I do not deny," retorted Nehemiah, stung at the suggestion. "But neither can I do what you ask. There is only one man among us with the power to do this."

"Ezra?"

"The same."

"Then go to him. Go and tell him the people of the city have petitioned you — that public opinion already outstrips his own zeal for the ways of Yahweh."

Shecaniah had already turned toward the door when Nehemiah thought of one more question. "Shecaniah," he called, "you realize that there can be no exceptions to this ordinance if it should come to that? Your mother, Fetneh..." Nehemiah left the question unfinished.

"It's as you say, Governor. There can be no exceptions."

"I will go to Ezra."

*   *   *

"Are you certain that Shecaniah speaks for the majority of the people?" It was the first question Ezra asked after Nehemiah had finished his presentation.

"Shecaniah would not have sought me out otherwise. I am sure of it. It speaks well for your Torah school — that there should be such whole-hearted devotion toward keeping Torah."

"Don't flatter me," Ezra said curtly. "The Feast of Booths is not quite two months past. What is this — the month of Kislev we are in now? Keeping Torah is still something of a novelty. The seed is hardly planted."

"And already bears fruit."

"Fruit, yes, but of what quality? To send wives away, children too; split families asunder — and by way of an ordinance invoked by my powers as a Persian overlord: Have you thought of what this commits you to if there is not widespread and voluntary compliance?"

Nehemiah pondered this. Clearly he had not considered the matter from this angle. Ezra continued. "If I proclaim an ordinance that in effect forces the divorce of all mixed marriages, and a family refuses to dissolve, this is no longer a matter of religious conscience. It becomes treason against a Persian law. What would you say to your friend Artaxerxes when he learns that we called upon *his* federal troops to wrench young mothers out of their homes, infants still at suck, forcing them into the countryside with only their tunics to cover them. It is barbaric — an offense even to Persian sensitivities."

Nehemiah remained silent, mentally playing out different variations of the scene Ezra had presented. None of them was appealing. No, he had not thought through these implications at all.

"This thing you seek — that Shecaniah seeks — cannot be enforced. Permitted, yes; permitted and even sanctioned. But enforced? Never."

"But if people knew you believed in it, that you would bless those who purified themselves, that would be enough. Look at what happened with other voluntary regulations we have passed. Ezra, the people hang off your every word. You have only to shed one tear and the people put on sackcloth. Tell me this is not the very thing you hoped would happen when you read the law that prohibits the taking of a foreign wife."

"I sought to make a shield against a future sin, not sharpen a sword that would cut families into pieces." Ezra sank back into his chair, chin on his chest. Finally he mumbled, "But I would be false if I pretended that I could not see this day. And now that it is on us, I am loathe to embrace it."

"Abraham's seed is not a thing to trifle with," said Nehemiah severely. But he had overplayed his hand.

"It's a holy people Yahweh wants, not holy loins."[53] And then more to himself than Nehemiah he added, "But it's the same everywhere. Men take the easiest path whenever it is offered. It's easier to find a new wife than to find a new heart."

"But you'll speak in favour of this idea?" Even as he said it, Nehemiah knew he was pressing beyond what was wise. Just then he did not care. This is my chance to make Jerusalem truly pure, he thought. The city of David once again white and spotless, her strong walls to keep out her enemies. This is my destiny!

"What I will do," Ezra replied in a voice that carried the weight of the world in it, "What I will do is seek Yahweh's face and his guidance. It is a terrible thing that faces us, Nehemiah — oh yes, I see your eager zeal for purity, or for what you think is purity. And yes, Yahweh loves purity. But divorce? To break a covenant with your wife for no other reason than that she is still as foreign as the day of her wedding — can that be the will of Yahweh? Would he break faith with us with such ease?"

"Surely you do not compare the promises of Yahweh to a marriage contract," Nehemiah said testily.

"But that's where you are wrong, my friend," Ezra said. "That is *precisely* the comparison that gives me pause."

"What answer shall I give Shecaniah," Nehemiah asked flatly.

"Tell him he will find me on my face in front of the temple doors, seeking the will of Yahweh in this matter.[54] You are dismissed. I must ready myself."

But I cannot do it today, thought Ezra, when he was alone. I have not the strength. And that is the problem. None of us has.

* * *

News of Ezra's whereabouts and purpose arrested Jerusalem. Merchants deserted their stalls, mothers neglected to cook, and even children ceased their usual boisterous antics in the narrow streets.

People talked of nothing else. "Ezra intercedes for us! He is on his face at the top of the temple steps. Do not disturb him. He seeks God's mercy and forgiveness for our sins and wickedness. What sins, you ask? Why, for the sin of having joined ourselves to a defiled people; the foreign tribes who still live in the land. We should never have married them, and now Torah has found us out. Ezra prays that God will overlook our sin."

Everyone who could walk tried to pass quietly through the temple square, wanting a glimpse of Ezra's slight frame lying prone on the temple terrace. By noon the square was thick with people who refused to leave. Ezra — the man who had brought them back to life — was now brought low, and it was the people who had caused his pain. The least they could do was stand with him, heads down, joining him as best they could in whatever supplications he was making on their behalf. No one dared approach him and not once did he rouse himself to take food or water. A holy dread seized those who stood. It was as if Ezra was their scapegoat and each man among them wished desperately that he could take Ezra's place and spare him the pain that was rightfully theirs.

Ezra was vaguely aware of the people. But he was too old, and at that moment, too preoccupied to care about their presence. As the day passed he grew less aware of them, entering some lonely spot deep within himself, where, stripped of all pretense, Yahweh might come. He had given up on words by the end of the first hour.[55]

Instead, he waited patiently for the images that he knew would soon fill his mind. It was a strange and intensely private habit that had been with him since the time when he'd made his first sacrifice. They were not visions in the way he understood the nabis received inner sight. The pictures that came to him were always natural scenes, scenes from his past, or the faces of how he imagined the patriarchs, whose stories he knew intimately, might have looked. At times the link between the prayer of his lips and the image in his heart was obvious. A prayer for the health of Jerusalem matched with an image of the city itself. He had never disclosed this peculiar trait to anyone. Only after years of pondering did he realize that the perspective of what came to him was always the same. They were the concerns of his heart, seen through the eyes of Yahweh. He had never heard the voice of God, in the way that Moses, Ezekiel, Isaiah and other great men were said to have been privileged to hear. But for him, the scenes that would enter unbidden into his head were enough, Yahweh joining him in his prayers. *'You are burdened for my city? I will show you my home as I see it. You petition me to watch over the young scribes to whom I have entrusted my Torah? I will show them to you through my eyes'.*

As Ezra grew older he had made peace with the people's need for public prayer, although privately he remained amused at the presumption that Yahweh needed their description of the trials and tribulations of the moment. So although he continued to pray aloud, and frequently in large gatherings, it was the moments when Yahweh gave him the pictures that he felt as if he were really praying. He lay, eyes shut, on the warm stones of the temple porch. What came to him were the faces of parents, anxious for their children. There was Eve, staring down at the still form of Abel; Abraham, in cold fear as he trudged up a mountain with Isaac; Jacob bent over in the agony of what he believed had befallen his favourite son, Joseph; David, tears streaking down his face, mourning the death of his rebellious yet still much loved son, Absalom.

But it was Samson's mother who came into his head and stayed. Her round, anxious eyes followed her son as he recklessly joined himself to the exotic delights of Delilah. His mother's face aged even as she watched her son with his oiled muscles and a pose of proud self-confidence, so sure that he could take Delilah to himself with impunity. The worry lines consumed her face in lockstep with the same steady pace with which Delilah consumed her son.

The story had not changed since the beginning of time; healthy, strong-willed children — on whom for the parents, the sun rose and set — led astray into the wilderness of bad marriages. Always it began with a naive belief that accommodation, on the essentials at least, would not be necessary. But then in would creep compromise, followed swiftly by capitulation.

How do you protect a child from the decisions he makes? It was a question that had choked the throat of every parent that had ever lived. Samson's wedding faded, replaced by another picture of his mother, old, grey and bent over from the weight of carrying a broken heart. Now she crouched low wailing at his sightless eyes and shackled limbs as the Philistines made sport of him. Hers was the nascent wail from Ramah, Rachel weeping for her children and refusing to be comforted because her children were no more.[56]

Ezra pictured the people he sensed were crowded into the temple courtyard, some now spilling onto the steps just behind him. They are chained as well, he thought.[57]

Samson's mother dissolved from his mind to be replaced by a picture of two old men, leaning into each other, crying silently at the folly of their children. He judges us, and rightly so, he thought. Yet he also weeps.

But then another wedding scene erupted, folding the two old men into a crowd of guests. At the centre stood a bride, pure and virginal, wrapped in a gold-edged cloak of her husband's making. Jewels stood at her throat and gold dripped from her ears. Ezra heard the strong voice of the groom solemnly declare the covenantal bonds as he claimed his wife, wrapping her into the mystery of two people becoming one flesh. Ezra knew the picture. It came from a vision given to the nabi Ezekiel who had died in exile in Babylon.[58] Ezra had personally copied the record of it and knew full well its meaning. Yahweh was the groom, Israel his bride, and the marriage vows were the binding covenant he would never break.

He winced as he pondered the implication of this latest picture. To break a marriage in order to keep one. Can any good come of such a thing?

But no picture came to answer him. Only hot tears and long wracking sobs that shook his body.

He was lifted to his feet by Shecaniah with the ease of a parent righting a small toddler. His eyes now open, he noticed that Shecaniah's brow was contorted into an intense look of worry, tinged with panic.

I've frightened them, thought Ezra, feeling guilty. Next time I should pray in a private place.

Shecaniah was speaking to him, but the voice came to him from far away. "The sin is ours, master, not yours. Woe that Yahweh should visit you with the stripes of our iniquities. It's we who should be punished, not you."

Comprehension seeped slowly into Ezra's mind. They think that Yahweh has laid me low in anger, he thought. He hadn't been aware of any seizure while lying on the ground, but he couldn't be entirely sure. Ezra tried to find something to say that might speak into the fear, but his mind was only slowly retreating back from the deep solitude.

Shecaniah was still speaking. "But it is not too late. We will make amends and purify ourselves. We can send them away — the foreign wives and the children of such unions.[59] It is not too late to obey Torah. We will obey your counsel; you have our support. Only say the words and we will obey."

His voice kept babbling on, filling the intolerable silence. But Ezra could not yet speak although by this time he had managed to stand. One last picture flashed through his head, arriving and departing in the same instant. It was the virgin bride, still in her wedding cloak, but no longer in the centre of her happy, smiling guests. Their faces were now angry, full of stony hate, pointing their fingers at her, raising their fists. "Go!" was what they were shouting at her. She was at the edge now of her own wedding banquet, slinking with shame and haste into the grey borders of the picture. She looked back over her shoulder one last time, staring straight into Ezra's eyes and holding them. *What is my guilt?* was what she asked him.

Ezra staggered under her glance so that Shecaniah had to catch him. He felt himself being turned so that he now faced out toward the packed square. Shecaniah's arm was around his back, propping him up. But it was Shecaniah, not Ezra, who spoke into the eager, upturned faces. "Men of Israel," he shouted. "This is the moment of decision. We can no longer escape our destiny. Here, in this square before the temple of our God, we can make our stand. And make no mistake. History will judge us by what we decide."

He turned toward Ezra and said quietly. "We are ready. Lead us, I pray to you; lead us in an oath of holiness. Give us the words to bind our hearts."

What do I say, thought Ezra. They ask too much of me. The square was now totally silent. Waiting.

"In the presence of Yahweh," he began, "and before the witnesses of all who stand with you. . . ." He stopped. It was as if a stone was stuck in his mouth, his tongue furiously working round and round to dislodge it. He started up again: "Those whose hearts are sure in this matter should show themselves, and be bound at this solemn moment." He drew a deep breath, pushing back against some awful weight that pressed against him. "And be bound at this solemn moment as by an oath from which there is no recourse. By the powers granted me, your desire to divorce is sanctioned."

* * *

Ezra approves! That was all that mattered, and all that Nehemiah needed to convert that one short phrase into an ordinance binding on all of Yehud. By next morning the proclamation had been written, and riders left the city at first light to read it in every village. What had started as an oath of purification settled on the land as a "Judicial Review for the Regularization of Marriages." It was a long, cumbersome title that Nehemiah very much liked the sound of when he practised it aloud. Over the protests of some, Nehemiah insisted that everything be done with both order and due process. The wholesale dissolution of marriages, motivated solely on religious grounds, was without precedence. Land titles would be affected, bride payments, many of them quite substantial, could be challenged and children's otherwise inviolate rights to inheritance were now questionable. Nehemiah recognized that his new proclamation was like pulling at a loose thread on a coat and he took great care that the whole woven cloak of civil code did not unravel into a terrible muddle. The rule of law must still prevail at the end of all this, he thought. It must not be said that I behaved like a despot, recklessly imposing my will without regard to the rights of contract. No, in this matter I must not be impulsive, or at least not seem to be.

All through the night, Nehemiah, drawing on his best advisors, laid out a plan that would not result in legal anarchy. In the end, what circulated was not new regulations, but rather a summons for a public meeting to which every family in Yehud must send a representative. It was a plebiscite at which time the will of the people would be solicited on a single question: Should foreign wives be sent away by the authority of Torah? So while, at least for the moment, the answer to the question remained open, attendance at the public assembly to discuss it was a civil, and therefore imperial, command. And so that no one would take the matter lightly, Nehemiah invoked strong penalties on those who did not attend. All their lands would be subject to forfeiture.

It's brilliant, he congratulated himself, watching the riders leave. No one will ever admit they were absent and not party to the vote since they risk losing their property. Regardless of who actually comes, or doesn't come, the will of the people will be unanimous.

The proclamation had set a date, three days hence, for the meeting. He settled in as well as he could to wait. There was no doubt in his mind about the outcome.

* * *

"What will you do?" Arémeté asked Meshullam bluntly. They sat across the remains of a late breakfast. The assembly would start the next morning.

"I shall talk Ezra out of the madness he commits us to," was his terse reply. "But at present I cannot reach him. He has secluded himself and admits no one."[60]

"And if you fail to persuade him? When you fail? What then?"

"I will not fail," he said heatedly. "This cannot be the will of Yahweh. It grates at everything we hold most sacred. Yahweh will give me the words when the time comes just as he is even now preparing the heart of Ezra to listen to me. Ezra will revoke his blessing. Nehemiah cannot proceed without it."

"I hope for both our sakes that you are successful," Arémeté answered with pronounced formality. *Mithra will not be mocked in this affair* was what she wanted to add. But she would not be cruel. There was enough cruelty in the air already.

* * *

"You've been summoned to appear at a public meeting tomorrow," Caleb informed Katannah without looking at her.

"I am not permitted to enter the temple courtyard," Katannah replied. "You know that. You were there when the words were read."

"An exception has been made," he answered. "The words that will be spoken tomorrow, directly concern you."

"Words," she answered. "They're all that matters to you anymore, aren't they, Caleb."

"Do not speak of the laws of Moses in that tone," he said. "They are sacred."

Sacred, she thought. Yet you hide behind them all these months the way a small child hides behind the skirts of his mother. But no sooner had the thought come to her than she felt guilty. He has no parents and the temple is all that he knows. Is it any wonder that he is so obedient?

"Caleb," she softened her voice. "You loved me once, and not so long ago. I know what you are being asked to do. All the foreign wives — we know our fate. But tell me, please; look me square in my eyes and tell me that I have been a hindrance to you — that I have even once tempted you to turn your back on your God. Name only one action, and I shall be satisfied."

There was no reply and when it became clear that none was coming, she began again, her voice wet with tears that she knew, in time, would find her face.

"Caleb, there is nothing I would not do for you, yes, even leave you if it was for your good, and you asked it of me. And I see it in your face already that you will send me away. And I will go. Your people will never accept you so long as I am your wife. And singing — in the service of this god of yours — it is your very life.

"I ask only one small thing. Leave me with my innocence. Let me at least live out my life having heard from your lips that I have not betrayed you. Tell me that, and I can bear the rest."

"The law of Moses," was his hoarse reply.

"More words!" she suddenly raged. "Words, words, words. It's always the Law of Moses that you invoke. 'Do this, don't do that'. Where are the words that give you permission to break my heart into a thousand pieces, spurn my love, turn your back on me and rip our family apart?"

She hurled her words into his astonished face. "Yes, family, Caleb. I'm pregnant. What did I ever do to this god of yours that he blesses your child with such cruelty?"

She turned and fled, not knowing or caring where she would spend the night, only knowing that she could never again lie beside the man she loved on the narrow bench they called a bed.

Caleb sat alone, not bothering with a lamp as night deepened. Finally he got up, removed his clothes and felt his way to the bed. He spread his arms out, clutching the empty space that was now all his.

Katannah found herself at Fetneh's house, though she did not remember making a decision about it. Fetneh opened her door, looked at Katannah's face and judged instantly what had happened. "Come in, child. There's food still on the table, not yet put away — and afterward a place to sleep." She fussed, making small talk, insisting on doing everything. Their change in roles went unnoticed by them both.

"I shouted at my husband," Katannah said softly. They were by this time sipping tea, cradling their round cups in both hands, watching the steam drifting lazily up.

"I've not met a woman yet who's not been driven to it at least once, for all the good it does," Fetneh chuckled. "Men are so thick."

Silence mingled with the steam from the cups, making a soothing haze that bathed the two women. "What will happen to you?" Katannah asked finally.

"Oh, I'm leaving; I've already told Jehiel as much. I've got family on my mother's side that will take me in right enough. And Jehiel is much too proud to send me away empty-handed. I'll make out fine enough."

"You seem so at ease," Katannah murmured, comparing Fetneh's calm to her own turmoil.

"Already begun to pack," was the reply. "It's time to go, Katannah. Let the Jews be Jews and let everyone else be happy." Fetneh gave a small laugh.

Katannah looked at her askance. "How can you be happy about this?"

"No child, not happy; content perhaps, in a strange sort of way, but not happy. I shall miss Jehiel, especially now that he has become such a — " she paused, " — such a man. All these years I've prayed to Ishtar for such a thing to happen."

"It's a strange way for her to have answered you."

Fetneh chuckled again. "Who am I to question the ways of Ishtar? It is enough that she has answered. Still, have care in what you pray for, I know that now for next time. But it's easier for me than for you. Loving your man from a distance is easier when you're old."

She paused again, then added, "It's Shecaniah I fear for."

"I have heard that he is at the centre of things."

"Yes, and so distant from me that I cannot even give him my blessing. He sees the world in such straight lines, like the buildings he puts up. Poor man; he misses much, as a consequence. I bear him no ill."

But Katannah, exhausted, had already closed her eyes. Fetneh went in search of a blanket.

You poor thing. You poor, poor lamb, she thought. Your only crime is that you have loved your Jewish husband with a pure heart. She tucked the coverlet gently around Katannah's face and stroked her cheek. I will take you with me. In the morning we'll go, before the meeting. You have suffered enough already.

* * *

It had taken the rider an extra hour to find the home of Nikaso and her husband, Manasseh. He had cursed every minute of lost time, and when he finally found the home, the froth that spilled from his horse's mouth hung in pink strands. He had been abused savagely as the rider forced his way through the twisted city streets.

"Water," said the rider, jerking his head toward the horse when the first servant ran up. "And where will I find Nikaso?"

"She is within."

The rider entered the doorway, calling out for Nikaso as he ran. She appeared quickly, Manasseh with her.

"A letter from your father," he said, "and a thousand pardons for my rudeness, but I was instructed that the matter is urgent. I am to await your orders."

He handed over the bound and sealed parcel of papyrus. Nikaso's hand waved him back. She broke the packet open and began to read, holding it so that Manasseh could read as well, over her shoulder.

My daughter,
News of Nehemiah's latest madness reached us here in Samaria
last night. Some do not believe he would stoop so low or make
a mockery of the very Persian code he himself is bound by. But
from one who knows him, such perfidy is no surprise.

  May Yahweh allow this letter to reach you in time. I cannot bear
the thought that you might be subjected to the public humiliation
that Nehemiah so earnestly wishes for you — and is the certain
outcome of the judicial inquiry he pretends to follow. Instead, leave
the city now, and by doing so let it be known that it is Nehemiah
and his twisted use of Torah that has been judged; judged and
found wanting. Come to Samaria, where there is still the will to
follow Yahweh and his laws, with a pure heart, where the odium
of politics does not corrupt.

  And tell your husband that he too is welcome; more than wel-
come, for I have great need of his skills and passion. I have secured
both the permission and the funds to build a new temple at the base
of Mount Gerizim[61] just as Moses commanded. And I have need of
a high priest whose family is of Aaron's to oversee the sacrifices. The
job is his if he will only come.[62]

  The rider who brings this letter is yours to command. And I have
others who will join you once you are outside those cursed walls.

By my own hand,

Sanballat.

"A generous letter in all respects," Manasseh spoke first. "And I do not believe his offer to me is anything more than a timely statement of his needs."

"He knows you cannot be bought," agreed Nikaso.

"Not with the job of senior priest, at any rate." She looked up into his impish face as he finished his thought. "Now if he'd offered me a library, that would have been different. For that my loyalties are for sale, provided it was big enough, of course."

"Manasseh, this is serious!" his wife protested. "Nehemiah's inquiry — "

"You mean his inquisition — "

"Whatever. Be serious about this. You know what tomorrow will bring down on our heads."

"Yes, but alas, it will not include the walls."

"Manasseh!"

He turned, grew serious and said, "What do *you* want to do?"

"I just want to be left alone! I want to ride my horse." She stamped her foot. "I want to have your children and greet you at the end of each day as you return from your scriptorium that you love so much. I want to live in peace. I am tired of Nehemiah and his grand designs. Who is he to say which of us is fit to worship Yahweh and which of us is not? It's absurd. The whole thing is absurd."

"Your father offers us a way forward. We would live peaceably enough in Samaria."

"You mean he offers us a way out. It befits neither of us to slink out of town in haste. It is only because he is so anxious for me that he counsels such a thing. No, if I go, it will not be in the dark."

"If *we* go, you mean."

She looked to make sure she understood him. "What do *you* want to do?" she asked him. In answer, he put both his hands on her waist, and pulling her into him, stared straight into her upturned face.

"I love two things in life," he began. "The first is you and the second is this city. And I will resist Nehemiah or any other thug who tries to take either of them from me."

"It will not be easy if we stay," she said.

"Nehemiah has been a gnat in our ear since the day we married, and we have survived. And some day, he will fly back to Persia."

"Things will change for you at the temple."

"Things have already changed. My two brothers fight openly about who will be next High Priest and I have no stomach to join their quarrel."

"But everyone is so obsessed with who is foreign, and who is not — the whole city thinks of nothing else."

"Yes, Nikaso, at the moment we have all been whipped into a frenzy, but I for one believe it will not last. It cannot. It has come upon us too quickly, like a fever. Nehemiah will take it with him when he leaves."

"But the inquiry; what will they do to us?"

"Nothing, except break their teeth on us. You are the daughter of a governor and I am the grandson of the High Priest. I do not even own land that Nehemiah can seize. Not even he is stupid enough to make trouble for us. Besides, you are *not* foreign. You are Samarian. And nowhere has the Torah forbidden our marriage."

He grinned at her. "Believe me, I know what Torah says as well as any man, and I have checked."

"Then we stay?" she asked him.

"If you are content, that would be my wish, yes. And in the end, we will be vindicated."

* * *

The rain started at midnight. It fell hard in sheets so that by morning it sluiced through the streets with no relent.[63] People were wet the instant they left their doorways, flinching as they sloshed through the ankle-deep water, now with a thick oily scum that stuck to their legs. Conversation was an added labour, best avoided if possible. Not only did their voices have to shout over the rain, but it also meant lifting their heads, exposing their faces to the stinging droplets. People arrived at the temple square sullen and soaked.

Nehemiah had worn his best vestments, thick with overlays, and regretted the decision within minutes of arriving. They now hung shapeless, sodden and cold, on his body. No one looks any better, he thought, looking around at the other officials who joined him on the temple terrace. But it was only a small comfort to a man who placed great stock in his image. Ezra, gaunt and pale from his three-day fast, had worn only a single tunic, his hair and beard lying in tangled strands plastered to his skin. Anyone with long hair suffered the same fate. The rain was no respecter of persons.

This will not take long, Nehemiah thought. No one wants to be here any longer than necessary. He started in, shouting into the rain that continued to fall so fiercely that the edges of the square were hidden.

"Men of Israel," he roared. "You know already our guilt — that many among us have taken foreign wives, mingling the seed of Abraham in unholy alliance."

"You are right," came their reply.

"We have been unfaithful to Yahweh." He waited, cueing the crowd for their lines.

"You are right," came the response, this time louder. The men caught on quickly as to what was expected of them.

"We have transgressed Torah."

Again the crowd gave their response and Nehemiah sensed that the mood was improving, as if the rain were an adversary to be shouted into submission. He nodded to Ezra, who stepped forward.

"Are you willing to confess your sin in this matter?"

"We are willing," came the shout back to him.

"Are you willing to make amends?"

"We are willing!"

"Are you willing to submit to the findings of the magistrates appointed by your governor for this purpose?"

"We will. We will. We will." It was a chant that took on the sound of a thousand marching feet. Ezra let it go for several minutes, listening to its throaty roar mix in with the rain. He raised his hands, calling finally for silence and asked his final question. He had not wanted to include it, but Nehemiah had insisted. Unanimity for what would follow was essential.

"Are there any among you that would counsel otherwise?"

"Yes!" Meshullam had been waiting at the bottom of the steps. "Yes, I counsel otherwise."

"Who speaks?" asked Ezra. He looked down and watched Meshullam mount the first of the ten steps that separated them.

"I do. Meshullam, son of Bani, who came with you out of Persia."

"I do as well." A thin voice came from somewhere to the left.

"And I, too, protest." A third voice was heard directly behind Meshullam but further back in the crowd. An angry murmur rattled through the square, but Ezra held up his hands again and the crowd silenced.

"Let all who would speak come forward. We will not silence anyone. This is a matter on which all must speak freely."

Meshullam waited, and to his great joy three other men pushed their way to join him on the step. He knew only two of them by name but just at that moment he smiled at them as if they were lost brothers.[64] They advanced up the steps, stopping one below where Ezra stood.

"Meshullam. And you have stood with me since the beginning." But Ezra's voice did not carry the accusation of his words.

"As I still do, teacher."

"You have a strange way of showing it," Ezra replied.

"Ezra, we both have given our lives to truth. Please, my dearest friend — my master who has been my father all these years — please do not close your ears to me. Be open to truth, however inconvenient."

"Then speak the truth," said Ezra. "Show me my error. A teacher must not be above his students. All of us bend the knee to wisdom."

"All that you have said about the taking of foreign wives is beyond doubt or debate. Torah is clear and Yahweh does not will it," began Meshullam.

"We are agreed then," said Ezra.

"But that is not the whole of Torah, it is not the whole heart of Yahweh in this matter. There are other laws — other truths that lie even deeper than the words of Torah."

"Name them for me, Meshullam. Name this law that lets us set aside the law of Moses."

"The law of the Garden," was his reply. "The law that was in the earth before there was even an Abraham to make a chosen people from. You know the story as do I. Marriage is not a thing of our making. It is not just some convenient comfort we have invented. Yahweh made it — made it in the same instant that Eve stood in front of Adam, formed from his own flesh. One flesh, Ezra. The law of one flesh. Adam said it to Eve. 'You are bone of my bone, and flesh of my flesh.' When two persons marry, they become one. How can such a thing ever be undone?"

"I know the story," said Ezra. He could hear the crowd shifting restlessly, shut out from the conversation, seeing only that four men, huddled on the steps, had somehow stopped the proceedings.

Someone finally shouted out, "You men are traitors. Are you even Jews?"

Meshullam spun round, trying to see the man who had flung the taunt. "Not Jewish?" he roared out over their heads. "Not Jewish, are we? Go look at the Jerusalem Covenant that hangs so proudly on your Governor's wall. My seal is on it."

"It says we should not marry foreigners," a voice came from the crowd, this time a different one.

"It says we will no longer give our children over to such things. It speaks to the future, not the past."

"Past, present, future; it is all the same to Yahweh." Nehemiah could no longer keep silent, his spittle mixing in with the rain. "And I will purify all of it."

"Yes, I have noticed," Meshullam spun to face this new attack. "You are quick to do the work of God and you also undo it with the same blunt, misguided zeal."

"What is your point?" said Ezra to Meshullam, ignoring Nehemiah. Not once had he taken his eyes off the face of the young man he thought of as a son.

"The holy covenant of marriage, is my point. We are the bride of Yahweh and he does not throw us over to choose another people. Whatever wrongs have been committed — how can our redemption lie in tearing apart two people whom God has made one? How can our God ask us for such a thing when he does not do it himself? It is a kind of murder, the spilling of innocent blood."

Ezra closed his eyes. The bride in his picture now stood before him asking him the same question. My son, my son, Ezra thought. Would that every man here today had your heart, and your courage. But they are like weak reeds, easily bent. And because of it, their wives will suffer. Forgive me, my son, for what I must do to save these people from vanishing from the face of the earth. For if there is no people of God, where then is the God of the people?

He opened his eyes and replied, "Without the shedding of blood there can be no forgiveness of sins, Meshullam. That too is a law set down in the Garden. And it is the one that must prevail today. Purity is all."

Meshullam dropped to his knees, and Ezra, moved by the gesture, drew forward, resting a hand on his bent shoulder. But all the love that held them could not shield them from the rasp of two convictions that would not yield.

"Ezra, tell me that Yahweh guides you in this affair. Tell me that he has blessed you with his words and I shall go away satisfied and humbled." He looked up earnestly into Ezra's face, ignoring the rain that stung his face.

"I cannot. Yahweh has not spoken. He has left me alone with the burden of deciding."[65]

"Then may Yahweh show you his mercy." Meshullam wept.

"May Yahweh show mercy to us all." Ezra drew Meshullam to his feet and laid his hands on the top of the younger man's still-bent head. "I release you from my service. Return to Persia. There are still Jews there who need teaching. Go."

"I will not break my marriage vows."

"Goodbye."

Ezra gave a short nod to Nehemiah to finish the proceedings. He turned and shuffled off into the rain.

* * *

The scope of Nehemiah's court of inquiry spanned all of Yehud and it required three months to regularize the "foreign" marriages. The fate of the wives and children who were investigated is not recorded.

The one hundred and twelve men listed as guilty of intermarriage include Jehiel, the father of Shecaniah, Caleb the cantor and Meshullam, son of Bani. We do not know for certain what Meshullam decided to do after his disagreement with Ezra. Manasseh, grandson of the high priest, is not mentioned in the list. The first-century historian Josephus places Manasseh in Jerusalem well after this story took place.

Nehemiah was finally recalled by King Artaxerxes to resume his duties as cupbearer. Thirteen years later he returned to Jerusalem for a second term as Governor. Much to his fury, the practice of marrying foreign wives had resumed.

Scripture is silent about the final days of Ezra. Jewish traditions say that he died while en route back to Babylon in the city of Khuzistan where columns of fire were often seen to hover over his grave at night.

This is the last story in the Old Testament history of the Jews.

ENDNOTES

1. Caleb's (Eliashib) wife is never named. Her name is imaginary.

2. Ezra 10:24. The actual name of this character is Eliashib but since the High Priest at the time shared the same name, I have changed it so as not to confuse the reader.

3. Ezra 10:2 names Shecaniah as the son of Jehiel. Ezra 10:26 identifies Jehiel as having married a foreigner. The actions of Shecaniah suggest that he was well respected within the Jerusalem leadership but held no official position that we know of.

4. Ezra 8:22,23.

5. This is not simply a literary allusion. Louis Ginzberg (1873–1953), famed for his four-volume book *The Legends of the Jews*, says, "If Moses had not anticipated him, Ezra would have received the Torah. In a sense he was, indeed, a second Moses. The Torah had fallen into neglect and oblivion in his day, and he restored and re-established it in the minds of his people." The use of the word "Legend" in Ginzberg's seminal work should not diminish the books' content. They may be equally thought of as "the traditions," or "the folklore" (*aggadah*), and the bulk of them have been gleaned from the Mishnah, the two Talmuds and the Midrash. He has also included certain stories from secular works that had been repudiated by the Synagogue but embraced by the Christian Church.

6. Aaron was brother to Moses and the first priest anointed shortly after the Israelites left Egypt.

7. In the context of describing the scope of the temple treasury that King Artaxerxes gave, he also issued the following instructions: "Whatever the God of heaven has prescribed, let it be done with diligence for the temple of the God of heaven. Why should there be wrath against the realm of the king and of his sons?" (Ezra 7:23).

8. Nehemiah 12:42. Jezrahiah is mentioned as the director of the two mass choirs that participated in the dedication of Jerusalem's wall.

9. In II Kings 2:11, Elijah did not die, but was taken up into heaven. The last prophecy in Malachi, chapter 4, promises that Elijah will return to God's people. In fact, Ezra was not the fulfillment of this prophecy; rather, John the Baptist, forerunner to Jesus, was confirmed as the second Elijah. In the angelic visitation made to John's father, the angel promises ". . . John will go on before the Lord in the spirit and power of Elijah, to turn the hearts of the fathers to their children and the disobedient to the wisdom of the righteous — to make ready a people prepared for the Lord" (Luke 1:17). But see also John 1:19ff for another understanding of this same prophecy.

10. Ezra was both priest and scribe (Ezra 7:12). The nouns, however, are interchanged as literary devices according to the scene being described. For example, it is Ezra the scribe who reads out the Book of the Law of Moses (Nehemiah 8:1), but it is Ezra the priest who confronts the people with their sin (Ezra 10:10).

11. Meshullam son of Bani (Hebrew meaning 'restitution for a child who died'): There are several characters in the Ezra/Nehemiah account who bear this name and they cannot be differentiated with complete certainty. The Meshullam of this story may be found in the following places:

- in Ezra 8:16, he is one of the "leading men," sent on special assignment for Ezra during the journey from Susa to Jerusalem; we can conclude therefore that he is a trusted confidant and adjunct to Ezra; we can also conclude that his marriage to a foreigner took place in Persia before he accompanied Ezra on his mission to Jerusalem.

- in Nehemiah 12:32, he is one of the leading men who accompanies Ezra in one of the processions that celebrated the completion of Jerusalem's wall.

- in Nehemiah 8:4, he stood at Ezra's right hand during the proclamation of Torah and was therefore one of the men who descended into the crowd to give personal instruction.

- in Nehemiah 10:7, he is a priest and signatory to what I refer to as the Jerusalem Covenant, a document that governed the civil affairs of Jerusalem.

- in Ezra 10:15, he publicly opposed Ezra's (his mentor) policy on the divorce of foreign wives.

- in Ezra 10:29, he is listed among the men who had married foreign wives.

What emerges is a character who would have been highly educated in Torah and possibly instrumental in the compilation of Jewish sacred writings that Ezra brought with him back to Jerusalem. He was notably active in the Jerusalem reforms. His marriage to a foreigner had not barred his career or influence while he was in Persia, and Ezra's reliance on him suggests a tacit approval of his marital status. That his wife was "foreign" suggests that she had not converted to Judaism, and, given Meshullam's status, it is plausible to assume that she came from equivalent highborn Persian society. There is no mention of children in the text. His convictions regarding the full extent of the reforms, however, were sufficiently strong as to make him publicly challenge his friend and mentor. The text is silent on whether he submitted to Ezra's edict and divorced his wife, or, as my story suggests, withdrew from the community.

Another Meshullam of note also figures in the Ezra/Nehemiah account, namely Meshullam, son of Berekiah, a descendent of David's royal family (I Chronicles 3:19). From Nehemiah 3:4 & 30, we learn that he helped build two portions of the wall, but that he had given his daughter in marriage to the son of Tobiah, an ardent detractor of Nehemiah's reconstruction.

12. Leviticus 21:17ff: ". . . (no priest) who has a defect may come near to offer the food of his God. No man who has any defect may come near."

13. Exodus 34:26. Deuteronomy 14:21.

14. Leviticus 19:28.

15. Leviticus 19:27.

16. Genesis 32:33. What is referred to is the story of how, when Jacob wrestled with God, his hip socket was injured. Out of respect for this holy wound, eating the sinew of the thigh from any animal was proscribed.

17. Deuteronomy 12:21.

18. This was no idle comment. One historian reported that from the time young boys could walk they were trained in riding the horse, shooting the bow and speaking truth.

19. Numbers 15:37–41 contains instructions for these tassels and in particular that at least one blue thread should be used. The most current version of this ancient clothing is a fringed prayer shawl, usually white but always with a tassel at each of the four corners made from blue threads.

20. Numbers 15:39 is the place where Caleb's words first appear.

21. A short story is inserted into a census list that is reproduced in both Ezra (2:61) and Nehemiah (7:61). It tells that the descendents of three priestly families could not sufficiently prove their priestly lineage and were removed from office by "the governor" lest they desecrate the temple by their presence. The dating of these elaborate and multi-generational genealogies is uncertain and thought to have been added to both books. The governor who issued the interdiction, therefore, could well have preceded Nehemiah. Regardless of when the three men were removed, the story speaks of rigid zeal for ethnic purity in all strata of society.

22. Nehemiah 3:4 and 3:20 describe the sections of wall that Meremoth built. In Ezra 8:33 Meremoth formally receives and issues a receipt for the temple funds brought by Ezra from Persia.

23. I Chronicles 24:6 tells us "the scribe Shemaiah, son of Nethanel, recorded their names in the presence of the King" (David). Presumably this, or some other similar document, was uncovered to reinstate Meremoth who was a descendant of Hakkoz.

24. Numbers 18:20 reads, "The LORD said to Aaron (the first priest), 'You shall have no inheritance in the land, nor will you have any share among

them; I am your share and your inheritance among the Israelites.'"

25. Ezra is credited (by L. Ginsberg) with having established what in Protestant traditions is known as the daily office: a published schedule of readings from Torah to be read at set times through each week so that all the holy writings would be heard at least once during the year.

26. The Feast of Booths, also known as the Feast of Tabernacles (Leviticus 23:33ff) or the Feast of Ingathering (Exodus 34:22), was one of three annual celebrations commanded by Moses that all Jews should observe. Other references are Deuteronomy 16:13, II Chronicles 8:13 and Deuteronomy 31:11. It is a seven-day harvest celebration, although the custom of living in small "booths" made with branches is a memorial to when the Israelites lived in temporary shelters during the forty-year sojourn to the Promised Land.

Once every seven years, the entire Torah was to be read aloud as part of this celebration. By the time of Ezra, the feast had not been observed for at least one hundred and fifty years — a considerable lapse in the keeping of Jewish law, considering how central the feast was meant to be in the corporate life of Israel.

27. The words of Moses — the Pentateuch — had been lost from Jewish public life at least once before. II Kings 22 & 23 tell the story of how King Josiah (641–610 BC) discovered the Law Books hidden in the temple and, on discovering them, read them aloud in their entirety on the steps of the temple. The lengthy liturgy was followed by public repentance and a renewal of the people's fidelity to Yahweh. The scene described would have lasted several days, perhaps longer.

28. Psalm 132:13.

29. A loose paraphrase of Psalm 137.

30. Psalm 126.

31 Nehemiah 12:43 comments that the noise of the celebration could be heard in the surrounding villages.

32 Caleb's song is based on Psalm 122.

33 The names that Jehiel reads are a partial list of those mentioned in Ezra 2 and again in Nehemiah 7. Scholarly consensus is that the lists were originally historical records, borrowed by both authors. There is also some overlap with two other family lists found in Ezra 8 and Nehemiah 10.

34. Taken from Deuteronomy 6:1–9.

35. Nehemiah 23:1–3: The dating of this particular reading from Torah is sufficiently obscure that I have placed it in this scene since it is the only specific reference to a passage of Torah that was read in public. At all other times, in both Ezra and Nehemiah, only a general statement is made that Ezra read from "the Law" but we are not told what sections he read at other times. Both books

indicate that the people progressed in their understanding of righteousness and it is plausible that the people's grasp of ethnic purity started with something as basic as who was to be excluded from a general assembly. The section of Torah read may be found in Deuteronomy 23:1–8.

36. That is, the sons of Esau, brother of Jacob and first cousins to the Jews. In 587 BC when Jerusalem was destroyed, the Edomites actively harassed those people fleeing Nebuchadnezzar's siege army. Relations between the two ethnic groups remained bitter from that point onward. The short oracle of Obadiah is directed against Edom and prophesies their destruction "... *because of the violence against your brother Jacob ... on the day you stood aloof while strangers carried off his wealth ...*" In the same way that exclusion of Ammonites and Moabites would have been a challenge for change, so also would more friendly dealings with the Edomites who occupied the lands just south of Yehud.

37. Nehemiah 9:6. This is the opening preamble to a long prayer that recaps the history of the Jews and concludes that, as a consequence of their hardened hearts, they are in essence still in captivity.

38. Nehemiah 8:6.

39. Nehemiah 8:4: A total of thirteen young men are listed as having stood with Ezra, and later dispersed into the crowd to provide more personal teaching.

40. Nehemiah 9:7.

41. Walter Wangerin Jr., in *The Book of God*, positioned the story of Genesis as part of Ezra's public ministry, and this footnote gladly acknowledges my debt to this outstanding author.

42. Nehemiah 9:13,14.

43. Nehemiah 8:17.

44. Two prophets, Jeremiah and Ezekiel, guided the Jews during the chaos of Israel's final days as a nation and subsequent deportation to Babylon. Their respective books remain major contributions to the Old Testament. Ezekiel is thought to have been among the first group of deportees and left Jerusalem at least a decade before Jerusalem was actually destroyed. Jeremiah remained behind, counseling (in vain) surrender to King Nebuchadnezzar. One of his letters to the Jews in exile reads in part: "This is what Yahweh Almighty, the God of Israel, says to all those I carried into exile from Jerusalem to Babylon: 'Build houses and settle down; plant gardens and eat what they produce. Marry and have sons and daughters; find wives for your sons and give your daughters in marriage, so that they too may have sons and daughters. Increase in number there; do not decrease. Also, seek the peace and prosperity of the city to which I have carried you into exile'" (Jeremiah. 29:4–8).

45. Jeremiah 29:17.

46. Jeremiah 29:17–20. Not only are those who were left in the land likened to rotten figs not fit to be eaten, they were singled out for further hardships that would come at the instigation of God himself. The full text reads: "Yes, this is what the LORD Almighty says: 'I will pursue them with the sword, famine and plague and will make them abhorrent to all the kingdoms of the earth and an object of cursing and horror, of scorn and reproach, among all the nations where I drive them.'"

In fact, part of those who were left in the land after Nebuchadnezzar's destruction did emigrate to Egypt, forcing Jeremiah to go with them. Noteworthy also are the verses that immediately follow this passage. Although the Jews in exile are also charged with not heeding God's voice, it is only their false prophets who are punished.

47. Jeremiah 33:5. "I will hide my face from this city because of all its wickedness."

48. The compilation of Jeremiah's oracles would probably have been undertaken in Persia. Some of his writings had actually been sent to the Persian exiles in the form of public letters. Jeremiah himself died in Egypt among apostate Jews who had forcibly removed him from Jerusalem. Jewish tradition holds that after Jeremiah died, his loyal scribe, Baruch, traveled from Egypt to Babylon and finished the book that bears his master's name. Certainly those Jews left in the land would have had neither the interest nor literary skill to retain the writings of Jeremiah. These, together with the oracles of Ezekiel, would have accompanied Ezra and been as new to the citizens of Jerusalem as was the Torah.

49. Nehemiah 9:38. The timing of this declaration within the ministry of Ezra is not certain, but it is a logical outcome of Ezra's month-long public discourse. Public enthusiasm for the keeping of Torah would have been widespread.

50. Nehemiah 10:2–27: This list includes twenty-two priestly families, seventeen Levites and forty-four civil leaders. Nehemiah's name (of course) is listed first. Noteworthy is that Meshullam is listed as a signatory, but Shecaniah is not.

51. The difficulty of mixed marriages cannot be fully appreciated outside some discussion about the population of various groups, and I shall try and deal with both in this footnote.

The general attitude of Torah was that mixed marriages from the ethnic groups occupying the land of Canaan were to be avoided (Deuteronomy 7:1–4, 20:10–18, Exodus 34:11–16) since inevitably Jewish fidelity to Yahweh suffered. The high priest was specifically enjoined from marrying a foreigner (Leviticus 31:14), and Manasseh's decision to marry Nikaso would have disqualified him from seeking the office. These parts of Torah, however, are all specifically in anticipation of the Israelites entering and dislocating various tribes and not a general prohibition against marrying a foreigner. In the Deuteronomy 20 passage, for example, marriages to ethnic groups that live in cities "a distance away" are dealt with differently from unions with peoples from cities that lay within Canaan.

Additionally, some notable mixed marriages take place within the scriptures, seemingly without any ill effects. Abraham sired his son Ishmael with his Egyptian concubine Hagar (Genesis 16:3). Joseph married the Egyptian Pharaoh's daughter Asenath and from that union came two of the tribes of Israel, Manasseh and Ephraim (Genesis 45:45ff). Moses married Zipporah the Cushite (Exodus 2:21). Within the royal family of David, several foreign wives are cited. The great-grandmother of David was Ruth, the Moabite (Ruth 4:18), who married Boaz. As for Boaz, his ancestors included none other than Rahab, the prostitute from Jericho who is given honour both in the genealogy of Jesus (Matthew 1:5) and in Hebrews (11:31). David's favourite son, Absalom (II Samuel 3:3), was the offspring of a foreign marriage, as might also have been the case with King Solomon, whose mother was Bathsheba, the widow of a Hittite.

In all these stories, the legitimacy of the unions is viewed in light of the religious attitudes portrayed rather than strict ethnic origins. The dilemma of mixed marriages as presented in the Ezra narrative reflects a departure from (or shall we say a new application of) the Torah passages that proscribe the taking of foreign wives. In Ezra 9:1–2, the lay leaders of Jerusalem alter the understanding of Deuteronomy 7:3–6 (which they partially quote) by replacing the phrase "holy people" with the phrase "holy seed." An understanding of a covenant people, into which any number of ethnic groups might be grafted, has been replaced by a much more legalistic understanding of physical ethnic purity without reference to anyone's heart or allegiance to Yahweh.

It is this older understanding of the Torah laws, with its emphasis on religious purity, together with Jeremiah's encouragement to freely mingle with the Babylonians (Jeremiah 29:4–8) that explains why the Jews of the exile could have felt free to intermarry yet at the same time retain such a devout loyalty to Yahweh.

But there is a second reason why the mixed marriages that took place in Persia might have been viewed as being different from the mixed marriages among the people who had always lived in Yehud. The harsh truth contained in both Ezekiel and Jeremiah is that Yahweh deliberately turned away from "those people who remained in the land" in favour of those who went into exile. Ezekiel 11 confirms not only that God has deserted the land, but that he will provide a sanctuary for those who have been scattered among the countries. It goes on to promise that God will not only bring them back to the land of Israel, but that there he will remove from them their hearts of stone and give them instead hearts of flesh. They will be his people, and he will be their God. Jeremiah 33 paints a picture of Jerusalem laid totally to waste, filled only with dead bodies and the surrounding environs desolate of men or animals. But as in Ezekiel's oracle, God also promises to bring Israel back from her captivity (in Babylon) and rebuild her as before.

This prevailing theme of rejection of those who were not fortunate enough to be sent to Babylon, while harsh and perhaps unpalatable, at least explains why attempts at piety and devotion to Yahweh by the people who remained in the land were generally unsuccessful. Ezra 4:1–3 describes how the Samarians' offer to help in the rebuilding of the temple was rebuffed because "they had no part with us." Within the greater sweep of God's history, that was quite true, however much they (and we) might wish otherwise.

Note on Populations:

Population estimates might help the reader understand the intense seriousness with which Ezra responds to the problem of mixed marriages. In his prayer (Ezra 9:6–15), he says, "we are left this day as remnant," and pleads with God not to destroy his people utterly. This is no metaphor.

The bulk of Israel's population (that is, the ten "northern" tribes) was essentially destroyed as an identifiable ethnic and self-governing group by the Assyrians in 722 B.C. By the time of this story, the people were referred to as Samarians and considered foreigners by Nehemiah and Ezra despite the Samarians' devotion to Yahweh. There are no reliable estimates of this population, although Assyrian records indicate that almost 30,000 Jews were deported as part of their occupation.

Just prior to Nebuchadnezzar's invasion (587 BC), the population of Judah (the southern kingdom) is tentatively estimated at 30,000. But by Nehemiah's time, those who still lived in the land (defined as roughly 770 square miles or roughly 20 miles wide by 30 miles long) could have been as few as 10,000, although some respected scholars use a higher estimate of 20,000. Whatever estimate is used, compared to the roughly million people that left Egypt to enter the Promised Land, God's chosen people had been brought low.

Depopulation of the land occurred in four ways:

1) an estimated 4,600 to 18,000 educated and skilled deportees were sent to Babylon in the years prior to Jerusalem's final destruction (Jer. 52:28-30 and II Kings 24:14–16).

2) an indeterminate number of "poor people" were similarly shipped back to Babylon immediately after Jerusalem was destroyed (Jer. 52:15)

3) an indeterminate number of Jews who, having been left in the land by the Babylonians, chose to relocate to Egypt, taking Jeremiah with them.

4) an indeterminate number of Jews either starved to death or were killed during the Babylonian invasion. Jeremiah's references, while

not numeric, point to horrific losses of life that could well have exceeded 10,000 people.

Various references all point to a view of Yehud's territory as being desolate: Zechariah 7:14 says that God scattered his people among the nations with such force that the land was left desolate so that no one could come or go. Ezekiel 33:23–29 is perhaps the most hauntingly poignant declaration of Yahweh's judgment on all his people who had not been sent into exile. It reads in part:

"This is what the Sovereign LORD says: As surely as I live, those who are left in the ruins will fall by the sword, those out in the country I will give to the wild animals to be devoured, and those in strongholds and caves will die of a plague. I will make the land a desolate waste, and her proud strength will come to an end, and the mountains of Israel will become desolate so that no one will cross them. Then they will know that I am the LORD, when I have made the land a desolate waste because of all the detestable things they have done."

The conclusion from all this is that, in the divine ordering of history, God reduced his chosen people to only those who had been sent into exile — the tiny group numbering between 4,600 and 18,000.

These "exiles," however, were promised God's divine protection. They represented the fulfillment of the prophecy in Isaiah 11:1 that says, out of the "stump of Jesse" will come a tender shoot that will eventually bear fruit. In Jeremiah 30:11,19 God promises, "though I (will) completely destroy the nations among which I scatter you, I will not completely destroy you . . . I will add to (your) numbers, and you will not be decreased."

By the time of Ezra/Nehemiah, this promise had come true! Ezra chapter two enumerates no fewer than 42,000 returning exiles, although this list probably covered several decades of repatriation. Total assimilation of the Jewish nation had been narrowly averted and a well resourced, educated Jewish people, now equipped with an extensive library of sacred texts and good leadership, was re-entering the Promised Land.

In all of Israel's history, mixed marriages within the Promised Land ended in syncretism and religious apostasy. While they may have been permitted, and even ordained in Persia as part of God's sovereign plan to rebuild his people, no such confidence could be counted on once the people had returned.

Both Ezra and Nehemiah in effect drew a circle around the "people of exile" and made every effort to keep this new remnant distinct. The destruction that Ezra anticipates (Ezra 9) would not come about through another invading army, but from within through marital alliances with the various peoples living in the land. Whatever spiritual fortitude the Jews had developed while in Persia that kept them distinct could not be counted on once they returned to their land. The spiritual torpor of the Jews who had remained behind is attested to by the prophet Malachi, who was probably still alive at the time of Ezra/Nehemiah. As far as God was concerned, the people's faith was both shallow and futile: *"Oh that one of you would shut the temple doors, so that you would not light useless fires on my altar!"* says Malachi 1:10, attributing the words to Yahweh.

But against the threat of assimilation, Ezra was also constrained by the clear bias in Torah against divorce. Ironically, one specific behaviour that Malachi highlights is the casual attitude towards divorce that had been adopted by the indigenous Jews. *"I hate divorce,"* God says in Malachi 2:16. *"Has not the Lord made them one flesh?"* Ezra is caught, therefore, between trying to protect the tender shoot from the stump of Jesse, newly arrived from Persia, and the attitude of scriptures that says at the very least, divorce is not a thing to be entered into lightly.

In the end, Ezra permitted (but did not initiate) what the people felt was necessary. But two things should be noted about the people's actions. First is that, what must have been from their perspective an act of extreme devotion to Yahweh, is from Ezra's prayer a desperate measure taken as a last resort simply to keep the nation alive. Secondly, Yahweh's opinion in the matter is not recorded. From this time period, we have only his words as proclaimed by his prophet Malachi, *"I hate divorce. So guard yourself in your spirit and do not break faith."*

References for this Footnote:

Terry J. Betts, "The Book of Nehemiah in Its Biblical and Historical Context," in *The Southern Baptist Journal of Theology,* Vol. 9, No. 3, Fall 2005. *The Oxford History of the Biblical World,* Oxford University Press, 1998, pp 288-291.

52. Nehemiah 13:24.

53. This is not just a clever turn of phrase. In Ezra 9:2, when the people describe the problem to Ezra, they use the phrase "holy seed" in an attempt to quote Deuteronomy chapter seven. The Deuteronomy phrase, however, is "holy people" and was meant to refer to the state of Israel's heart, not their particular bloodline.

54. Ezra 10:1.

55. The full text of his prayer may be read in Ezra 9:5–15.

56. This metaphor, redirected in this case, is from Jeremiah 31:15, and is used again in yet another lament in the story of the birth of the Christ child.

57. Ezra 9:8. Ezra maintained a consistent stance that the people remained in bondage, despite being free from the captivity of the foreign land.

58. Ezekiel 16:8ff.

59. Ezra 10:3. Children are specifically included.

60. Ezra 10:6. Ezra did in fact remain in a private chamber, taking neither food nor water for the three days.

61. This footnote is a repeat of Footnote #10 in the previous story "The Left Hand of God" and is reproduced here for the convenience of the reader.

Mount Gerizim (the mount of blessings) together with its twin mountain Ebal (the mount of curses) is located about fifty miles north of Jerusalem and ten miles to the southeast of Samaria. Jacob's well (John 4:6) is located in the valley between them, where Jesus encountered the Samaritan woman (John 4:20). The ancient town of Shechem is at the base of Mount Gerizim. Mount Gerizim became the centre for Samarian worship, and a temple was built at its base in the fourth century BC.

In Deuteronomy 27:1–9 Moses instructs the Israelites to cross over the Jordan and build an altar of natural stone on Mount Ebal. The words of the law were to be chiseled into rock dolmens placed prominently on the mountainside. This location was understood to be the central place of worship. The two mountains are again mentioned in Joshua 8:30–35 and Deuteronomy 27:11–13. These scriptures describe a national liturgy in which the people positioned themselves on both mountains, creating a natural amphitheatre. Those on Mount Gerizim would shout the "blessing formulas" while those on Mount Ebal would respond with appropriate "cursing formulas."

Adherents of the Samarian (later, Samaritan) sect worshiped Yahweh, adhered to Torah and claimed Moses as their prophet. They also asserted that in the original versions of Torah, Moses had chosen Mount Gerizim as the central place of worship, and not Mount Ebal, as our English language texts read. Samarian tradition holds that it was Ezra who deliberately changed the words of Torah to undermine the Samarians' claim to be legitimate Yahweh worshippers and part of the Jewish community. Whereas in Jewish traditions Ezra is revered as a prophet second only to Moses, in Samarian history he is an infidel, guilty of having changed the words of Torah. The meaning of Samaritan is "keeper of the faith," and their Jewish roots are traced back to the northern tribes of Ephraim and Manasseh.

While certainty is impossible, there is some weight to the Samarians' claim. It seems unusual that the Mount of Curses would be the place where Moses ordained central worship, rather than the Mount of Blessings. Textual evidence is divided. A report issued by the United Bible Society concluded that "…the original text of Deuteronomy 27:4 cited Mount Gerizim but we are tentative in our conclusions" (D. Barthelemy ed. *Preliminary Report on the Old Testament Text Project*. New York: United Bible Society, 1979).

62. The first-century Jewish historian Josephus (Book II, ch. 7,8) says that Manasseh was eventually commanded to divorce his foreign wife or not approach the altar. Not wishing to lose his 'sacerdotal dignity on her account', he tells her father, Sanballat, of his dilemma who offers him the job of High Priest at a temple he will build at Mount Gerizim. The story, however, is rife with historical inconsistencies and some scholars discount it entirely.

63. Ezra 10:9 especially mentions the rain that fell so hard it shortened the proceedings.

64. Ezra 10:33 lists four men who spoke out against the proceedings; they were Jonathan son of Asahel, Jahzeiah son of Tikvah, Shabbethai the Levite and Meshullam. Whatever one thinks about their opinions, their courage was remarkable.

65. Unlike the books of prophecy, the mind of God remains hidden in both Ezra and Nehemiah. We have only the oracles of Malachi, who was probably still alive at the time of this story, who declared on behalf of Yahweh: "*I hate divorce. I, Yahweh, act as the witness between you and the wife of your youth, because you have broken faith with her, though she is your partner, the wife of your marriage covenant*" (Malachi 2:13ff).

The Left Hand of God is Rob Alloway's third collection of Bible stories. His first volume is *Balaam's Revenge* (1999) and was followed by *Babylon Post* (2005). He is a contributing columnist to *ChristianWeek* magazine. In addition to his written work, he gives readings, chapel talks and occasional lectures on Old Testament literature. Rob lives in Toronto, where he is currently working on a fourth collection of stories.

Contact Information: alloway@alloway.org

Printed in the United States
132077LV00001B/43/P